"*I am concerned with only one thing,*" says Joyce Carol Oates, "*the moral and social conditions of my generation.*" These are spelled out with exquisite compassion and compelling detail in her novels and stories.

Joyce Carol Oates is "a storyteller with a unique viewpoint rooted in her sense of the explosive power and mystery in human beings.... For her interest in violence and rural scenes, Miss Oates has been compared with Faulkner.... I am also reminded of D. H. Lawrence, in whom an awareness, similar to Miss Oates', of complex and unnamed vitalities gives an electric touch to fictional scenes. And, young as she is, Miss Oates is not unworthy of such comparisons."

—NEW YORK TIMES BOOK REVIEW

Upon the Sweeping Flood

and other stories

by Joyce Carol Oates

A FAWCETT CREST BOOK

Fawcett Publications, Inc., Greenwich, Conn.

UPON THE SWEEPING FLOOD

Contents

UPON THE SWEEPING FLOOD

Oh! that Id had a tear to've quencht that flame
    Which did dissolve the Heavens above
    Into those liquid drops that Came
        To drown our Carnall love.
Our cheeks were dry and eyes refused to weep.
Tears bursting out ran down the skies darke Cheek.

Were th'Heavens sick? must wee their Doctors bee
    And physick them with pills, our sin?
    To make them purg and Vomit, see,
        And excrements out fling?
We've griev'd them by such Physick that they shed
Their Excrements upon our lofty heads.

EDWARD TAYLOR, 1683

Stigmata

Though his father had been at St. Jerome's Home for the Aged for five or six years now, Walt Turner had never seen the home before—he had seen his father, of course, at various Christmases, at various houses of brothers and sisters, and the old man had journeyed down out of these saintly hills one fall to attend a Sunday High Mass sung by his second oldest son, newly ordained a priest: but Walt had never visited him at the home and had never imagined visiting him, since he did not like his father particularly. And he had guessed that a visit to the home, with those faint mountains and hills peering in the old man's window, and that blue sky that was so fraudulently pure it offended one's credulity, would be, as his sister Clara had reported sadly, "a visit to him in Heaven —all he does is smile."

Walt had driven alone up to the home, in spite of his distrust of this secondhand car, refusing a ride with his brothers—who drove carefully and looked at the scenery and talked about their jobs and their children and their father—and as he approached the nursing home the impact of its high, rigid, ascetic opulence struck him so that he felt the car slowing as if weakened by the vision. St. Jerome's, as its worthy brochure had shown, was built on a hill: a kind of drumlin, perhaps, at any rate a freakish hill that lifted high above the level of the immediate area. It was jarring: a photograph or a vision made real.

7

Oh, there were frills of nature attendant upon it, fir trees
and slimly elegant shrubs; there were foothills and real
mountains behind it suggesting its location in nature; but
the building itself, a heavy rectangular structure that
surrendered nothing to art, that, constructed of some
deliberate anonymous colorless rock, looked centuries old
and simultaneously unrelated to time, showed by the very
bluntness of its reality the illusion that nature conspired—
there were meek dying trees beneath that green, and
hills fated to erode beneath those slivers of leftover snow,
and mountains so vague they might be erased by hand.
And had not nature's great contribution to history, the
wooden cross, become transformed into brilliant silver,
gleaming over there above the chapel? It was human
creation that would survive all worldly accidents.

Walt turned up the long gravel drive. The big building
waited coyly atop its hill: the drive leaned this way, now
that way, as if teasing. As it rose slowly, Walt began to
see the parking lot behind the home; there were a large
number of cars parked there. And he noticed in his rear-
view mirror that a station wagon was just turning in from
the road. He drove faster. On the bumper of the station
wagon was a sticker with orange fluorescent letters—a
politician's name? But it was months too early for that.
Walt drove faster and heard with satisfaction gravel being
picked up and churned around his wheels. He supposed
the driver behind him had taken in, carefully, this car
and was wondering about it—St. Jerome's, though planned
as near-charity, was aristocratic, after all, and bluntly
expensive. And who else would there be to wonder at
him? There would be reporters and doctors and one or
two psychiatrists and a university professor from down-
state, not to mention his two frail sweet sisters whose
letters he did not answer and his two successful brothers
whose offers of money he refused (the third brother was
now in Rome, regretted violently that he could not
come). Walt parked along the edge of the driveway; his
heart was pounding. The station wagon passed him,
headed for the parking lot, and he found himself staring
at the orange sticker: OBSERVE EASTER.

Walt was met inside by a young nun in a brown outfit, who smiled the way his father smiled. He introduced himself with an absurd yet faintly proud sense of being important; he had noticed, sitting about the foyer on cheap modern chairs, men who must certainly be reporters. Other people drifted by, dumpy women in furs, young women holding back straining children, visitors to lesser patients who looked about wonderingly. Was it possible a miracle might occur, and in this building? Walt's blood throbbed foolishly as he ascended the stairs.

But it was for nothing: his father was not in his room. A nurse explained politely, another young woman in a brown outfit, hardly more than a girl. No, not out in the sun porch either, this was his time of devotion; she spoke in short, snatched enthusiastic phrases. "But your family is inside waiting. Won't you wait with them?" She was obviously shy and pleased and embarrassed.

As Walt knocked, he heard his brother Art's voice, a solemn murmur that must be dragging down the corners of his mouth. The door opened—a dazzling flash of white like a glimpse of another world, beautifully white walls—his sister standing there, chic in a dark tweed suit with black fur about its collar. "Walt, dear," she cried. She embraced him and he held his breath against the odor of cologne, though he liked Clara immensely: had she not always taken his side, the side of the youngest, the weakest, the nastiest? "It's so good to see you again," she said in her family-gathering voice. The others were on their feet and crowding in; welcomes were general. There were Carolyn and her husband, Carolyn now getting old —nearly forty—but smiling bravely, defying all wrinkles, trusting to a new complex sort of make-up: but Carolyn was a fine woman, a fine mother, wasn't that true? Walt accepted her embrace and saw over her shoulder the embarrassed expressions of his brothers. Then, as he was released to them, their expressions clicked into proper looks of solemn, cautious welcome, the professional greeting among older brothers. "Walt," Art said, shaking hands and cuffing his shoulder; Ronald did the same. "If only Tom had been able to come!" Clara said. In the awkward group they jostled about for a while, lighting cigarettes, helping Walt off with his coat; Carolyn and her husband exchanged domestic murmurs, nothing important, the sort of thing expected between husband and wife; Art—who was putting on weight, a round, well-fed, red-faced stranger—went back to his position by the window, where the fine glare burned around his head and blurred his features. "Here, sit down. I suppose you've driven all the way?" Clara said, leading him somewhere. "We're staying in town, at the hotel. *The* hotel. There's only one but it's rather nice—big and white, with a veranda. It was built in 1850." Walt made his way through the odor of cologne and cigar smoke and sat down. "So where is he?" he said. "Holding a press conference or something?"

He saw that look of pain shoot in several directions, ricochet off one face and hit another, become absorbed finally in Clara's shrill chatty voice. "He's at his devotions now," she said. "All the old people spend quite a bit of time at their devotions, especially during Holy Week. But Father more than anyone—you understand." Walt showed no understanding but lit a cigarette and everyone watched him drop the match into a dirty ash tray.

The room was smaller than he had expected: the brochure had hinted at larger rooms. This room, despite the esteem of its inmate, was hardly more than a cell—with a large window, it was true, viewing the parking lot; its walls were starkly white, a white so relentlessly clean and featureless that it turned Walt's eyes continually away from it and to the security of flesh—the familiar unfamiliar faces of his family. Their mother had died years ago and so there was only a brother missing, Tom, who was tall, angular, bony-faced, with a gift of venomous wit—Tom in Italy now humbling himself in a study of marriage law, Tom who had wanted to teach college: Walt missed him. How much easier these people were without him lurking in the background to ridicule and love them—how much straighter they stood! "If only Tom had been able to get permission!" Clara said, looking at Walt.

"The discipline is too strong," Carolyn's husband suggested without enthusiasm. Walt could not remember if he was Catholic—maybe a convert. Didn't they have five children? Everyone murmured over this, perhaps agreeing, perhaps disagreeing. "A bulwark against anarchy," Ronald said. He wore a gray vest that bulged gently about his abdomen. "But it is too strong!" Clara said. "What are you talking about, anarchy? His own father is a saint and the Church won't let him come! What are you talking about?" Clara's nose seemed to grow sharper; a dull red flush overtook her cheeks. "For God's sake don't start on that, that saint business," Art said. He looked at Walt. "We've been instructed about that. They've made it clear nobody's a saint when he's living, and there's no evidence—no final—" "But in your heart what do you feel?" Clara cried triumphantly.

An excited, embarrassed silence fell upon them. Walt's fingers were cold. "Oh, for Christ's sake," he said. "So you believe in this." They were too fond of him, or too dignified, to answer; Ronald, twelve years Walt's senior, blinked benignly at him as if at a child. It was odd that Walt's remark should hang in the air so clearly, as if it were cherished by them, examined by them, distinguishing him from them and their successful lives. . . . Walt, his face burning with anger and shame, felt catapulted back in time, sitting again at that big dinner table in the old parlor, with a napkin on his lap. Food being passed elegantly, in white dishes; his sisters' young faces, hair recently washed, his brothers in suits and ties, his mother with her heavy pearls, his father, there at the head of the table with his back reflected in the glass of the mahogany china cabinet: his father! While they murmured happily, with the full fierce impersonal glare of their father's love falling upon them without distinction, like the sun's rays on the blind earth, Walt had groveled backward like a crab, staring down at his food and his dirt-edged fingernails, thinking that he was not related to them, could recognize nothing of himself in them, why did they pretend love for him? His mind shifted backward steadily, away from the candlelight, he retreated inside his bowed

head from that half-smile on his father's lean, attractive
face. His father smiled that smile to all of them, Art who
was so good in math, and Walt who had been caught
stealing comic books in the drugstore!

"It isn't the reporters I mind," Carolyn was saying.
"I thought I would. But it's the psychiatrist, the one from
Chicago. Did you meet him? He's staying at the hotel."
"He seemed cordial," Art said. "But they don't believe—
any of them!" Carolyn said. "And," said Art carefully,
"it's better that way—they'll be forced to believe. Why
do you think they allow them here to examine Father?
They've been analyzing him for a week. —The bishop has
finally come around, Walt, did you hear that?" Walt
shrugged his shoulders. He had crossed his legs and noted
now, with indifferent curiosity, that the cuffs of his trousers were dirty. "There's going to be a procession of the
faithful on Friday, if everything is well," said Art. "If he
starts to bleed on time," Walt said.

"Walt, how is Linda?" Carolyn said. She wore a hat
with a sea-green feather twisting about it; it seemed to
tense with the anticipation of putting Walt down.

"Fine, last time I saw her."

They looked at him sadly. "She was a sweet girl, but
maybe a little too young. Immature," Clara offered.

"Not was but is. *Is* a sweet girl." Now that they watched
him so closely he gloried, despite himself, in their attention. "And it hadn't anything much to do with her.
Don't blame her."

"I wasn't blaming her," Clara said sharply.

"Well, don't. I know you all do." He leered at them,
grinning. That would pierce their benevolent hearts. Or
had they learned from their father that august generous
indifference, that godly calm that stifles all anger, all love?
He believed he could see something of their father in
each of them, even in Clara—poor nervous Clara, a girl
forced into a woman, with bracelets and rings and clouds
of perfume, to whose pretty smile so many young men
had been drawn, eager at first, later perplexed, bored,
retreating to firmer women. And especially in Art, the
oldest, who leaned back against the window sill sucking

at a cigar, with the same look of tender concern their father had directed toward his own cigars, or his food, or Clara's recitations at family reunions of sprightly verse from *Alice in Wonderland*. "I used to think it would be strange to be a father," Walt said. "But it isn't anything, is it? That's the hell of it. It meant something to Linda, having the baby—but not to me. That's the way it is, isn't it?"

They looked at him blankly; this was too personal. With a frown Art stretched his arm so he could consult his watch: "Twenty past five. He stays in the chapel from one until five-thirty. On his knees, a man that age. Do you know he's been fasting all this year? Since last Easter, Walt." Walt shivered, not at this sinister information, but at his own name; what kin was he to such insanity? "He insisted that communion every morning would be enough for him to live on, but they wouldn't allow it—there was quite a controversy, all the way up to the chancery office. It was thought to be too extreme— I think I agree—"

"He's such an old man now, Walt, wait till you see him! He's lost so much weight," Clara said.

"But if *he* feels communion would be enough, they should let him fast," Carolyn pointed out. The sisters did not look at each other but toward each other, obliquely; their glances crossed in mid-air. "He knows more than they do. I *don't* care if they are the Church, this is something special, obviously. It's a direct revelation from God."

"It isn't going through channels, that's sure," Ronald said.

"But if he were to die—!" Clara whispered.

"He's got to die," said Walt. "Then he's got to be resurrected Sunday morning. Isn't that how it goes, and isn't he under contract to a television network for it?"

"Look, why the hell did you come?" Art said. Their father's look slid off his face and he stared over at Walt. "Just what are you doing here?"

Walt glanced away—at the unfinished bureau, the

crucifix above it. His hands became loose and self-conscious. "I don't know."

"I know you've been under a strain, Walt, with the divorce and all," Art said slowly. "I don't want any quarrels. Not here. There's too much at stake. It's just that you don't seem to realize what this is—what's really happening and how important it is."

"Walt, the whole world is waiting," Clara said.

The horror of this remark calmed Walt. It was true that he believed in nothing, benevolence neither divine nor human, he expected nothing but age, perhaps cancer, perhaps a failing heart, since nature runs only one way; he expected no more abortive gestures of love; he was too ironical to care, really, about the college degrees he had never been able to use. He had begun to drink too much, as if fulfilling a role; it was true that his mind had no refuge: thoughts before sleep could center on nothing, neither the future nor the past nor the distant past, that sunless perplexing area of his childhood. On his mother? But she was dead too long, it was not a person he remembered but an image, an American formula. And yet, he wanted to assure them, there was something in him to which they could address themselves —if they wanted— They could speak with him singly, honestly, they could reveal the truth about their secret lives and he would listen—greedily, gratefully— He was not hard, his heart was not dead, he was waiting and vulnerable. He muttered, "Sorry."

Carolyn was speaking slowly and elaborately about the political machinations in the diocese when the door was opened rather roughly, given these still surroundings— and a heavy white-faced nun stared in at them. "Could you please wait downstairs? Could you— You must leave, something has happened to your father—" The women cried out; Walt got to his feet. Another nun appeared, an older woman. "Yes, your father has collapsed in the chapel but he is being attended. He is being attended. The doctors are going to bring him back up here and so we would like the room empty—you'll be able to visit him soon— No, it's nothing critical, he has regained consciousness. You understand he will have the best of medical care." The women breathed audibly, trembling, the brothers moved tentatively toward the door: all stared at the nuns. "We weren't prepared for this," the older nun said suddenly, "since it—it began last year on Friday— And today is only Thursday— We weren't prepared—your father was not prepared, exactly, but he seems well—he is conscious, perfectly conscious— Pray for him. Pray for him," she said in excitement. "He is praying for us. God has visited this blessing upon him for us, for all of us, your father prays for all the world—" Her fierce, controlled hysteria followed Walt out into the hall. Ahead of him his sisters and brothers walked along in frightened obedience, like children; staring at their stiff backs, Walt was sickened with fear—was it possible that this miracle was going to happen? A miracle advertised in cheap Catholic pamphlets, a miracle insisted upon by factions within the Church—hinted at in his own newspaper, a sophisticated large-circulation daily? He saw the figures of old men in doorways, watching them as they passed, envious old men in bathrobes and slippers whose sunken mouths showed their despair over being no more than ordinary dying old men.

:

They checked Walt into the hotel and had dinner there that evening with Father Mann—an old priest with a heavy, drooping head and an apologetic smile—and a writer introduced as a "special friend of the Church," a well-fed young man who did not take notes but listened to their conversation as if he were recording it. "Your father has concentrated his life upon Christ and the passion of Christ," the priest told them gently. They were at dinner, eating perfunctorily; an odor of baked fish rose about the table. "It was for this reason that he wanted to come to St. Jerome's. We know the unhappiness this caused—you felt that a man's children should take care of him in his old age. All this is true, true," he said, nodding, as Walt remembered the shrill quarrels that had shot back and forth from child to child, nervous refutations of earlier remarks, or accusations, insistences upon love, duty. No one had really wanted him since all were afraid of him, and yet all—except Walt—had wanted him desperately and viciously, afraid to surrender him to anyone else. "All this is true ordinarily, but you have always known that your father is no ordinary man. The miracle of his faith, the physical miracle, is but a symptom —you understand. A sign, a manifestation of inner faith. Here at St. Jerome's he was able to withdraw as far as possible from the world; he could contemplate Christ and the bitter crucifixion of Christ without having to return, except incidentally, to the world. . . ."

"He never recognized the world," Walt said.

"Never recognized it?" The reporter leaned forward.

"Never recognized it, yes, a good expression," Father Mann said slowly. "Perhaps he spoke of his faith to you? Yes, he is a saintly man, a holy man—by contrast with us who are secular," he added carefully. "It's believed, you may have heard, that the manifestation of Our Savior's wounds came to him earlier than last year. As long as three years ago. . . . One of the nurses has told us she remembered your father falling sometime during Holy Week and suffering headaches, but of course nothing was suspected, nothing supernatural. And last year the wounds appeared unmistakably, on both hands, his feet, in his side; they bled slightly for about three hours on Good Friday but your father did not seem to regain consciousness until Sunday morning. He came back to us as if from a great distance, and the wounds faded. . . . A miracle." The old man looked moved by his own words; his jaw had begun to tremble finely. A small piece of fish, newly cut from the rest, lay cooling on his plate. "Except for the miracle of the Mass there's never been anything like it, in my life— Never so clear a sign of God's love, so obvious a blessing. The sharing of Christ's suffering by a human being, an ordinary man—this will be acclaimed as a miracle, this will be a lever for conversion and strengthening of faith all over the world."

"But why today? Why has it happened today?" Clara interrupted.

"God's time is not necessarily our time," the priest said coldly.

There was a long, intricate quarrel over the check, but Walt, who excused himself to head for the bar, did not notice who won. In the half-deserted lounge he sat at a small table in the rear, grateful for the dark. His eyes had begun to sting. He drank slowly, while the yawning bartender read through a newspaper, turning the pages noisily in the lurid red glow from a neon sign. A little after ten, Clara joined him. She had changed from the suit to a dark wool dress; gold jewelry tinkled about her wrist. "I'm going to try to make it with them for six o'clock services," she said, "but I couldn't sleep just now, I don't want to take more pills. . . ." She chattered on with the nervous coquettish energy that Walt had always pitied, knowing it must end slumped before a dressing table mirror, nose a little shiny, powder smeared subtly by perspiration, lips heavy. She skipped from topic to topic, person to person, circling but steadily nearing the center of their worlds, the accident that bound them there together, at a small cheap-surfaced table in this dreary lounge— "I'm afraid that this will injure him," she said seriously. Her innocence alarmed Walt. "You mean you don't think he's suffering?" Walt asked. "Suffering? Suffering?" Clara murmured, looking in her purse for something. In the dull red light she looked suddenly young; she allowed him the calculated impact of her simplicity. "Why, yes, he's suffering . . . some. . . . That's part of it, I've done some reading and I was talking to the Mother Superior, she" . . . "But how does he suffer?" Her fingers paused inside her purse. Walt could see a tangle of objects, silver and gold, leather, the neat oval gleams of Clara's enameled nails. "Like Christ," said Walt with a grin. But Clara had begun to retreat. She took out a compact, opened it, and looked at herself dutifully, licking her lips; then she snapped it shut and replaced it. Her expression had the look of assurance that comes from having just been checked in a mirror. "But I hope it doesn't injure him so that he's different, so that he doesn't know us any more," she said. "I've been up to see him, Walt, more than anyone, once a month, and he's so remote—always so remote—I could hardly talk to him. Oh, he wasn't impolite; you know Father, he's incapable of hurting anyone. . . . But he was so distracted that I felt later he wouldn't remember I had come. Or he wouldn't remember who had come." "Then why do you come to see him?" said Walt. "Because I love him," Clara said. "But why do you love him?" said Walt. "Because I love him," Clara said sharply. "He's our father." They sat in silence for a while. Walt noticed a waitress with silver-blond hair uplifted and ballooning over the top of her head. She teetered skillfully on high heels. "I can't bear to think of anything happening to him," Clara went on apologetically. "Anything to change him. What if he forgets? I can't sleep sometimes, or I wake up at night, thinking—what if he forgets me? Because I've always waited for him—I've always thought he might— Well, he might tell me something," she said, confused, "he might talk about home, when we were children, or he might ask me how I am, what my life is now— How could I have ever given everything over to some other man, some stranger, when—I thought he might tell me something, some secret about myself." They stared in embarrassment at each other. The kinship between them was so strong that Walt, to control his sudden nervousness, had to light a cigarette. "Do you understand?" Clara said. "Do you understand?"

Around three that morning, unable to sleep, Walt thought of calling his wife—his ex-wife—and had picked up the receiver, was dreamily awaiting the outside line, when he saw his reflection in the bureau mirror like a policeman popped up to accuse him: it was always a surprise to see that he was no longer really young; that last year between twenty-nine and thirty must have exhausted his youth. He had black hair, cut close against his head so that it looked like a cap, giving him an appearance of innocence—jocularity. His eyes, which were drooping like his brother Tom's, belied any innocence; they took in most things, including themselves, without enthusiasm. Yet he had a gift for irony, and if he prized it rather too much—if he sought in himself an academic salvation through it—it was because there was nothing else for him, really nothing. He had never believed in himself, any more than he had believed in the world: alien shapes, lines, colors, conversation, toothed smiles that convey whole dialogues, patterns of living, even passion— all had drifted by his sight with the watery instability of distractions in dreams, mere trifles to divert the mind from its true object. But what was this object? He had never been able to discover it, as his father so easily had; and perhaps it was only after struggle, relinquishing a part of their heritage, that his brothers had blinked away the glorious threat of this ideal and had surrendered to the complex material charms of the world. For these charms were complex and frightening, it was no coward who succumbed to them. Walt could appreciate the courage it took to sink oneself in the world, in the ponderous ways, yet he could not make the leap—any more than he could make the leap to the pleasant ghostly universe his father inhabited, gentlemanly man! He saw his fright in the mirror before he felt it: the telephone was speaking to him. "No, sorry, I've changed my mind." He put the receiver back. And he felt, then, half smiling at the telephone, that he had, indeed, escaped—a clever escape —and that his father, if he had known, would have been pleased.

Walt woke after eight, feeling drugged, and drove alone up to St. Jerome's. The air was cold, there was no hint of spring; slivers of ice lay in the ditches. Cars were already in the parking lot, and about the damp front steps groups of people stood, families, breathing in the cold air. A young man with an acne-ravaged face and a maroon scarf approached Walt. "You are a member of the Turner family?" he said. "No," said Walt. Evidently they were waiting for the doors to be opened. He looked around at the mild faces, country people like domesticated animals, calmed by impending excitement. Some, older women, were saying rosaries to themselves. Walt heard

the man with the scarf and another man, who wore a
hat, talking behind him. "Supposed to be an inside story,"
one said. "Born without eyes, the skin just growing over.
Radiation poisoning. It's going to break in a week." "Is
this the same one, the one in California?" the other said.

The meek crowd moved along up the wide stone steps,
watching their feet. Inside, the building was gleaming
with cleanliness: the floor shone, windows shone in the
brittle light, the nuns' shoes, when they peeked out from
beneath the heavy brown skirts, were polished a shiny
black. Walt met his sister Carolyn upstairs. She took his
arm. "They've put Father in another room, in the sun
porch," she whispered. Her face was pale and not very
pretty: she had sacrificed lipstick for Good Friday. "He
knows us, Walt. He knows us." Her whisper became
throaty with triumph; Walt felt her shiver. "The tourists
are here," Walt said brutally. "They're downstairs." "The
audience of the faithful," Carolyn said, as if reading a
sign on the wall. Walt looked up: there was a sign there,
but it said NO SMOKING.

When he entered the antiseptic-smelling room—which
was crowded quietly in the background—Walt understood
that he had been preparing for this meeting for months.
Carolyn urged him on as his heart thudded, and, yes,
there was his father—no stranger after all, but his father,
their father, familiar man!—that face leapt to Walt with
the serenity of habit, the face of Walt's dreams, day-
dreams, and nothing in him protested as he approached
the bed and sank to his knees on the tiled floor. . . . Was
he supposed to pray? He supposed it was proper to pray
a little, to mutter harmlessly, and to cross oneself; he
crossed himself with care. He peered up at his father,
who did not seem to notice him. There the old man lay,
real as life! Weight gone out of his chest; his cheeks
sunken (as if the stubborn rotted old teeth had finally
been pulled); his face was pale, mottled slightly, mild,
peaceful, charmed with itself or with this blessing, his
eyes fastened upon something in the air, his throat quiver-
ing as if sustaining an inaudible dialogue. White, frail
hair, that of a professional old man; and arms poking

out of bony shoulders, narrow as rods, hands turned upward to catch the precise gleam of bright spring air from the great windows on the side wall—palms covered with blood! Beneath them, on a paper-thin bluish plastic sheet that protected the bedclothes, little beads of blood. Walt felt a queer, half-pleasant paralysis, his legs were dead, his eyes fastened themselves greedily upon that shining blood and—to be recalled later with shame— he drew in a breath, slowly, sniffing to catch the odor of blood, legitimate blood. He smelled only antiseptic. "But the feet," he wanted to cry, "and the bleeding side— where are they? If I don't see them I won't believe!" But he simply got to his feet, allowed Carolyn to lead him away. He thought he was smiling, grinning, but the family, the nuns, the strange men looked at him tenderly, with understanding.

The phenomenon continued throughout the day, the old man in a trance, and several hundred frightened visitors were allowed, singly, in the room to drop to their knees, pray, stare, and leave; but the bleeding did not abate, neither that evening nor the next day, and the audience of the faithful continued. There was an alarming swell on Saturday afternoon. Walt waited out these hours at the hotel, in the lounge, reading newspapers about the miracle at St. Jerome's, which the Church, though refusing comment, was viewing "with benevolent interest." There were side articles about other miracles, most of them in Italy, one in southern France. Opinions of doctors, who were baffled, opinions of other authorities, one of them—Walt read with anger—who attributed the bleeding to psychosomatic blisters! Walt did not see his brothers and sisters, they were at the home, near the old man, so he began to mutter to himself as he drank. Sometimes his mind, jolted naked by the insanity of this experience, called for flight, escape: if he did not escape soon he would be doomed. He forgot to eat and the inertia of half-pleasant nausea overtook him. On Saturday afternoon he was sick off and on for hours, waiting patiently on the edge of the bathtub, then he drank a little more until dinner. He came upon Ronald in the hotel lobby: Ronald looked aged, his hair had fallen loose about his forehead. But he smiled and gripped Walt's shoulders passionately. "He knows us!" he said. "The way he looks when we kneel by him—when you knelt too, did you see it? He recognizes us!"

Walt woke the next morning, oddly relaxed. Then he remembered that it was Sunday; all was over. Resurrection. He felt drained, pleased, his stomach ached with hunger. Perhaps his father would die before next Easter. Perhaps he would die. He ordered breakfast from room service, showered, shaved, hung out the door looking for someone familiar—saw no one—saw, out the window, people dressed for Easter Sunday, resplendent in the sunshine. On an impulse he opened the window, grunting. There was a sound of remote bells.

He ate ravenously—eggs fried in butter, bacon, toast with jelly of two sorts, grape and apple. Cups of hot coffee, sweetened with cream. He watched the food lovingly as he ate, later he brushed his teeth and watched himself in the mirror with approval, then he dressed himself with a sense of pleasure and freedom: some catharsis had taken place after all, the miracle had touched him. He sped out of town to St. Jerome's, which jutted out of the earth in a glory.

The foyer was radiant with lilies. Walt passed them, through the aisle they bounded, frail white proud things that had blossomed out of the nursing home air itself. He exchanged greetings with young nuns, with strangers, men and women decked in fine warm clothes, little girls in patent leather shoes. It occurred to him, ascending the stairs for the last time, that he had not yet thought about his father—facing him now would be more difficult than facing him on Friday; when he was transfigured, another person, what did one say to such a being? But the Sunday air buoyed him, cheered him. Doors were opened upon domestic scenes—families sitting around beds, around old men in wheel chairs. Radios played, television sets were on. By one doorway a pile of breakfast dishes, plate smeared with hardened egg, were set carelessly on the floor—such was the vagabond holiday mood of Easter!

But the door to his father's old room was closed, locked, and Walt wandered on, puzzled, down the corridor to the sun porch . . . which was blocked off by bureaus and bedframes dragged down from the attic, surely, and seeing this, Walt's blood seemed to slow. There were his brothers standing by a railing, looking down over a stairway, smoking. And Carolyn on a leather couch, legs crossed and stockings straining with muscle—legs nearly as girlish as ever. Ronald came up to Walt gravely. "Well, have you heard? It isn't over." "Isn't over?" Walt said. He saw immediately, in his mind's eye, a calendar; perhaps there was a confusion of dates. "The bleeding hasn't stopped," Ronald said, looking significantly at Walt. Walt wanted to say, "God's time is not necessarily man's time," but Ronald was so frightened—so *disappointed*—that Walt only stared abruptly down at his feet, as if something had dragged his gaze that way. "No one knows what's wrong," Ronald said. "Clara's in there with him, they can't get her to leave. It's been hell, Walt, you don't know—we think Clara might be—might need— You're so goddamned lucky, aren't you, off in your corner when things get tough!" Ronald's sickish face was puffy and distorted, like that of a bulldog. "Leave us to worry about it like you've always done!"

Walt pulled away and approached Ronald from another side, as if executing a dance step; this seemed to work. "What have they done about it? Do the newsmen know?" he whispered. "It's been kept a secret," Ronald said. "They expect it to stop soon. Today. For God's sake why hasn't it stopped? It's only supposed to bleed a few hours on Friday." "Is he in pain?" said Walt. But Ronald shrugged his shoulders. "Money couldn't get him any better care. I've got to get started back, my wife called, she's worried as hell," he said, "and if Art wants a ride, and Carolyn and. . . . The responsibility of it. . . . Could you take Clara home? It's sure to stop today, it started earlier and maybe that's why it kept on longer." "How's Clara?" said Walt. "Oh, God, Clara . . . You remember the time she ripped some evening dress with her heel, putting it on? The same thing . . ." "Does he talk?" said

Walt. "Yes, he talks," Ronald said abruptly. "Art," he said, holding out his arm, "what time do you have?"

Walt stared at the closed door. He felt dizzy, isolated. Everything spun away from him, even time: here he was back on Friday again, forced to enter that door, approach that bed, kneel, cross himself, sniff at the blood. . . . He argued gently with a nun who came at him out of nowhere, was admitted, saw with shock Clara's disorderly figure jerking to its feet as he entered the room. And there was his father in bed, the same position! Nothing had changed except that the room was empty now of people, filled sweetly with lilies. Clara, on the other side of the bed, stared resentfully across at Walt. The old man was covered now with a brown blanket—lovingly darned at one corner by a solitary, smiling old nun—his hands still out, though bandaged thickly, face propped up against the pillows. There was a small metal crucifix propped up against a fold in the blanket. The old man squinted at Walt as he approached. The room was silent; only from afar could they hear the pleasant muffled sounds of televisions, conversations, children's cries. At the bedside Walt saw the old man's lips move. Walt stared, transfixed, he awaited his name . . . the old man said something but Walt's ears were deafened by blood, he had to stoop like a little old man himself and say, "I didn't hear." The old man's throat quivered and the lips moved again. "I hurt," he said. Walt, still bent, stared at nothing—at the pillow. "I hurt," his father said again.

Walt stared. Again he felt the sensation of being alone, of being lost, as if ordinary time and the ordinary people it involved had been sucked violently away from him; even Clara, ravaged by despair, looked on without involvement or comprehension. It was at that moment, judging finally that old, handsome, dying face, that Walt understood what had happened to his father. Safe in his old age, before that safe in his tranquility, he had refined himself out of life—he had had, so easily, six children; he had given them nothing, not his own identity, not identities of their own, he had not distinguished one from the other; he had moved as a ghost among the mild, ghostly illusions of this world as a young man and, now, an old man; he had never been a man; and he was being educated now in the pain of being human. "Why, this is a punishment," Walt said at once, almost laughing at the surprise of his discovery. "This isn't a blessing, who told you that? This is a punishment. A punishment." He looked up: Clara stared with hatred at him. And his father, was that not a sly look, sly and knowing behind the wincing pain? "You're being punished!" Walt cried.

There were others around him, nurses, and a man he had not seen before; they propelled him around. "A punishment! Or a penance—your word for it!" he shouted into the face of one of the nuns. *"He* knows! Ask *him!"* he said, jerking around to point with his jaw back at the old man. At the opened door they scuffled, Walt looked around again at the bed. Tears burned his eyes. "Punishment that you deserve! Goddamn selfish old bastard, now you're getting it! God's on the right track! Got your number—never loved us, did you? Took all our love from us and—" They had pushed him out the door but he continued, laughing, seeing the faces of his brothers rush toward him— "Took it and kept taking it, a goddamn sewer! a drain! down a toilet, anything we gave you! Now you're getting it good!—He is, he's getting it good," Walt was crying at his brothers, "he's lying in there and told me how he changed his mind and doesn't want the miracle any more, he told me it with his eyes, he says he hates God, hates Christ, says Christ had it easier than he does, if there was a real Christ—which he doubts! Told me it with his eyes!" He felt a sharp pain through his sleeve—a needle? He spun around and grabbed something—the doctor's jacket—and with rage borne out of revenge for his father, for the joke played upon him, began to tear violently. Tears spilled out over his face, onto his own threshing hands.

Walt was not allowed in St. Jerome's again, so he waited down at the hotel, in his room, lying on his rumpled bed. He found out that Ronald and Art had gone— that was Monday afternoon. No change in his father. He

tried to get in touch with Carolyn but there was never
anyone in her room, his notes were never answered. . . .
On Wednesday he paid part of his hotel bill, aware that
the management was suspicious of him; he paid with a
check that was worthless, but they would not know that
immediately; he was elated with his own cunning. But as
if to give him away, his hands trembled as he made out
the check. Upstairs he waited the hours away, lying on
his bed. He forgot to drink. His eyes grew sore as if
weakening from disuse. On Thursday he understood the
peculiar inertia, the heavy calm that had dulled his brain
for so long, when he was told of his father's death.

A professional-looking stranger who had knocked
gently, whose eyes, in spite of the message of gravity to
be given, could not help but wander about the smelling,
cluttered room. If there were toast crusts on the floor there,
those eyes would seek them out! The stranger spoke
gently to Walt. "He managed to get out of the room
during the night and found his way down to the visitors'
rest room, the men's room, the room by the stairs. . . .
Strips of sheet he tore from his bedclothes—did harm to
himself— If you'd like to get dressed and come with me—
He was found in the morning—" Walt lay on the bed, his
legs outstretched. Though he had heard only part of the
man's speech, he could see his father's skinny body dan-
gling in the air as clearly as if the old man had hanged
himself in the hotel closet, pushing the hangers to one side.
Walt felt neither surprise nor relief. "Did the bleeding
stop, then?" he said. "Your father was out of his mind with
the pain, he wasn't responsible for what he did," the man
said. "My father was responsible for what he did," Walt
said with dignity.

The man waited for him outside. Time went slowly, it
took time to dress. He ran his razor, dry, over his jaw,
lost interest, turned around in the white cramped bathroom as if looking for something—forgot what it was—
The white walls blurred and dazzled his vision; a roaring
began in his ears. What legacy had his father left him?
His father had recognized him! He had known him, had
talked to him—he had left him a legacy of death, spiteful

death, but a work of art! Walt turned his palms up close to his face and stared at them. No blood. Nothing. No marks, no scars, no hints of anything, not even blisters. Clean as a life never quite lived. There were wrinkles there, and hints of soft, blue veins beneath, far beneath, pinkish-gray skin that looked, upon examination, more like wood than flesh—the same hands he remembered looking at, idly, one day as a child, as if those innocent palms might tell him something about the life to come.

The Survival of Childhood

After class, Carl Reeves was accompanied by the student with the well-fed voice who had contributed most to that day's discussion of poetry. The young man, conscious of the dignity and value of words, delivered his sentences like rounds of ammunition. They walked down the hall together, the professor tall and rather gaunt, the student soft, round, amiable: Carl thought they must look like a parody of companions, or brothers, making their way through the throngs of students, bound together by a single interest. "The question of the meaning of life," the student murmured. Carl knew that if he were to glance at the student he would find the boy's eyes, shrewd behind his glasses, cast downward out of respect for the genius of Shakespeare. "Yes. It is a very profound question. And man's insignificance in the universe— That too."

"Yes," Carl said automatically. He had approached the department mailboxes and now he saw that there was something in his box, a letter. "Excuse me," he said. The student waited uncertainly while Carl took the letter out of his small, dusty box. His lips opened at once with surprise.

The letter was from his brother Gene. As he opened it impatiently, visions of unhappiness and destruction crowded his mind—fires, deaths, his father fallen with a stroke, his brother Gene maimed in a fight, the old house itself in which he and his five brothers and sisters had been born finally collapsing in, burdened by the incredible weight of time and suffering. His eye automatically scanned the letter for certain key words, signals of disaster, but found none.

It began with a large HELLO CARL.

The old bastard runs the store fell down the other night and broke his hip; now I take turns sitting with him, his wife sniffing and moaning around and crashing dishes together in the kitchen. The store is the same. We got more room for the POST OFFICE part now, a whole counter. If you write a letter I will get it right away, on account of handling the mail like I am.

Ma is the same. Pa though aged a lot. When you were here last Christmas he was just beginning a long bad cold. He ain't really got over it yet, and it almost November now. What the hell. A sonbitch kitten crawled in under the well cover & fell in & drowned. In town they got a new entryway for the HIGH SCHOOL, of red brick.

Maybe you remember a certain girl was asking of you. She had: dark hair worn up on her head, probably with some kind of twist of something in back, but I can't remember.

Say hello to your wife. I hope all is well. Ma & Pa say hello too.

Gene

Carl was annoyed at his trembling. But his brother had never written him before, had never spoken to him in any but the most perfunctory, indifferent way since they had grown up. The letter was a shock, a mystery.

"Dr. Reeves?"

The student edged toward him. "Really, Mr. Dwyer," Carl snapped, making no effort to conceal his irritation, "can't you see I'm busy?" The rebuff landed on the student's face, spread itself out visibly in all directions, slumping his shoulders, hollowing his chest, giving his

legs a loose, shuffling look. He hurried away. Carl put
the letter in his pocket and went down to his office.

Gene was the youngest of the children, four years
younger than Carl himself, and he had always evoked
in his parents and brothers and sisters fierce conflicts of
love and hate. When Carl thought of him—and he did
think of Gene often—there came to his mind not the blunt
bored expression with which Gene had endured the
previous Christmas, but a child's expression, a child's
face. Of course Gene had never really outgrown his child's
face: a look of measured simplicity, innocence, which
probably hid only vacuousness. Gene was the wild boy,
the one relatives talked of sadly, familiarly, as if he were
not (as everyone sensed) dearer to them because of his
wildness. But he, Carl, had beaten him finally—beaten
the wild boy, the loved boy, the boy who had, on that
cold morning some twenty years ago, stared silently at
Carl while the sheer sharp crack of the rifle shot still
hung in the air, vibrating and ringing about them. Carl
lowered the rifle, tears of ferocity came to his eyes. "I
was shooting at the trunk. The old trunk," he had cried.
In his mind, soaked with the heavy damp mist of that
morning, he insisted the old tree trunk had stood alone,
waiting for him, and only after he squeezed the trigger
blindly did his brother's face appear—pale and poised
and silently astonished—between him and it. "I was
shooting at the trunk. You stupid fool, stupid fool," Carl
cried furiously. "You want to get yourself kilt? Do you?"
Gene, about nine but runty for his age, stared vacantly
at Carl; he had pulled off one of his mittens—red mittens
their mother had knitted—and wiped at his eyes with his
bare, grimy fingers.

Later, at breakfast, Carl's hot oatmeal tasted like
scum in his stale mouth, sticking to his teeth, his tongue,
gathering hot and hard in his stomach. Across the table,
nudging elbows with an older sister in the perfunctory,
perpetual, almost impersonal conflict of childhood, Gene
sat eating, licking his spoon, moving his pink tongue
around the spoon in delight. Carl had waited and waited.
His father would whip him, maybe beat him with the

stock of the gun itself. The gun would be taken away—
given to Gene. The kitchen was filled with the sounds of
eating and arguing and chair scraping: brother and
brother, sister and sister, brother and sister, often interrupted by the impatient whine of their mother or a shout
from their big, brusque, black-bearded father, a giant of a
man who was unaware, most of the time, of the children
he had sired. Carl had waited, but Gene said nothing.
Walking the two miles to school that morning, Gene had
gone ahead with their older sister, a girl fifteen, and that
was unusual; but that was all. Neither of them ever
spoke of the incident again.

The memory of Gene as a child stayed with Carl that
day. It was absurd to think of having "beaten" Gene:
Gene was a country boy, he was not intelligent or sensi-
tive, he had some imagination—at one time he liked to
draw—but he was not on Carl's level. Carl had nothing
in common with his brothers or sisters. He had escaped
the curse of his family, bad luck inherited with stubborn-
ness, opaqueness, an inability or refusal to understand
the world. His father, for instance: what slow, ignorant
strength he had commanded in his youth and manhood,
what graceless cruelty, not refined by thought, he had
worked upon the helpless woman who had loved him!
Yet all his strength had burned out, come to nothing,
like lightning striking the ground and disappearing. Carl
used to think that his father had never understood the
process of human reproduction, the simple, causal chain
of action that leads to childbirth and then to ties, bonds,
responsibility; perhaps—even—love. His children were
accidents, as storms, floods, mud slides, cattle diseases,
insects were accidents: nothing more. Even now, decades
later, Carl could not think of that man, the father of his
childhood, without emotion. The old bald man who dod-
dered and wheezed around the drafty house now was
someone else; he did not matter, he did not even demand
pity.

But there were accounts unsettled. Carl was tortured
by memories of his childhood, which came to him as he
drove home through the colorless day with a sharp,

delicate pang of clarity. His life here in this expanding
industrial city, teaching grammar and literature to factory
workers' children whose hard eyes showed distrust, was
so different, so altered, from his past life, that the reality
of his link with those back-country people, with the
back-country boy he himself had been, staggered his mind.
Yet sudden memories, sudden visions, forced themselves
upon him: the old house, the well (into which a kitten
had fallen!), the tilting barn, the cornfields in which they
had worked, boys and girls alike, the sound of their
father's bellows, their father hammering out horseshoes
in the barn. Men came with their horses, sat around
spitting in the dust. Their boys came with them, fought
with Gene and Carl and Roy and Bob in the big hay
barn, throwing corncobs and green pears. Saturdays they
drove into town, the boys sitting in the back of the pickup
truck. When he was fourteen Gene had gotten into a
knife fight with one of the town boys, and Carl and his
mother had been running somewhere—one of his sisters
behind them—and they came out of the alleyway and
into the street and saw Gene, a lean, muscular, taut-faced
boy, with an expression of such viciousness, such ageless
fury, that Carl's hands had jerked upward by themselves,
to protect his face, his knowledge. . . . Gene's arm was
bleeding near his shoulder and there was dirt all over him.
Down the street a small crowd stood, a boy sobbing a
few yards in front of them. "You goddamn yellow bastard, you come down this way!" Gene had yelled madly.
He raised his knife again—an old fishing knife his father
had, inexplicably, given him instead of the other, older,
more deserving boys. "Bastard! I'll cut out your gizzard
and make you eat it!" Gene's chest had shuddered with
the violence of his breath, his feet in frayed sneakers
seemed to dance by themselves, kicking at the dirt. He's
older than I am, Carl had thought. Here he got older
than I am, and me eighteen already.

That evening Carl tried to explain his mood to his wife.
His solemn recitation to her of certain events in his past
and his desire to hear her interpretation of Gene's letter
pleased her: she often accused him of "leaving her out of

his life," of having no time for her. "But why do you think it's strange?" she said. "He just wanted to write. Isn't that natural? He says a girl was asking about you."

"Yes," said Carl. "I don't understand that. But you know Gene. . . ."

"No, I don't know Gene."

She seemed to be accusing him. Perhaps it was that he himself did not know Gene, did not have a right to speak familiarly of him. She had always resented both his family and the fact that he himself did not cherish them, rarely spoke of them. In the days of their courtship Carl had told her about his escape from the deep country, his ascendency from hell: Julie, eager to please at that time, had been sympathetic. Yet even then she must have been startled by his hatred of his family. Their own failure to have a child, the first of their many strange, vague failures, had since set between them barriers of a sort that could not, even in moments of sudden intimacy, be conquered. Where had that early, sympathetic Julie gone? And, behind her, the old memories of Carl's family and their big creaking house, the dirt roads lined with wheat, the hot blue skies, his blustering father, silent mother, his brother Gene gulping down breakfast on the day he was to run away from home, his face breaking out into smiles—where had all these visions gone?

"We'll drive up to see them," Carl said impulsively. "Next weekend."

"Yes. If you want to," his wife said slowly.

"He might want help. Why else would he write?"

"Help?" said Julie. "You think he wants help? Gene? From you?"

Her words stung. She must have sensed the old rivalry between him and his younger brother. It might have existed about the house, breathed into the musty, damp air, that Christmas they had spent there several years before. An ugly, tedious visit: Gene had been abrupt, as if he knew that Carl's reasons for returning were to shock his wife with the poverty of his family and to enjoy a strange mixture of self-pity and relief at having escaped. But he had been charming to Julie; he had talked to her of his brief career teaching high school. Most of the time, however, he was out with his friends— men like himself, unmarried, between the ages of twenty-five and thirty—and Carl and Julie had to talk to Carl's parents and brothers and sisters who dropped in, strangers from outlying districts of the world.

They made plans to drive up the following weekend; these were displaced by an invitation to dinner, and automatically resumed for the next weekend; but as the days passed, both understood they would not be going. It was about a month after Carl received Gene's letter that he looked up in response to a rap on his opened door and saw his brother standing there.

Carl got to his feet. He could feel his heart begin to pound absurdly. "Come in, Gene," he said. "Please. This is a—such a surprise. You might have let me . . ."

Gene, now twenty-nine, still had his child's face, but it was, Carl saw shrewdly, altered by something—not necessarily age—and had taken on an expression of savage, perplexed vitality. Gene was not a tall man, but his compact leanness and his oddly formal blue eyes had always suggested great confidence in his own strength, his own charm. His hair was white-blond, worn too long as usual; he looked alien and threatening in the familiar doorway of Carl's office. "You're a bastard not to answer me," he said.

"What's wrong?" said Carl.

Two girls passed in the hall and stared at Gene, at his faded overalls and dirty plaid jacket. Carl said, "We'll leave here. All right? I know a place where we can talk."

The dingy little tavern faced the railroad tracks, looking out on a gray, colorless, rust-ornated expanse of metal and dried weeds and junked machines. Carl's shirt and tie, the professional stamp of his suit, evoked silent scorn in the bartender and the two men who sat at the bar and perhaps in Gene as well. They sat in a back booth and drank beer for a while. Carl studied his brother closely. Gene was in command of himself as usual; even the movements of his hands, his fingers, addressed themselves to an assumed admiration in Carl.

So Gene had always addressed himself to admiration, to envy, and to love in others: Gene in school, pompous in his hard worn triumph over the boys, his teasing of the big girls, his understanding of their excitement. "So?" Carl said.

Gene licked his lips. "So? What about the girl?"

"Girl?"

The brothers watched each other suspiciously. "The girl I wrote you about! Goddamn it, you never answered. What a bastard you are, after all, all that education you got yourself!"

"But what girl? What do you mean?"

"The one in the dream," Gene said. "Ah, hell. Wait." He lit a cigarette fiercely. "The one I wrote you about. Asking if you remembered her."

Carl found himself imitating his brother's coarseness. "No," he said. "I don't remember her. So what?"

"I'm in some trouble," Gene said.

They stared at each other. "Another girl?" said Carl.

"It's not what you think," Gene said. "Look. Don't laugh at me?"

"I won't laugh, Gene."

"I got some trouble, somehow," Gene said. "It's a god-damn thing. I'm not that kind of person, really. You know. Sure I feel sorry for bastards got to cough their guts out from working in the mines up there—sure—and them spindly-backed wives of theirs, and their skinny children. Who the hell wouldn't? None of it's changed at home—from when you were there, I mean. Other things change—for instance you—but not that." Gene smiled, shrugged his shoulders. "You remember old Taylor's barn on fire that time, the horse burning to death? How old were we? And how I would get that mixed up in my mind later, where I was the horse. In dreams now and then." He looked at Carl suspiciously. "You don't think I'm crazy, do you?"

"Of course not," said Carl. If anyone from that wretched family would go crazy it would not be Gene but Carl himself—Carl with his early, neurotic sensitivity, his awe and fear of the world. Gene had always faced matters simply, blandly. "You don't have the right kind of mind for it," he said.

Gene seemed to accept this. "Sure," he said. "I know. But still, I got this trouble. You know how I had some bad times, the two years I was away from home— We never talked about it much; you were in college then. I guess we weren't too close. For brothers, I mean." Carl felt oddly touched by this. "Well, we never talked the way we ought to," Gene said. "We were the closest out of the family, I mean out of the rest of them, but still— still—we never talked. I could have told you some things."

"What sort of things?"

"Things I did, things that happened to me." He fell silent. Carl was afraid that he had forgotten what he was about to say. Then he glanced up. "This thing now. . . ."

"What is it?"

"Just a dream. A dream about a girl."

"But what is it?" Carl said, leaning forward. "What is it, that it bothers you so?"

"I had the dream a while before I wrote you. I didn't spose it would do any good, to write. In the dream there's a girl—a woman. It starts off with me somewhere, waiting, and a kind of fog around, the way it is in dreams; and she starts coming toward me, a shadow, but blown up so I can see her head. Just the shadow of her head."

"What about it?" said Carl.

"What about it?" said Gene. "Goddamn it, I had that dream for weeks! Do you know what that's like? A nail got inside your head!" He stared hatefully at Carl. "You never dream things like that, do you, you with your goddamn education!"

"I'm sorry," Carl said. They sat for a while without speaking. Then Carl cleared his throat. "So it's worse now?"

"Hell, yes," Gene said. "And you don't know her? Who it could be?"

"Is the dream still the same?"

"It's closer—she's closer now," Gene said. "I don't have it every night. I don't want it but I look forward to it—I'm excited about it— I can't think of much else.

I'm afraid of it but I wait for it. She's a little clearer now. I spose before long I'll be able to see who it is."

"One of your girls, maybe," Carl said.

"No," said Gene. "I don't think so. Though I was a bastard about them. . . . Well," he said, finishing his beer, "thanks for listening. I got to get back."

"You're staying for dinner, aren't you?"

"Hell, no," said Gene. He drummed on the table, his eyes drifted past Carl as if he had forgotten him. "I got to get back. They've got a nutty thing going about robbers, expecting them to come out of the woodwork. There was a robbery the other week, a woman and two kids killed. A bum, I guess, along the highway." He pursed his lips. "Anyway, I'm not crazy. You believe that."

"Sure," said Carl.

"I'm not getting—you know—queer."

"No."

They waited. Carl wanted to say more, wanted to thank Gene for this confused, weak appeal. But when he did speak it was to say something entirely unexpected. "But you don't want to go to a doctor?"

"A doctor?" said Gene. He looked frightened. "No—no— It would cost too much, and I don't think—A doctor couldn't help it."

"I suppose not," said Carl.

That evening Carl discussed the matter with his wife. "We were never close. Yet we were close—in a way. Sometimes he'd draw all day long with charcoal or crayon, and I liked to watch. I was probably a little jealous. I thought he was good at drawing but I don't know now, probably he was nothing special. I was a little jealous of him. . . . Later on, when he was about twenty, he was able to get a job teaching art in high school. They had just begun offering art courses; it was something new. There was a period when he did nothing but water colors, the same scenes over and over again— I remember one of our fishing places down by the creek. He told you about the job, didn't he? How he was fired? One of the girls

kept bothering him and then she made up some story—
it got all around— She said—"

"I know. I don't want to hear it again," Julie said.

Carl went on, a little loudly, "Anyway, I never heard
his side of it. Or much about what he did the two years
he was away. I wanted to know but I never wanted to
ask him. He looked different when he came back—of
course he was older, but— It's a strange thing to have a
brother. The relationship is strange."

His wife smiled. "And to have a wife?" she said.

"Yes, yes, that too," Carl said vaguely. But his mind
had drifted to other matters. At thirty-three he was aware
of, had adjusted to certain inadequacies in himself. His
childhood had turned his gaze inward, limiting it, wisely,
to that small sphere within which lay the potentiality of
his success, and he had not been deluded, as his mother
had, by mythical bonds of responsibility and selflessness
that would have drained his energy, distracted his vision
of himself. He had recognized as a child the terrible iso-
lation of the self-conscious individual within a world of
complex links—of relationships of blood, of emotion, of
economic accident; he had recognized the hollowness
within these links, the illusions that sustained them. Sitting at the old round table, chewing their food, his family
had been held together by a terrific force—what could
it have been? Why had they not flown off in all directions,
hurled apart, lost to one another in the vast depths of the
world? The boy whose dark eyes moved from one strange
face to another, identifying and resisting identification,
felt the mockery of their blood bondage so strong that
he had to resist throwing his head back and laughing
wildly, insanely, so causing his father's fierce black eyes
to turn upon him. . . . The memory was very strong. Now
Carl stared at his wife: she was leafing through the telephone book, her head bowed. Her hair had been combed
back behind her ears, giving her a careless, dowdy look,
though she was not yet thirty.

She looked up as if she felt his gaze. She smiled.
"What are you thinking of?"

"Nothing," Carl said. "Nothing important."

He did not so much resent as feel guilty over her frequent pleas—so determinedly casual—for entry into the privacy of his mind. They had shared eight years together, but he had spoken long before their marriage of the final, secret area of experience and of dreaming that each of them would preserve, that the other must not try to violate. His married friends had warned him of the occasional loneliness in love, the inexplicable loneliness in even a good marriage. Discovering it, he had not been, like Julie, surprised or hurt. But he had not felt the loss of that ghostly child as she had. Dinners had ended, broken up, by her shrill rising voice, demanding of him the admission of his final lack of concern—his lack of despair, his failure to share her despair. Carl had not had the cowardice to lie. He could not follow her to despair, to grief over an anonymous child, a never-to-be-born product of their bodies and their love: he could not exactly share the agonized horror of that cry, that relentless familiar cry, as Julie felt, in whatever room, out of his sight, the first hot seeping of blood in her loins. He said now, "I was just thinking of Gene."

She was visibly relieved at his answer.

Next weekend he drove up to the old house. He had known he would have to go, since he resisted so strongly. Filling the lonely driving hours with imagined conversations, admissions of something close to love—perhaps not love—perhaps love—he came close, at times, to understanding why he was returning at all. For some reason his brother's life was concerned. But it was more than that: he must return to them, endure them, so that he might finally be free.

When he arrived at the old house his mother met him rather quietly, as if his coming were no surprise. Gene was not home; he was "out somewhere" with his friends. "Is Pa still sick?" he said. She nodded: a small, frail woman who had been worn out years ago. "I'll find Gene first, then I'll be back," Carl said. He was shivering with excitement. "I'll be back." She smiled. To her confused mind, perhaps, Carl's sudden appearance now was no more surprising than it might have been when he was a child, obeying the summons to dinner, to bedtime, running in from the fields to the back porch. Carl saw this with sorrow. The house, with its smell of mildew and food, was disappointing; smaller than he had recalled and not so shabby, not so worthy of nostalgia. Someone had fixed the front porch. . . . "I'm glad to see you, Ma," Carl said as they embraced again. He was about to leave when he thought of something. "Let me see Gene's room, Ma. It won't take a minute."

She blinked at him. "Gene's room," Carl said. "Can I see it? I'll just—" He had started past her, but she caught his arm. She whispered furiously, "Oh, he won't let you. He won't let you." Carl stared. "I don't understand," he said. "Is Gene here after all? Is he here?" "It's locked," his mother said. Now they were conspirators and she leaned to him, whispering secretly. "He keeps it locked. He won't let me in. Cleans it himself," she said, clearing her throat angrily.

Carl saw that the door to Gene's room was indeed locked—with a barn padlock. "Why does he do this?" he said. His mother, shuffling up behind him, began tittering in a ferocious, accusing, humorless way, pointing at the lock. "Cleans it himself! Keeps his mother out!" she cried. "A boy his age!" "I'll see about this when I get back," Carl said. There was something about the lock, something about the finality of that closed door, that he did not like. He felt Gene to be in danger.

He found Gene a while later at a roadhouse on the highway. It was a small, forlorn tavern set back from the road with a broad expanse of frozen mud about it. Gene was sitting at a corner table with two other men. Carl recognized them vaguely, or recognized their families' features in their dull faces. Gene did not stand as Carl approached, but Carl could read his astonishment beneath the careful indifference of his expression. "Look who's here, come to see me off!" Gene said. His hair was wild.

"See you off?" Carl said. The men laughed and he sat with them, trying to hide his anger. He ordered a beer and faced his brother. He saw that Gene looked peculiar

—not older, but thinner, wasted. "Well, how the hell are you?" Gene said abruptly. He lit a cigarette and stared.

"It's you I'm concerned about," Carl said.

Gene shrugged. "What's the difference?" he said. "A horse afire then or going nuts now, what's the difference? It's not worth bothering about."

"I think it is," Carl said.

"It's no business of yours."

"It is my business," Carl said calmly, as if he knew what he was talking about. Gene hesitated, about to agree; then his expression changed.

"Never thought you'd drive all the way up here, just to see me off. But anyway, this makes it easier." He grinned so that Carl could see his stained teeth. "I sure as hell wouldn't of done it, if I was you. Wouldn't come near— it might be catching."

One of the men winked at Carl. "He ain't been home to supper," he said.

"I had it here," Gene said. "I'm done with eating. Makes me sick." He gulped drunkenly at his beer, as if for the look of it. "I been explaining it to these guys. I would of wrote a letter to you, but you don't answer them. I got this way when I was chased around a railroad once," Gene said, grinning. "This old guy and me, we woke up to a railroad cop coming at us with a piece of iron or something. Wham! he hits that old bastard on the head—that's the end of him! His skull got mashed in, teach him a lesson. And up I run, little Gene away from home. No cat dipped in kerosene runs faster than little Gene, let me tell you, or no rabbit tearing along in front of the dogs runs with more skill, more jumping-up-over of junk! And I run and run and never once stopped. . . ."

They all laughed uneasily. Carl made a sign for them to be quiet. He felt confused, betrayed—this trip to see Gene had turned out wrong. Instead of there occurring between them a sudden revelation of—perhaps—admiration, there was only this persistent brittle sarcasm of Gene's, apparently intended to insult him. Carl wanted to push the other men away; he wanted his brother to himself. Suddenly he felt, staring at Gene's spiteful expression, his young, ravaged face, that Gene had perhaps saved him from something. Gene had resisted, magically, a young death on that gray morning long ago; he had bloodied his face in skirmishes, initiated himself to the harsh-faced girls of the countryside, he had left home, he had returned home; he had experienced the strange events of which he had just now spoken. Carl had never known the necessity to do these things because they had been done for him.

"And the old man?" said Gene. "How'd he look to you? Nice old miserable old bastard, ain't he?"

"Pa? I didn't have a chance to see him. I came right out after you."

Gene, shaking out a match, stared at Carl with his hand frozen in mid-air. "Didn't even see him?" he said slowly. But in the next instant he tossed the match to the floor; he exhaled smoke luxuriously. "Well," he said, "you'll be wanting some sleep. You can fix up on the parlor couch for the night. The old rooms are filled with junk. You can listen to him cough tonight, like I do."

He stood swaying. Carl resisted the impulse to take hold of his arm. Outside, they argued about whether Gene should drive his car home or ride with Carl; the argument ended when Gene, quite unexpectedly, and wearily, tossed his cigarette away and got in Carl's car. They drove home in silence. When Carl hesitated at a crossroads Gene said contemptuously, "To the left! Don't make out you forgot!"

There was no light burning for them when they arrived at the house. Gene got out and stamped up the porch without waiting for Carl. Carl followed him, depressed and bewildered. Why had he come? Who had wanted him—who would have ever missed him if he had not come? He had expected some sympathy from Gene, perhaps some gratitude; but he saw now that he had made a mistake.

Inside, Gene thrust an armful of blankets at him and pointed to the couch, a sway-backed, sagging thing that had been stained with dirt and grease when Carl was still a child. Carl threw the blankets down angrily. "You self-pitying little bastard," he whispered. "Here I drive up to help you, if you need help, and I get to listen to you whine. What is it? What is this talk about going crazy, about dying? I want an answer from you."

Gene grinned at once. "You just come up to see me off!" he said.

"What are you talking about? What's wrong?"

"Look, I got to get up at six-thirty," Gene said. He stared past Carl's head. He had begun rubbing his nose, slowly and deliberately. "I ain't got time. . . . Yeah, well, okay. Okay, wait a minute." He left the parlor. Carl, trembling, heard him unlock his door. He snapped on the light and sat on the couch. When Gene returned he was holding something up before him and squinting at it. "Well, here's a picture," he said. He was calm, as if there were nothing unexplained between them. "Here. It's her." Carl took it from him: an aged photograph of a young woman, dressed in a long skirt and an old-fashioned white blouse, so white it had blurred part of the picture, with her hair pulled severely back from her face. She was pretty in a delicate, ordinary way, and Carl believed there was something familiar about her.

"But what is this?" he said.

"This is it," Gene said. "I had the dream a hundred times, maybe. It wouldn't quit. When I woke I would remember parts of it, sometimes the shape of her face, though I never really saw it in the dream. It was never more than an outline, something seen through a fog." Carl stared at him. It was incredible that his brother should speak so calmly now, when his words indicated insanity. "So. I got the idea one day that she might be in an old photograph. I don't know why. I just got the idea. So I went through Ma's junk in the attic and found it. After that the dream got clearer—I could see her eyes."

"You mean this is it? But why the hell her? Why her?"

"She's a cousin of Grandma's. Ma's mother. She's buried out there with the rest of them. I went out to look at the grave a few times. She had four children and she's buried next to her husband, and the four children are around them. One's a little marker—for a baby. I stayed around there a while. I thought maybe something would get clear. Then I came home."

"But what is all this?" Carl said.

"I don't know," Gene said. He took the photograph back. He dismissed it from Carl's life with a gesture. "Well. Will you be warm enough tonight? I don't feel so good; from being there so long I feel kind of sick or else we'd talk. We do have some things to talk about."

"Yes," said Carl.

"Things around home, things we've both seen and done, and people we know. We'll do that tomorrow."

They said good night seriously and formally.

The next morning at about six o'clock a single rifle shot marked Gene's death. Carl, jerking up on the couch, knew at once what had happened. He met his mother shrieking in the halls; his father—an old, old man with loose, trembling flesh—whined for help, limping around in his long underwear. When Carl opened the door he made sure that, by standing in the doorway, his parents could not push past him.

Gene lay on the bed, on his back, fully dressed, with one side of his face blown away. The old rifle he hugged to his chest, its barrel disappearing into a raw red hole at his chin. The room smelled of rifle smoke and of dampness. It was just dawn: the cold sunlight touched the steamed windows, reflecting a white, placid world. Carl stared in silence. What lay on the bed was no longer his brother, and he felt a revulsion that had nothing to do with the fact of death, or its physical horror, but attached itself to the phenomenon of change—of metamorphosis—that death had worked in Gene. He was in the presence of a stranger.

Then he saw, on the peeling walls of the room, a galaxy of faces drawn in black: what had been in the first instant of his entry a confused jumble of lines and shapes now gave way, as the cold seconds ticked by, to a queerly ordered jumble of faces that stared at him and his whimpering parents. On the uneven wall, on the dirty, peeling wallpaper, the expressionless and anguished faces of Gene's mind watched them without interest: long, angular faces of men with black holes for eyes, faces of women framed by wild, listless hair, faces of children confronting bluntly and terribly the cold dawning light of the winter morning. Their clarity was chilling—obscene— He could not look any longer. He turned away to his mother's shrieking, as if her ugly sorrow might comfort him.

After the funeral the old house was filled with visitors and relatives—sons and daughters and their own children, cousins, even one or two old, old uncles. Children ran about on the newly repaired porch, appeared crawling out of the cellar windows, tried to get into Gene's locked room. Carl's mother led him out to the kitchen. "Sit and eat," she said. The parlor hummed with excitement; she must return to it. Carl, picking at his food, sat with his eyes open and staring at the table. Things had happened too quickly for him. He had taken part in them, precipitated them, helped others to understand them; but he himself had not absorbed their meanings. He felt old and fragile, more fragile than his own father, who sat as the center of attention in the living room, dramatizing instinctively his sorrow, putting aside for the occasion his wracking cough, his shuffling, shambling whine. . . .

Carl got his coat and went outside. It was half raining, half snowing, as he drove to the store where Gene had worked. He was astonished at the squalor and dinginess of the place, about which, long ago, he and other children had played, sucking on penny candy, staring at automobiles passing on the road. The store was in an oversized stone building, murky with age, quite alone on the highway; there were the remains of a small coal yard on one side, an untended field on the other. The highway, a black-top road that sagged at either side to a turmoil of mud and ice, led off into a straight, misty, indefinite distance.

Inside, an old woman shuffled toward him in her bedroom slippers. She wore a man's old black sweater. "Yes?" she said. "Cold enough for you, mister?"

"I'm Gene's brother," Carl said.

The woman came into the light. She stared at him as if he had just confessed a crime. Her hair was gray and wispy, sticking out in small curious clumps about her aged face. Carl realized that he looked bad; he had not shaved, his clothes were rumpled, and his face—surely— was the face of a sick man.

"What do you want?" she said.

"I'll take over his job for today."

She shivered. She backed away, indicated a counter. "So it's Carl Reeves," she whispered. "Yes, yes. Yes," she sighed. "My husband is sickly and I'm here alone. Did Gene tell you to do this? He sat with my husband while I waited on women. We took turns with him. He fell on the cellar steps and hurt his hip. You know how it is with old people—with us old people." She lifted her hands helplessly.

Carl took off his coat, ran his fingers through his hair. He went behind a counter piled with clothing. The old woman too went behind a counter, ceremoniously, and faced him across the slanted, nicked glass that distorted the stale candy within. Carl felt lightheaded and absurd. He did not know what he was doing here. The woman must not have trusted him to stay here alone, or perhaps she was lonely herself. "I took care of the mail myself," she said. "Not much of it. It was like Gene to think of it, though, having you come. . . . But what a poor way to go. My own brother committed suicide," she said wearily, "but he was older, and sick, he thought he had cancer. He had little things in his throat, little bumps. He laid down across the road one night and that was how he done it."

The day passed slowly. There were few customers. Outside, the drizzle turned to mist and back to drizzle again. Carl felt he should be exhausted, but actually his perception was keen; his mind was keen, racing wildly at times, lured back into the past and the near past by a long wavering string of associations he could not control.

The coarse black mittens on the counter there, waiting coyly to be sold—for how many years?—put him in mind of something, maybe a young boy with his nose newly clean, made decent by a sly use of those mittens. Yet his sense of the present was painful and analytical, and it seemed to him that he could pursue both past and present simultaneously, that one led inexorably into the other, that he was the focal point for their meeting, he himself, and that this was somehow a matter for despair. Vaguely his wife summoned him; and he was astonished to realize how small a part of his life had been spent in marriage, how small a part of his long life belonged to the present. Tension between past and present accumulated in him. He felt old, aged, and yet this weight of mortality did not suggest peace to him—it did not even suggest that sort of comfortable, whining mortality his father had escaped to, relieved of the terrible burden of manliness and strength. His father had made it; his mother, serene in her life of trouble, had made it. This old woman's brother, lying with eyes fiercely shut on a country road, waiting for hours, perhaps, thinking who knows what thoughts of impending salvation? And Gene had made it too, though messily, blasting his good looks away, cheating worms, decay, rot, disturbing the peace of an early winter morning with the violence of his escape.

Carl thought of him now as a victim. He had been not only a victim of the world, but of the world's judgment upon him—a judgment he had accepted without question. But they had all misjudged him—neighbors, relatives, parents, Carl himself—mistaking with grim satisfaction the boy's centripetal flight, judging it ironic that Gene, out of all the family, should return home to care for his parents, instead of judging his action as admirable. Gene's nervous, savage energy had burned itself out, they supposed, again with satisfaction; and look now to what he has come! He sorts out mail in the country store! They had mobbed him, praised him, loved him, but they had not understood him. And Carl, with his self-congratulatory intellect, was most guilty. Seeing those anguished faces on Gene's wall, he had realized the depth of the occasional surface awareness in his brother, the real depth of that hint of angry sympathy, of forlorn, raging despair for the horror of life at this edge of the world.

Carl looked out the streaked front window at the rain. It fell slowly, weightlessly dissolving into the earth, so that at times it seemed to move in both directions, lifting upward, sinking downward, a phenomenon of immobility —of entropy. Carl could not feel that the view mattered much, or that anything mattered much. Automobiles and pickup trucks passed on the road occasionally, and occasionally people came into the store, stamping without haste through the rain. Farmers with big noses, burned faces, pale eyes, sometimes women in cotton scarves. They did not recognize him. What talk there was centered itself with relish upon the latest death, and already there were rumors of a girl left somewhere—unmarried—"You know how he was!" Then they would hush (the old woman must have made a complex, effective signal toward Carl's back).

So Gene had consumed enough of life, and perhaps something in the air of this old store—or of the old home—or of the countryside itself, a wilderness broken up into a long, straggling, disorderly community a hundred miles from the nearest large city, had suggested that he deserved rest, that he had earned, at twenty-nine, his final escape. He would protest this fatal sensitivity, he would denounce his vision, laugh scornfully at his susceptibility to the accustomed despair in the faces of what people he knew! He would rage at his decline, seize and hold up to the merciless morning air his illusion; but he could not exorcise it despite its folly. Perhaps the weight of the dead, the waiting dead, had stated their case so surely, so winningly, that the seducer, Gene, surrendered at last to seduction, gave up the painful and tedious suspension of his life. Well, he had made it. He had made it!

In the late afternoon Carl began his drive home. What thoughts he had were confused and unimportant, as if his mind were holding itself back, preparing itself for a final

exertion. He reached the industrial outskirts of the city
in the evening, reached home forty-five minutes later. His
wife embraced him quietly; he held her with a bitter,
savage strength. Why wasn't she surprised at his emotion?
"It isn't too late for our marriage," he said. "You'll see.
I'll make you understand." He had no reason to believe
any of this, but at the moment his words were forceful
and touching, and something in his tone, their sudden
emotion, perhaps in the night itself, went through their
hearts. Much later, lying beside her in bed, Carl woke
from a light sleep. He stared at the dim window, he tried
to remember what had happened, what he had done,
most of all what he had just dreamed. How had it begun
with Gene? A sudden dark figure in a dream, just one
shadow out of a jungle of shadows that emerge out of
one's mind, released by sleep. . . . But he did not need
to worry. He knew that. He was not capable of a dream
like Gene's, and he must not think too much about his
failure.

The Death of Mrs. Sheer

One afternoon not long ago, on a red-streaked dirt road in the Eden Valley, two men in an open jalopy were driving along in such a hurry that anyone watching could have guessed they had business ahead. The jalopy was without species: it bore no insignia or features to identify it with other cars or jalopies, but many to distinguish itself in the memory—jingling behind was a battered license plate, last year's and now five months outdated, hanging down straight from a twist of wire, and other twists of this wire (which was not even chicken fence wire, but new shiny copper wire), professional and concise, held the trunk door nearly closed and both doors permanently closed. Dirty string and clothesline laced important parts of the car together too, notably the hood and the left front fender, the only fender remaining. Though parts here and there creaked and the lone fender shuddered, everything really moved in harmony, including the men who nodded in agreement with the rapid progression of scrubland. Their nods were solemn, prudent, and innocently calculating. They looked vaguely alike, as if their original faces had been identical and a brush stroke here, a flattening as with a mallet there, had turned them into Jeremiah and Sweet Gum.

Jeremiah, who drove, was about thirty-four. He was a tall thick-chested man, with a dark beard ragged about his face and pleased-looking lips shut tight as if he had a secret he wouldn't tell, not even to Sweet Gum. His forehead was innocent of wrinkles or thought. It was true that his hair was matted and made him look something like one of the larger land animals—most people were put in mind of a buffalo, even those who had never seen buffaloes but had only looked at pictures of them. But his eyes were clear and alert and looked intelligent, especially when anyone was talking to him. Jeremiah, years ago, had passed up through all grades except seventh, his last, just by gazing at his teacher with that look and sometimes nodding, as he did now. They were approaching an old wooden bridge and Jeremiah nodded as if he had known it was coming.

Sweet Gum's throat jumped at the sight of that bridge: Sweet Gum was only twenty and had never been this far from home, except to the Army and back (he told the story that he had decided against the Army, even after they gave him supper there, because he didn't like all the niggers around). He had a fair roundish face, that of a cherub dashed out of his element and so baffled and sullen for life. His hair, bleached by the sun, grew down shabby and long on his neck, though the ridge where the bowl had been and his mother had stopped cutting was still visible, jutting out two or three inches up his head, so that he looked ruffled and distorted. He had pale eyes, probably blue, and soft-looking eyebrows that were really one eyebrow, grown gently together over his nose. His cheeks were plump, freckled, his lips moist and always parted (at night there was wet anywhere he put his head, after a while). Like his cousin Jeremiah he wore a suit in spite of the heat—it was about ninety-eight—with a colored shirt open at the throat. Sweet Gum's suit was still too big for him, a hand-down that was wearing out before he grew into it, and Jeremiah's suit, a pure, dead black, was shiny and smelled like the attic. Ever since Jeremiah had appeared wearing it, Sweet Gum had been glancing at him strangely, as if he weren't sure whether this was his cousin Jeremiah or some other Jeremiah.

They clattered onto the bridge. "Whooee," Jeremiah

laughed without enthusiasm, as boards clanked and
jumped behind them and the old rusted rails jerked up as
if caught by surprise. The bridge spanned nothing—just
dried-up, cracked ground with dying weeds—and both
men stared down at it with all their features run together
into one blur of consternation. Then Jeremiah said, "All
passed. All passed," and they were safe again.

"*God* taken hold of us here," Sweet Gum said, so
frightened by the bridge that he forgot Jeremiah always
laughed at remarks like that. But Jeremiah did not seem
to notice. "God's saving us for our promise," he muttered, so that Jeremiah could hear it or not, just as he
wanted. Back in his mind, and even coming out when
his lips moved, was the thought: "First promise to do.
First promise." If the Devil himself were to come and
take Sweet Gum out into the desert with him, or up on a
mountain, or pyramid, or anywhere, and tempt him to
break his promise to his Uncle Simon, Sweet Gum would
shout "No!" at him— "No!" to the Devil himself.

As if to mock Sweet Gum's thoughts, Jeremiah twitched
and rubbed his nose suddenly. "Christ, boy," he said, "I
got a itch— Am I going to kiss a fool all the way out
here?"

Sweet Gum turned red. "You keep your goddamn kiss-
ing to yourself!" he snarled, as if Jeremiah were no one
to be afraid of. Had the duty of fulfilling a promise already begun to change him? He felt Jeremiah's surprise
with pride. "Nobody's going to kiss *me*," Sweet Gum
said with venom.

Probably no one on Main Street in Plain Dealing saw
Jeremiah and Sweet Gum leave, though many would see
them leave for the last time a few days later. By now
Sweet Gum sat in a real sweat of anticipation, his suit
drenched and his eyes squinting past a haze of sweat as if
peering out of a disguise. As soon as the startling sign
PLAIN DEALING appeared by the ditch, Jeremiah said
quietly, "Now, I don't want no upstart rambunctiousness
ruining our plans. You remember that." Sweet Gum
was embarrassed and angry, yet at the same time he

knew Jeremiah was right. Behind Jeremiah his family stretched out of sight: all the Coke family, grandfathers and fathers, sons, cousins, brothers, women all over; it made Sweet Gum and his mother and little brother look like a joke someone had played. Of course maybe someone had played a joke—Sweet Gum's mother was not married, and through years of furious shame he had gathered that his father, whoever he was, was not even the father of his brother. *That* bothered Sweet Gum as much as not knowing who his father was.

They drove through town. It was larger than they had expected. The main street was wide and paved; at either side long strips of reddish dirt stretched out to buildings and fields far from the road. There were open-air markets for vegetables and fruit and poultry, a schoolhouse (without a flag on its flagpole), a gas station and general store and Post Office put together (groups of boys and young men straggled about in front of this building, and Sweet Gum stared at them as if trying to recognize someone), houses (all built up on blocks, perched off the ground), and, even, catching the eye of both men, a movie house—in a Quonset hut with a roof painted shiny orange and a bright, poster-covered front. Sweet Gum stared as they drove by.

Jeremiah shortly turned the car into a driveway. Sweet Gum wanted to grab his arm in surprise. "This place is where *he* stays, you found it so fast?" he said faintly. "Hell, no," Jeremiah said. "Can't you read? This is a 'hotel.' We got to stay overnight, don't we?" "Overnight?" said Sweet Gum, looking around. "You mean in a room? Somebody else's room?" "They fix them for you. You get the key to the door and go in and out all you want," Jeremiah said. He had parked the car on a bumpy incline before an old, wide-verandaed house—peeling white, with pillars and vines and two old men, like twins, sitting in chairs as if somebody had placed them there. "Why are we staying overnight? *That's* what I don't like," Sweet Gum said. "It ain't for you to like, then," Jeremiah said with a sneer. He had climbed with elastic energy out of the car and now began smoothing his suit and hair and

face. Out of his pocket he took a necktie: a precise-
striped, urban tie, of a conservative gray color. "You
ain't going to leave me, are you?" Sweet Gum said,
climbing awkwardly out of the car.

They went to the counter inside and stood with their
hands out on it, as if waiting to be fed. A middle-aged
woman with a sour face stared back at them. "No lug-
gage, then pay in advance," she said. "Pay?" said Sweet
Gum. Jeremiah jabbed him in the ribs. "How much is
it?" Jeremiah said carefully, making a little bow with
his head. "Three for the two of you," the woman said.
Sweet Gum hoped that Jeremiah would roar with laughter at this; but instead he took out of his pocket a billfold
and money, and counted it out to the woman. One dollar
bill and many coins. "Might's well sleep in the car as pay
all that," Sweet Gum muttered. No one glanced at him.
Jeremiah was staring at the woman strangely—standing
at his full height, six foot three or so—so that when the
woman turned to give him the key she froze and stared
right back at him. Jeremiah smiled, dipped his head as if
pleased. The woman withdrew from the counter; little
prickly wrinkles had appeared on her face. "Ma'am,"
Jeremiah said formally, "maybe I could put to you a
little question? As how we're guests here and everything?" "Maybe," said the woman. Jeremiah paused and
wiggled his short beard, as if he were suddenly shy.
Sweet Gum waited in an agony of embarrassment, looking at the floor. But finally Jeremiah said, rushing the
words out: "Where's *he* live? Where's *his* house?"

His words vibrated in the hot musty air. Jeremiah's
face was wet with new perspiration as he listened to them
with disbelief. The woman only stared; her lips parted.
Sweet Gum, sensing error, wanted to run outside and
climb in the car and wait for Jeremiah, but his legs were
frozen. Finally the woman whispered, *"He?* Who do you
mean, *he?* My husband? My husband's right—" "No,
hell!" Jeremiah said. "I mean *Motley.*" With a clumsy
try at secrecy he leaned forward on the counter, craned
his neck, and whispered: "Motley. Nathan Motley.
Him." "Why, Nathan Motley," stammered the woman,

"he lives around here somewheres. He— You relatives of his, back country? Why do you want to see him?"

Sweet Gum could bear it no longer. "Who says there's a why about it?" he snarled. "Why? Why what? What why? *You* said there was a why about it, we never did! We just drove into town five minutes ago! Where's there a *why* about—"

Jeremiah brought his arm around and struck Sweet Gum in the chest. Not with his fist or elbow, but just with his arm; somehow that was degrading, as if Sweet Gum were not worth being hit properly. "That'll do," Jeremiah said. The woman was staring at them. "Get outside and get the *things*," he whispered to Sweet Gum contemptuously, "while I see to this woman here, you scairt-like-any-goddamn-back-country bastard."

Outside, four or five young men of Sweet Gum's age stood around the jalopy. They had hands pushed in their pockets, elbows idle, feet prodding at lumps of dried mud. Sweet Gum, glowering and muttering to himself, walked right down to the car. They made way for him. "How far you come in this thing?" one boy giggled. Sweet Gum leaned over and got the satchel out of the car. He pretended to be checking the lock, as if it had a lock. "Going to lose your license plates back here," somebody said. "This making way to fall off. Then the cops'll get you." Sweet Gum whirled around. "Cops? What the hell do I care about cops?" He lifted his lips. The boys all wore straw hats that looked alike, as if bought in the same store. Sweet Gum had the idea, staring at them, that their deaths—if they should fall over dead right now, one after the other—would mean no more than the random deaths in a woods of skunks and woodchucks and rabbits and squirrels. Somehow this pleased him. "Ain't worrying my young head over *cops*," Sweet Gum said. He knew they were watching as he strode back up to the hotel. Someone yelled out daringly, "Backwoods!" but Sweet Gum did not even glance around.

In a tavern that night Sweet Gum had to keep going back and forth to the outside and stand trembling on the

seashell gravel, waiting to get sick; then if he did get
sick, good enough, it was over for a while; if not, he
went back inside. Each time the fresh air revived him
and made him furious at Jeremiah, who sat slouched at
the bar talking to a woman, his big knees out in opposite
directions. Sweet Gum wanted to grab Jeremiah and say
it was time they were about their business. But when he
did speak, his voice always came out in a whine: "Ain't
we going to locate him tonight? What about that room
they got waiting for us? That woman—" Jeremiah turned
away from the conversation he was having—with a strange
thick black-haired woman, always smiling—and, with his
eyes shut tight, said, "You see to your own bus'ness. I'm
finding out about *him*." "But—" "Find out some yourself, go over there," Jeremiah said, his eyes still shut,
and waving vaguely behind Sweet Gum. Then he turned
away. Sweet Gum drank beer faster and faster. Once in
a while he would sniff sadly, wipe his nose, and take out
the black cloth change purse in which he had put the
money Uncle Simon had given him for "food." Despair
touched him: had he not already betrayed his uncle by
drinking instead of eating, by wasting time here, by getting sick so that by now people laughed when he got
up to hurry outside? If he *did* have a father, maybe that
man would be ashamed of him; and what then? Sweet
Gum sometimes dreamt of this—a strange man revealing
himself to be his father, and then saying plainly that he
was disappointed in his son. A man back from the Navy,
or from a ranch farther west. Sweet Gum wanted to begin,
to go to Motley, to find him somewhere—where would he
be hiding, up in an attic? crawled under a house?—and
get it over with and return home, have his uncle proud
of him and give him the reward, and turn, in two days,
into a man. His chest glowed with the thought: he would
become a man. But his inspiration was distracted by Jeremiah's big, sweating indifferent back and Sweet Gum's
own faint, sickish gasey feeling. "Goin' outside, ain't
comin' back," he muttered, purposely low so that Jeremiah would not hear and would wonder, later, where he
was. He stumbled down from the stool and wavered

through the crowd. Someone poked him, Sweet Gum looked around expecting to find a friend, found nothing instead—faces—and someone laughed. A woman somewhere laughed. Sweet Gum's stomach jerked with anger and he had to run to the door.

When Sweet Gum woke, lying flat on his stomach in the gravel, he could tell by the smell of the night that it was late. Everything was quiet: the tavern was closed and looked dark and harmless, like an abandoned house. Sweet Gum spat and got up. A thought touched him, really a recollection; and, with sweet memories of abandoned houses, he groped for a handful of seashells and pebbles and threw them at the window nearest him. It did not break and he threw again, more energetically: this time the window shattered. Sweet Gum nodded and went out to the road.

He went back to the hotel but found the door of the room locked. He could hear Jeremiah snoring inside. Yet instead of being angry, he felt strangely pleased, even pacified, and lay down on the floor outside. As he fell asleep he thought of Jeremiah, one of his many cousins, a Coke rightfully enough—a Coke who had killed a man before he was twenty-five and whose clever talk made all the girls whoop with laughter and look around at one another, as they never did with Sweet Gum.

After breakfast the next morning Jeremiah and Sweet Gum and the black-haired woman drove in Jeremiah's car through town. The woman sat by the door, where Sweet Gum wanted to sit, and as they drove up and down Main Street she shrieked and waved and roared with laughter at people on the street. "Don't know 'em!" she yelled at someone, a man, and shrugged her shoulders high. "Never seen 'em before!" Even Jeremiah thought that was funny. But after a while, when they had driven back and forth several times, Jeremiah announced that they had to be about their business: they were on a proposition and their time wasn't all their own. "Hell, just one more time around," said the woman loudly. She had a broad, splendid face, so shiny with lipstick and make-up and pencil lines that Sweet Gum's eye slid around helplessly and could not focus on any single part. "Ain't got time for it," Jeremiah said, "we got to be about our business. Which way is it?" "Drive on. Straight," the woman said sullenly. She had a big head of hair, a big body, and a hard, red, waxen mouth that fascinated Sweet Gum, but whenever he looked at her she was looking at something else; she never noticed him. All she did was push him away with her elbow and thigh, trying to make more room for herself but doing it without glancing at him, as if she didn't really know he was there. "Keep straight. A mile or two," she said, yawning.

A few minutes later, out in the country, they stopped in front of a house. It was a small single-story house, covered with ripped brown siding, set up on wobbly blocks. "He don't do no work that *I* know of," the woman said. "He's got his finger in some backwoods whisky— y'know, whisky from the backwoods." She winked at Jeremiah. Sweet Gum's heart was pounding; Jeremiah kept jiggling his beard. In the cinder driveway an old brown dog lay as if exhausted and watched them, getting ready to bark. There was a wild field next to the house on the right, and an old decaying orchard—pear trees— on the left. Across the road, a quarter mile away, was a small farm: Sweet Gum could see cows grazing by a creek. "All right, honey," Jeremiah said, "you can start back now." "Walk back?" said the woman. "Yes, we got bus'ness here, between men. Ain't I explained that?" "What kind of bus'ness?" said the woman. "Men's busi- ness," Jeremiah said, but kindly; and he reached past Sweet Gum and put his big hairy hand on the woman's arm. "You start walking back and like's not we'll catch up in a few minutes and ride you back. Don't worry Jeremiah now, honey." The woman hesitated, though Sweet Gum knew she had already made up her mind. "Well," she said, "all right, if it's men's bus'ness. But don't . . . maybe don't tell Nathan it was me put you on him." "We won't never do that," Jeremiah said.

Jeremiah wasted more time by waving at the woman

and blowing kisses as she walked away, but finally he calmed down and got out of the car and straightened his clothes and pressed down on his hair; he took out the necktie once more and tied it around his neck. Sweet Gum, carrying the satchel, climbed over the door on Jeremiah's side and jumped to the ground. The dog's ears shifted but the dog itself did not move. On the porch of the house sat a child, and behind him were piles of junk—firewood, old boxes, barrels, coils of rusted wire. The screen door opened and another child came out, a boy of about eight. He wore jeans and was barefoot. He and the smaller child and the dog watched Jeremiah and Sweet Gum arrange their clothing, slick down their hair by spitting into their palms and rubbing their heads viciously, and stare straight before them as if each were alone. Finally it was time: they crossed the ditch to the house.

The dog whimpered. "Son," cried Jeremiah to the older boy, "is your pa anywhere handy?" The boy's toes twitched on the edge of the steps. He began stepping backward, cautiously, and the other boy scrambled to his feet and backed up too, retreating behind the piles of junk. "Tell your pa we're here to see him," said Jeremiah. He walked ahead; Sweet Gum, hugging the satchel, followed close. Faces appeared at a window, another child or a woman. Then the screen door opened cautiously and a man stepped out.

He was about forty, gone to fat now, with a reddish apologetic face. The way he scratched the underside of his jaw made Sweet Gum know that he was apologetic about something. "You Nathan Motley?" Jeremiah cried. "What's that to you?" the man said, clearing his throat. Behind the piles of junk two boys crouched, watching. "Here, boy," Jeremiah said to Sweet Gum, "open it up." Sweet Gum opened up the satchel and Jeremiah took out his pistol, an old rust-streaked revolver that had belonged to his father. He aimed it at the man and fired. Someone screamed. But when Sweet Gum could see again, the porch was empty even of children—the screen door had fallen shut. "Goddamn," said Jeremiah, still holding the pistol aloof, "you spose I *missed* him?"

Sweet Gum had his pistol now—not his own yet, but it would be when he returned home. "I'm going around here," Sweet Gum said. He ran around the house. In the driveway the dog had drawn its muddy feet up to its body and lay watching them with wet, alert eyes. Sweet Gum had just rounded the back corner when he saw someone diving into a clump of bushes in the wild field behind the house. Sweet Gum let out a yodel: this was all familiar to him, nothing frightening about it, it was exactly like the games he had played as a child. "Here! Back here!" he yelled. He fired wildly at the clump of bushes. Behind him, in the house, there were screams and shrieks —Jeremiah was stomping through the house, bellowing. When he appeared running out of the back door his tie was thrown back over his shoulder as if someone had playfully pulled it there, and he still looked surprised. "This is hot weather for a hunt," he said when he caught up to Sweet Gum. They ran through the stiff grass, in brilliant sunshine, and about them birds flew up in terror. The field smelled of sunburned grass. "I'm headed this way, you keep straight," Jeremiah grunted. Sweet Gum ran on, slashing through bushes, pushing aside tree branches with his gun. "You, Motley!" he cried in despair. "Where you hiding at?" Something stumbled on the far side of a clump of bushes; Sweet Gum fired into it. In a moment Jeremiah appeared, mouth open and sucking for breath, as if he were swimming through the foliage. "Where's that bastard? He ain't over on my side, I swear it," Jeremiah said.

"If he gets away it ain't my fault," Sweet Gum cried. He was so angry he wanted to dance around. "He was standing there for you and you missed! Uncle Simon asks me, I got to tell the truth!"

Jeremiah scratched his head. "I got a feeling he's over this way. Let's track him over here." "I never seen him on my side," Sweet Gum said sullenly. "Nor me on *mine*," Jeremiah answered. They walked along, slashing at the tops of weeds with their guns. Birds sang airily about them. After a minute or two they slowed to a stop. Jeremiah scratched his beard with the barrel of the gun. "Spose we went back to the house," he said suddenly. "He's got to come back for supper, don't he? Or to sleep tonight?" Sweet Gum wished he had thought of that, but did not let on. "Hell of a idea," he grumbled. "First you miss him that close, then want to quit tracking him." "You track him, I'll go back alone," Jeremiah said. "Naw," said Sweet Gum, hiding his alarm, "I ain't staying back here alone." They turned and followed their paths back through the field.

Then something fortunate happened: Sweet Gum happened to see a hen pheasant start up in a panic. Off to their left, in a big long stretch of high grass. Sweet Gum fired into the grass. "There he is, he's hiding in there! He's hiding in there!" Jeremiah started forward, yelling, "Where do you see him? Do you see him?" He pushed past Sweet Gum, who fired again into the weeds. "He's laid flat," Sweet Gum said, "crawling around on the ground—" In the silence that followed, however, they heard only the usual country noises, insects and birds. "Motley, are you in there?" Jeremiah asked. His voice had a touch of impatience. "Where are you?" They waited. Then, incredibly, a voice lifted— "What do you want?" Sweet Gum fired at once. Both he and Jeremiah ran forward. "Which way was it? Was it this way?" Sweet Gum cried. He and Jeremiah collided. Jeremiah even swung his gun around and hit Sweet Gum, hard, on the chest. Sweet Gum sobbed with pain and anger. "*I* found him! *I* saw the pheasant go up!" he snarled. "Shut your mouth and keep it shut!" Jeremiah said.

"But what do you want?" the voice cried again. It was forlorn, a ghostly voice; it seemed to come out of the air. Sweet Gum was so confused he did not even fire. "Let's talk. Can't we talk?" Jeremiah stood, staring furiously into the grass. His face was red. "Ain't nothing to talk about," he said sullenly, as if he suspected a joke. "We got a job to do." "Somebody hired you?" the voice said. Sweet Gum lifted his gun but Jeremiah made a signal for him to wait. "Hired us for sure. What do you think?" Jeremiah said. "Somebody wants me kilt, then?" said the voice. "Somebody paying you for it?" "I just explained that!" Jeremiah said. "You having a joke with me?" And he lifted his pistol and took a step into the high grass. "No, no," the voice cried, "I'm not joking— I . . . I want to hire you to—I got a job for you to do . . . both of you— I'll pay—" *"How* can he pay, if he's dead?" Sweet Gum yelled furiously. "He's making fun of us!" "He ain't either, you goddamn backwoods idiot," Jeremiah said. "Shut your mouth. Now, mister, what's this-here job you got for us?"

The patch of weeds stirred. "A job for two men that can shoot straight," the voice said slowly. It paused. "That take in you two?" "Takes in me," Jeremiah said. "Me too," Sweet Gum heard his voice say—with surprise. "How much you paying?" said Jeremiah. "Fifty dollars a man," the voice said without hesitation. "Hell, that ain't enough," Sweet Gum said, raising his pistol. "No, no, a hunnert a man," the voice cried. Sweet Gum's arm froze. He and Jeremiah looked at each other. "A hunnert a man," Jeremiah said solemnly. "Uncle Simon's giving us fifty both, and a gun for Sweet Gum—that's him there— and a horse for me that I always liked; spose you can't thow in no horse, can you?" "And no gun neither!" Sweet Gum said in disgust. "Can't thow in no gun, and I'm purely fond of this one!" "But you can have the gun," said the voice, "after he's dead—and the horse too— Why couldn't you keep them, after he's dead? Didn't he promise them to you?"

Jeremiah scratched his nose. "Well," he said.

The patch moved. A man's head appeared—balding red hair, pop eyes, a mouth that kept opening and closing —and then his shoulders and arms and the rest of him. He looked from Jeremiah to Sweet Gum. "You two are good men, then?" His arms were loose at his sides. What was happening? Sweet Gum stood as if in a dream, a daze; he could not believe he had betrayed his uncle. "Aw, let's shoot him," he said suddenly, feverishly. "We come all this ways to do it—"

"Shut your mouth."

"But Uncle Simon—"

There was silence. The man brushed himself calmly. He knew enough to address Jeremiah when he spoke. "You two are good men, then? Can be trusted?"

"Ain't you trusting us now?" Jeremiah said with a wink. The man smiled politely. "What experience you got?"

At this, Sweet Gum looked down; his face went hot. "*I* got it," Jeremiah said, but slowly, as if he felt sorry for Sweet Gum. "Got put on trial for killing two men and found Not Guilty."

"When was this?"

"Few years," Jeremiah said. "I'm not saying whether I done it or not—was cautioned what to say. I don't know if the time is up yet. Two state troopers come and arrested me that hadn't any bus'ness in the Rapids— where we're from—and I got jailed and put on trial; for killing two storekeepers somewhere and taking seven hundred dollars. Was put on trial," Jeremiah said with a sigh, "and different people come to talk, one at a time, the jury come back and said Not Guilty for robbery; so it went for the other too—murder too. *But* they didn't let me keep the seven hundred dollars; they kept that themselves and fixed up the schoolhouse. New windows and the bathrooms cleaned and something else. Makes me proud when I go past—I got lots of cousins in the school."

"You were Not Guilty? How was that?"

Jeremiah shrugged. "They decided so."

The man now turned to Sweet Gum. But Sweet Gum, ashamed, could hardly look up. He could see his uncle, with that big wide face and false teeth, watching him and Jeremiah as they stood in this field betraying him. "What about you, son?" the man said gently. "This ain't your first job, is it?" Sweet Gum nodded without looking up. "Well, I like to see young people given a chance," the man said—and Sweet Gum, in spite of his shame, did feel a pang of satisfaction at this. "I like to see young ones and experience go together," the man said.

He turned to Jeremiah and put out his hand. Jeremiah shook hands with him solemnly; both men's faces looked

alike. Sweet Gum stumbled through the grass to get to
them and put his hand right in the middle. His eyes
stung and he looked from man to man as if he thought
they might explain the miracle of why he was acting as
he was. But Motley, with color returning unevenly to his
face, just grinned and said, "Let's go back to the house
now."

An hour later Jeremiah and Sweet Gum were heading
out of town. Jeremiah drove faster than before and kept
twitching and shifting around in the seat, pressing his
big belly against the steering wheel. "No one of us mis-
likes it more than me," he said finally, "but you know
Uncle Simon ain't much expecting to live too long. Three-
four years." With his mouth open, Sweet Gum stared at
the road. There was a small dry hole in the side of his
head into which Jeremiah's words droned, and Sweet
Gum had no choice but to accept them. Inside, the words
became entangled with the shouting and cursing with
which Uncle Simon blessed this ride. The old man sat in
his rocking chair on the porch, stains of chewing-tobacco
juice etched permanently down the sides of his chin,
glaring at Jeremiah and Sweet Gum who, thirty and
forty years younger than he, were rushing along hot dirt
roads to hurry him out of his life. And his teeth were
new: not more than five years old. Sweet Gum remembered when Uncle Simon had got the teeth from a city
and had shown the family how they worked, biting into
apples and chewing with a malicious look of triumph.
Uncle Simon! Sweet Gum felt as if the old man had put
his bony hand on his shoulder.

"Boy, what's wrong with you?" Jeremiah said nervously.

"Sent us out after something and we ain't preformed
it," Sweet Gum said. He wiped his nose on the back of
his hand.

Jeremiah considered this. Then he said, after a moment, "But kin don't mean nothing. Being kin to somebody is just a accident; you got to think it through, what

other ones mean to you. Uncles or what not. Or brothers, or grandmas, or anything."

Sweet Gum blinked. "Even a man with his father? If he had a father?"

That was the thing about Sweet Gum: he would always get onto this subject sooner or later. Usually whoever it was he spoke to would shrug his shoulders and look embarrassed—but Jeremiah just glanced over at him as if something had shocked him. "A father's maybe different," Jeremiah said, and let Sweet Gum know by the hard set of his jaw that he was finished talking.

They made so many turns, followed so many twisting roads, that the sun leaped back and forth across the sky. Sweet Gum could always tell the time at home, but out on the road it might as well be nine o'clock as three o'clock; nothing stayed still, nothing could be trusted. The old car was covered with dust and it got into their noses and mouths, making them choke. Sweet Gum wondered if his punishment for betraying his uncle had already begun, or if this wouldn't count because the murder hadn't taken place yet. "Remember this turn, don't you?" Jeremiah said, trying to be cheerful. Sweet Gum showed by his empty stare that he did not remember having seen this patch of hot scrubby land before— he recognized nothing on the return trip, as if he were really someone else.

As soon as they crossed the bridge to the Rapids, Sweet Gum gulped, "I can't do it."

Some boys were running in the road after the car, shouting and tossing stones. "Hey, you, Jeremiah Coke, you give us a ride!" they yelled. But Jeremiah was so surprised by Sweet Gum that he did not even glance around. "Hell, what's wrong now? Ain't we decided what to do?"

Sweet Gum's lips trembled. "Sent us out and we ain't preformed it for him," he said.

"Goddamn it, didn't you shake hands with Motley? Come loping acrost the weeds to stick your hand in, didn't you? Hired yourself out for a hunnert dollars. Do you do that much bus'ness every day?"

"No," said Sweet Gum, wiping his nose.

"Ain't a man his own bus'ness? Christ Himself was a bus'ness; he was selling stuff. Wasn't He? He never took money for it, wanted other things instead—more important things—a person's life, is that cheap? Everybody's a bus'ness trying for something and you got to farm yourself out to the richest one that wants you. Goddamn it, boy," Jeremiah said, "are you going back on Motley when you just now gave him your word?"

"Gone back on Uncle Simon," Sweet Gum said.

"That'll do on him. I'm asking you something else. The least thing you do after you break one promise is to keep the next one. A man is allowed one change of mind."

Sweet Gum, already won, liked to keep Jeremiah's attention so fiercely on him. When Jeremiah looked at him he felt warm, even hot: but it was a good feeling. "Well," said Sweet Gum sighing. They were just then turning off onto their uncle's lane.

There the old house was, back past a clump of weed-like willows, with the old barns and the new aluminum-roofed barn behind it. Sweet Gum was surprised that he didn't feel frightened: but everything seemed familiar, as it did when he was chasing Motley, and strangely correct —even righteous—along with being familiar.

The car rolled to a stop. Jeremiah took his pistol out of the satchel and shoved it into the top of his trousers, past his big stomach; it looked uncomfortable but Jeremiah wouldn't admit it by taking it out. Sweet Gum climbed over the door and stood in the lane. The dirt quivered beneath his feet; he felt unreal. He giggled as he followed Jeremiah back the lane. They crossed to a field, half wild grass, half trees. When Jeremiah got down on his hands and knees, Sweet Gum did the same. They crawled along, Sweet Gum with his head hanging limply down, staring at the bottoms of Jeremiah's boots. If Jeremiah had wanted to crawl back and forth all day in the field Sweet Gum would have followed him.

Jeremiah stopped. "There he is. Sitting there." He

pulled some weeds aside for Sweet Gum to look out, but
Sweet Gum nodded immediately; he did not have to be
shown. His brain was throbbing. "Here, aim at him,"
Jeremiah whispered. He pulled Sweet Gum's arm up.
"I'll say the word and both fire at once. Then lay low;
we can crawl back to the car and drive up and ask them
what-all went on." Sweet Gum saw that Jeremiah's face
was mottled, red and gray, like Motley's had been. Jeremiah aimed through the weeds, waited, and then, queerly,
turned back to Sweet Gum. "You ain't aiming right!
Don't want to shoot, do you? Have me do it all, you
little bastard!"

"I ain't one of them!" Sweet Gum screamed.

The scream was astounding. A mile away, even, a bird
must have heard it and now, in the following silence,
questioned it—three bright notes and a trill. Sweet Gum
was so numb he couldn't think of the name of that bird.
Jeremiah was staring at Sweet Gum; their faces were so
close that their breathing surely got mixed up. That was
why, Sweet Gum thought, he felt dizzy—old dirty air
coming out of Jeremiah and getting sucked into him.
Rocked in inertia, dazzled by the sunshine and the silence,
the two men stared at each other. "No, I ain't one of
them," Sweet Gum whispered. "Please, I ain't." Then a
voice sailed over that Sweet Gum recognized at once.

"Who's over there? Who's in the field? Goddamn it if
I don't hear somebody there." There was a furious rap-
ping noise: Uncle Simon slamming the porch floor with
his old-fashioned thick-heeled boots, angry enough to
break into a jig. Jeremiah and Sweet Gum crouched
together, sweating. They heard the old man talking with
his wife, then his mutter rising without hesitation into
another series of shouts: "Who is it? Stand up. Stand up
and face me. Who's hiding there? I'll have my gun out in
a minute. —Get the hell out of here, Ma, go back inside.
I *said*—"

Jeremiah, sighing mightily, got to his feet. "Hiya, Uncle
Simon," he said, waving the pistol. "It's Sweet Gum here,
and me." He helped Sweet Gum to his feet. Across the
lane the old man stood on the edge of his porch with one

fist in the air. Was that the Uncle Simon who had cursed them all day, hovering over the car like a ghost? The old man looked younger than Sweet Gum remembered. "Just us over here," Jeremiah said, smiling foolishly.

"What the hell are you up to?" Uncle Simon yelled. At this, the old woman came out again, her hands wiping each other on her apron as always. "Jeremiah himself and Sweet Gum hiding over there, playing at guns with their own Uncle Simon," the old man said viciously. "A man with three-four years to go an not a month more. See them there?"

The old woman, almost blind, nodded sullenly just the same. Sweet Gum wanted to run over to her and have her embrace him, smell the damp clean odor of her smooth-cracked hands, be told that everything was all right—as she had told him when two cousins of his, boys hardly older than he, had been arrested for killing a government agent one Hallowe'en night. And that *had* turned out all right, for the judge could not get a jury— everyone liked the boys or were related to them—and so the case was dismissed. "Like niggers in a field! Look at them there, crawling around like niggers in a field!" Uncle Simon yelled.

Jeremiah was the first to break down. Big hot tears exploded out of his eyes, tumbled down his face and were lost in his beard. *"He* talked us into it," he said, "me and Sweet Gum was trapped by him. *He* talked us all kinds of fast words, and long sentences like at church; and explained it to us that he would tell the state police. I had enough trouble with them once, Uncle Simon, didn't I? —And he tole us it would be a hunnert a man and we could keep the horse and the gun anyways. We got so mixed up hearing it all, and them police at the back of my mind—" Jeremiah's voice ran down suddenly. Sweet Gum stared at his feet, hoping he would not be expected to continue.

"Who? Motley? A hunnert a man?" What was strange was that Uncle Simon stared at them like that—his rage frozen on his face, and something new taking over. "A hunnert a man?"

"And to keep the horse and the gun anyways," Jeremiah said in a croaking voice.

The old man put his little finger to his eye and scratched it, just once. Then he yelled: "All right. Get back in that car. Goddamn you both, get in and turn it around and get back to Plain Dealing! I'll plain-deal you! I'll ambush you! Use your brains—tell that Motley bastard you took care of it out here—shot your poor old uncle— and want the reward from him now. Say you want your reward, can you remember that? Jeremiah, you stay back; don't you come on my lane. You stay back in the field. I don't want to see your goddamn faces again till you do the job right. Do I have to go all that ways myself, a man sixty-five or more years old, would be retired like they do in the city if I was a regular man? Yes, would be retired with money coming in, a check, every month— Ma, *you* stay back, this ain't anything of yours! And say to Motley you want your reward,— and let him give it to you—one hunnert a man—then fire at him and that's that. How much money you make from it?"

Sweet Gum said, so fast he surprised himself, "A hunnert a man."

"How much?"

Sweet Gum's brain reeled and clicked. "A hunnert-fifty a man and a gun for me. And a horse for Jeremiah."

"Put in a horse for you and another one for Jeremiah. That's that." The old man spat maliciously toward them. "Now, get the hell back to the car. You got some work to do with Motley."

"Yes, thank you, that's right, Uncle Simon," Jeremiah said. He gulped at air. "We're on the way to do it. Two horses? Which one is the other? The red mare or what?"

"Your pick," the old man said. He turned sullenly away as if he had forgotten about them. Sweet Gum wanted to laugh out loud—it had been so easy. He did laugh, he heard himself with alarm, and felt at the same time something begin to twitch in his face. It twitched again: a muscle around his eye. Nothing like that had ever happened to him before, yet he understood that

the twitch, and probably the breathless giggle, would
be with him for life.

Jeremiah's jalopy broke down on the return trip, without drama: it just rolled to a stop as if it had died.
Jeremiah got out and kicked it in a fury and tore off the
fender and part of the bumper; but Sweet Gum just stood
quietly and watched, and by and by Jeremiah joined him.
They strolled along the road for a while. Sweet Gum
noticed how Jeremiah's fingers kept twitching.

Though they were on a U.S. highway, there was not
much traffic—when a car appeared Sweet Gum would
stand diffidently by the road and put up his hand, without
apparent purpose, as if he were ready to withdraw it at
any moment. After an hour or two an automobile
stopped, as if by magic; the man said he was driving
right through Plain Dealing.

When they arrived in front of Motley's house it was
suppertime. Sweet Gum and Jeremiah went up the driveway; Jeremiah took out his pistol and looked at it, for
some reason, and Sweet Gum did the same—he noticed
that he had one bullet left. Hiding a yawn, Jeremiah
approached the porch and peered in the window: there
the family sat, or at least the woman and children,
arguing about something so that their faces took on
slanted, vicious expressions. Jeremiah stood staring in
the window until someone—the oldest boy—happened
to see him. The boy's face jerked, his features blurred
together, his bony arm jerked up as if he were accusing
Jeremiah of something. Then the woman caught sight
of him and, pulling her dress somehow, straightening the
skirt, came to the door. "Whatcha got there? He's in
town right now. You them clowns come out here before,
ain't you?" The woman looked ready to laugh. "Nat told
me about you; says you were kidding him with play-guns.
How come I don't know you? Nat says—"

"Where is he?" said Jeremiah.

"In town," the woman said. "He's at the club probably. That's the Five Aces Club, acrost from the bank.
He tole me not to wait on him tonight so I didn't, but he
never tole me to expeck some guests for supper. As a

fact, he never tells me much," she laughed. "Bet you tell
your wife where you are or whatcha doing or who's
coming out for supper. Bet you—"

"How do you spell that?" Jeremiah said patiently.

"Spell it? Huh? Spell what?"

"The place he's at."

"Acrost from the bank, the Five Aces—I don't know,
how do you spell five? It's a number five, they got it on
a sign; you know how five looks? That's it." Both Jeremiah and Sweet Gum nodded. "Then 'Aces,' that's out
there too—begins with A, A s or A c, then s on the end—
it's more than one. Acrost from the bank. But why don't
you come in and wait, he'll be—"

"We surely thank you," Jeremiah said with a faint
smile, "but we got bus'ness to attend to. Maybe later on."

It took them a while to walk back to town. Jeremiah's
fingers were busier than ever. Most of the time they were
scratching at his head, then darting into his ears or nose
and darting back out again. Sweet Gum walked behind so
that his giggling would not annoy Jeremiah. They passed
houses, farmers' markets, a gas station with an old model-
T out front filled with tires. They passed a diner that was
boarded up, and the movie house, in front of which the
boys with straw hats stood around smoking. When Sweet
Gum and Jeremiah passed, the boys stared in silence;
even the smoke from their cigarettes stiffened in the air.

Town began suddenly: a drug store, an old country
store on a corner. In a clapboard shanty, a dentist's
office advertised in bright green paint. There were no
sidewalks, so Jeremiah and Sweet Gum walked at the side
of the road. "Down there looks like the bank," Jeremiah
said, waving his pistol at something ahead; Sweet Gum
did not see it. They walked on. "We come a long way,"
Jeremiah said in a strange remote voice, like a man em-
barking on a speech. "Done a lot this past week or
however long it's been. I never known till now that I was
born for this life—did you? Thought it'd be for me like
anyone else—a farm and cows maybe and a fambly to
raise up and maybe chickens, the wife could take care
of them; I mostly had the wife picked out too. Won't

tell you which one. But now I know different. Now I see
it was in me all along, from before I kilt them two men
even—I thought I done that by *accident,* had too much to
drink—something in a dream—but no, now I know
better; now I got it clear." A few cars passed them:
people out for after-supper rides. A girl of about two,
with thin blond hair, leaned out a window and waved
sweetly at Sweet Gum. "Now I know," Jeremiah said, so
strangely that Sweet Gum felt embarrassed in spite of
his confusion, "that there isn't a person but wouldn't
like to do that, what I did. Or to set a place afire, say—
any place—their own house even. Set it all afire, house
and grass and trees alike, all the same. Was there ever
a difference between a house people live in and trees
outside that they name? Them trees *make* you name
them, think up names for them as soon as you see
them, what choice does a man have! Never no choice!
Get rid of it all, fire it all up, all the things that bother
you, that keep you from yourself, and people too—and
people too— Sweet Gum, I got to tell you now, with us
both coming so far like we did, that I'm your pa here,
I am, Jeremiah your pa after all these years, all the way
from the beginning!"

They continued walking. Sweet Gum blinked once or
twice. Jeremiah's words bored through that tiny hole in
the side of his head, flipped themselves around right side
up to make sense: but Sweet Gum only hid a sudden
laugh with his hand, stared at the sweaty back of Jeremiah's old funeral suit, and thought aloud, "Is that so."
"That so, boy, all the way from the beginning," Jeremiah
said, stifling a yawn. "This-here is your own pa walking
right in front of you."

Sweet Gum should have said something, but he could
not think of it and so let it pass. They were approaching
the 5 Aces Club now, heading toward it as if it were a
magnet. Sweet Gum heard voices behind him and glanced
around: the group of boys was following them, idly and
at a distance; a man in overalls had joined them, looking
sour and disapproving. Sweet Gum forgot them as soon
as he turned again. They passed a laundromat with orange

signs: OPEN 24 HOURS EACH DAY WASH 20¢ DRY 10¢ A few people were inside in spite of the heat. In the doorway children kicked at one another and did not even glance up at Jeremiah and Sweet Gum. Then there was a 5¢ 10¢ 25¢ AND $1.00 STORE, gold letters on a red background, windows crowded and stuffed with merchandise; but it was closed. Then the club itself, coming so fast Sweet Gum's eye twitched more than ever and he had to hold onto it with his palm to keep it from jumping out of his head. "Spose he's in there," Sweet Gum whimpered, "spose he gets to talking. Don't let him talk. Please. Don't let him. Shoot him right off. If I hear talk of horses or gun or twice as much money—"

The club had had a window at one time, a big square window like something in a shoe store, but now it was completely hidden by tin foil. There were advertisements for beer and cigarettes everywhere: beautiful pink-cheeked girls, men with black hair and big chests and clean white gleaming teeth. Long muscular thighs, smooth legs, slender ankles, silver-painted toenails, tattooed arms and backs of hands; and curly-haired chests and dimpled chests, chests bare and bronze in the sun, chests demurely proud in red polka-dot halters—everything mixed together! Faces channeled themselves out of blue skies and rushed at Sweet Gum with their fixed serene smiles. "That *there* is heaven," Sweet Gum thought suddenly, with a certainty he had never before felt about life—as if, about to leave it, he might pass judgment on it. His stomach ached with silent sobs, as much for that lost heaven as for the duties of this familiar, demanding world.

Jeremiah had opened the door to the tavern. "You, Motley, come out here a minute." Someone answered inside but Jeremiah went on patiently, "Motley. Some bus'ness outside."

Jeremiah let the door close. Sweet Gum clutched at him. "Is he coming? Is he? Was that him inside?" he said. "Don't let him talk none. Shoot him first or let me—shoot him—"

"We ain't going to shoot him yet."

"But what if he talks of more horses or another gun? What if—"

"He ain't. Get back, now—"

"I'm going to shoot him—"

"Goddamn you, boy, you stand back," Jeremiah shouted. "Why's it always you at the center of trouble? Any goddamn thing that bothers me these days, *you're* in the middle!"

"Don't let him talk none. If he—"

"We got to talk to him. Got to tell him we come for the reward."

"Reward?" Sweet Gum's sobs broke through to the surface. "Reward? I don't remember none, what reward? What? He's going to talk, going to—"

Jeremiah pushed him away and opened the door again. "Motley!" he yelled. Sweet Gum's head was so clamoring with voices that he could not be sure if he heard anyone answer. "He's coming, guess it's him," Jeremiah said vaguely. "Stand back now, boy, and don't you do no reckless shooting your pa will have to clean up after—"

"I'm going to shoot him," Sweet Gum cried, "or he'll talk like before— If he talks and we hear him we got to go back and be in the field again. We got to hide there. And Aunt Clarey, I always loved her so, how it's for *her* to see us hiding there? Even if she can't see much. If he comes out and talks we got to—"

"Boy, I'm telling you!"

"Don't you call me boy!"

The door opened suddenly, angrily. Sweet Gum raised his pistol, took a giant step backward, and was about to shoot when a stranger appeared in the doorway, a big pot-bellied bald man with a towel used for an apron tucked in his belt. "What the *hell*—" the man roared.

Sweet Gum, shocked, staggered back. Inside his head the clamoring arose to a mighty scream and, in defense, he turned to Jeremiah. Everything focused on Jeremiah, the sun itself seemed to glare on his bulging eyes. Sweet Gum cried: "*You!* It was *you* I been hunting these twenty years!" But somehow in his confusion he had turned around, or half around, and when he fired he did not shoot Jeremiah at all, or any man at all, but instead a woman—a stranger, a stocky woman with a sunburned, pleasant, bossy face, dressed in jeans and a man's dirty white shirt. She fell right into the basket of damp laundry she was carrying. Blood burst out of nowhere, onto the clothes, and also out of nowhere appeared two children, shrieking and screaming.

Sweet Gum backed away. A crowd, an untidy circle, was gathering about the fallen woman. Sweet Gum, dazed, put the barrel of the pistol to his lips and stared, still backing away, stumbling. He had been cheated: he could not get things clear: his whole life had flooded up to this moment and now was dammed and could not get past, everything was over. He could have wept for the end of his young life (mistakenly, as it turned out, for in less than three years he would be working downriver at the tomato canning factory, making good money), spilled here on the dirt road, splashing and sucked away, while everyone stood around gawking.

First Views of the Enemy

Just around the turn, the road was alive. First to assault the eye was a profusion of heads, black-haired, bobbing, and a number of straw hats that looked oddly professional—like straw hats in a documentary film; and shirts and overalls and dresses, red, yellow, beflowered, dotted, striped, some bleached by the sun, some stiff and brilliant, just bought and worn proudly out of the store. The bus in which they were traveling—a dead dark blue, colored, yet without any color—was parked half on the clay road and half in the prickly high grass by the ditch. Its old-fashioned hood was open, yanked cruelly up and doubled on itself, and staring into its greasy, dust-flecked tangle of parts was the driver, the only fair, brown-haired one of the bunch. Annette remembered later that as her station wagon moved in astonishment toward them, the driver looked up and straight at her: a big indifferent face, curious without interest, smeared with grease, as if deliberately to disguise himself. No kin of yours, lady, no kin! he warned contemptuously.

Breaking from a group of children, running with arms out for a mock embrace, a boy of about seven darted right toward Annette's car. The boy's thick black hair, curled with sweat, plastered onto his forehead, framed a delicate, cruelly tanned face, a face obviously dead white beneath its tan: great dark eyes, expanded out of proportion, neat little brows like angels' brows—that unbelievable and indecent beauty of children exploited for art —a pouting mouth, still purple at the corners from the raspberries picked and hidden for the long bus ride, these lips now turning as Annette stared into a hilarious grin and crying out at her and the stricken child who cringed beside her, legs already drawn up flatly at the knees—

In agony the brakes cried, held: the scene, dizzy with color, rocked with the car, down a little, back up, giddily, helplessly, while dust exploded up on all sides. "Mommy!" Timmy screamed, fascinated by the violence, yet his wail was oddly still and drawn out, and his eyes never once turned to his mother. The little Mexican boy had disappeared in front of the car. Still the red dust arose, the faces at the bus jerked around together, white eyes, white teeth, faces were propelled toward the windows of the bus, empty a second before. "God, God," Annette murmured; she had not yet released the steering wheel, and on it her fingers began to tighten as if they might tear the wheel off, hold it up to defend her and her child, perhaps even to attack.

A woman in a colorless dress pushed out of the crowd, barefooted in the red clay, pointed her finger at Annette and shouted something—gleefully. She shook her fist, grinning, others grinned behind her; the bus driver turned back to his bus. Annette saw now the little boy on the other side of the road, popping up safe in the ditch and jumping frantically—though the sharp weeds must have hurt his feet—and laughing, yelling, shouting as if he were insane. The air rang with shouts, with laughter. A good joke. What was the joke? Annette's brain reeled with shock, sucked for air as if drowning. Beside her Timmy wailed softly, but his eyes were fastened on the boy in the ditch. "He's safe, he's safe," Annette whispered. But others ran toward her now—big boys, tall but skinny, without shirts. How their ribs seemed to run with them, sliding up and down inside the dark tanned flesh with the effort of their legs! Even a few girls approached, hard dark faces, already aged, black hair matted and torn about their thin shoulders. They waved and cried, "Missus! Missus!" Someone even

shouted, "Cadillac!" though her station wagon, already a
year old, was far from being a Cadillac. As if to regain
attention, the little boy in the ditch picked up something,
a handful of pebbles, and threw it at the car, right beneath
Timmy's pale gaping face. A babble of Spanish followed,
more laughter, the barefoot woman who must have been
the boy's mother strode mightily across the road, grabbed
the boy, shook him in an extravagant mockery of punishment: sucked her lips at him, made spitting motions,
rubbed his head hard with the palm of her hand—this
hurt, Annette saw with satisfaction, for the child winced
in spite of his bravado. At the bus the American man's
back swelled damply and without concern beneath his
shirt; he did not even glance around.

Annette leaned to the window, managed a smile.
"Please let me through," she called. Her voice surprised
her, it sounded like a voice without body or identity,
channeled in over a radio.

The boys made odd gestures with their hands, not
clenching them into fists, but instead striking with the
edges of their hands, knifelike, into the air. Their teeth
grinned and now, with them so close (the bravest were at
her fender), Annette could see how discolored their
teeth were, though they had seemed white before. They
must have been eating dirt! she thought vaguely. "Please
let me through," she said. Beside her, Timmy sat in
terror. She wanted to reach over and put her hand
over his eyes, hide this sight from him—this mob of
dirty people, so hungry their tongues seemed to writhe
in their mouths, their exhaustion turned to frenzy.
"Missus! Missus! *Si, si,* Cadillac!" the boys yelled, pounding on the front of the car. The women, men, even very
old people—with frail white hair—watched, surprised
and pleased at being entertained.

"Please. Please." Suddenly Annette pressed on the
horn: what confidence that sound inspired! The boys
hesitated, moved back. She toyed with the accelerator,
wanting to slam down on it, to escape. But suppose one
of them were in the way. . . . The horror of that falling
thud, the vision of blood sucked into red clay, stilled her

nervousness, made her inch the big car forward slowly, slowly. And in the back, those unmistakable bags of groceries, what would be showing at the tops? Maybe tomatoes, pears, strawberries—perhaps picked by these people a few days ago—maybe bread, maybe meat— Annette's face burned with something more than shame. But when she spoke, her voice showed nothing. "Let me through, please. Let me through." She sounded cool and still.

Then she was past. The station wagon picked up speed. Behind her were yells, cries no longer gleeful, now insulted, vicious: in the mirror fists, shouting faces, the little boy running madly into the cloud of dust behind the car. He jerked something back behind his head, his skinny elbow swung, and with his entire body he sent a mud rock after the car that hit the back window square, hard, and exploded. With her fingers still frozen to the steering wheel, Annette sped home.

Beside her the child, fascinated, watched the familiar road as if seeing it for the first time. That tender smile was something strange; Annette did not like it. Annette herself, twitching with fear, always a nervous woman, electric as the harassed or the insanely ill are, saw with shock that her face in the mirror was warm and possessed. That was she, then, and not this wild, heart-thumping woman afraid of those poor children in the road. . . . Her eyes leaped home, her mind anticipated its haven. Already, straightening out of a turn, she could see it: the long, low orange brick home, trees behind the house not yet big enough for shade, young trees, a young house, a young family. Cleared out of the acres of wheat and wood and grass fields on either side, a surprise to someone driving by, looking for all the world as if it and its fine light green grass, so thin as to look unreal, and its Hercules fence had been picked up somewhere far away and dropped down here. Two miles away, on the highway that paralleled this road, there were homes something like this, but on this road there were only, a half-mile ahead, a few farmhouses, typical, some shacks deserted and not deserted, and even a gas station and store; otherwise nothing. Annette felt for the first time the insane danger of this location, and heard with magical accuracy her first question when her husband had suggested it: "But so far out. . . . Why do you want it so far out?" City children, both of them, the hot rich smell of sunlight and these soundless distances had never been forbidding, isolating. Instead, each random glance at the land strengthened in them a sense of their own cleverness. Children of fortune, to withdraw from their comfortable pasts, to raise a child in such safety! —It was fifteen miles to the nearest town where Annette did her shopping and Timmy went to school, and fifty miles to the city where her husband worked.

Annette turned in the driveway, drove slowly into the garage. Still in a trance, angry at herself, she got out of the car but stood with her hand still lingering on the steering wheel. A thin, fashionably thin young woman, for years more woman than girl, in a white dress she stood with a remote, vague smile, hand lightly on the wheel, mind enticed by something she could not name. Perplexed, incredulous: in spite of the enormity of what threatened (the migrant workers were hardly a mile away), she felt slowed and meaningless, her inertia touched even Timmy, who usually jumped out of the car and slammed the door. If only he would do this and she could cry, "Timmy! *Please!*" calm might be restored. But no, he climbed down on his side like a little old man, he pushed the door back indifferently so that it gave a feeble click and did not even close all the way. For a while mother and son stood on opposite sides of the car; Annette could tell that Timmy did not move and was not even looking at her. Then his footsteps began. He ran out of the garage.

Annette was angry. Only six, he understood her, he knew what was to come next: he was to help her with the packages, with the doors, open the cupboards in the kitchen, he would be in charge of putting things into the refrigerator. As if stricken by a sudden bad memory, Annette stood in the garage, waiting for her mind to clear. What was there in Timmy's running out? For an instant she felt betrayed—as if he cherished the memory of that strange little boy and ran out to keep it from her. She remembered the early days of her motherhood, how contemptuous she had been of herself, of what she had accomplished—a baby she refused to look at, a husband neurotic with worry, a waiting life of motherhood so oppressive that she felt nausea contemplating it: is this what I have become? What is this baby to me? Where am I? Where am *I*? Impassioned, a month out of college and fearful, in spite of her attractiveness, that she would never be married, Annette had taken the dangerous gamble of tearing aside her former life, rejecting the familiar possessions and patterns that had defined her, and had plunged, with that intense confident sharp-voiced young man, into a new life she was never quite sure had not betrayed the old, stricken the old: her parents, her lovely mother, now people to write to, send greeting cards to, hint vaguely at visiting to. . . .

Sighing, she began to move. She took the packages out of the car, went outside (the heat was not brilliant), put them down, and, with deft angry motions in case Timmy was secretly watching, pulled down the garage door and locked it. "There!" But when she turned, her confidence was distracted. She stared at the house. Shrubbery hiding the concrete slab—basements were not necessary this far south—rosebushes bobbing roses, vulnerable, insanely gaudy, the great picture window that made her think, always, someone was slyly watching her, even the faint professional sweep of grass out to the road—all these in their elaborate planned splendor shouted mockery at her, mockery at themselves, as if they were safe from destruction! Annette fought off the inertia again, it passed close by her, a whiff of something like death; the same darkness that had bothered her in the hospital, delivered of her child. She left the packages against the garage (though the ice cream in its special package might be melting) and, awkward in her high heels, hurried out the drive. She shielded her eyes: nothing in sight down the road. It was a red clay road, a country road that would never be paved, and she and her husband had at first

taken perverse pride in it. But it turned so, she had never
noticed that before, and great bankings of foliage hid it,
disguised its twistings, so that she could see not more
than a quarter mile away. Never before had the land
seemed so flat.

She hurried. At the gate the sun caught up with her,
without ceremony. She struggled to swing the gate around
(a few rusty, loosened prongs had caught in the grass),
she felt perspiration breaking out on her body, itching
and prickling her, under her arms, on her back. The
white dress must have hung damp and wrinkled about
her legs. Panting with the exertion, she managed to get
the gate loose and drag it around; it tilted down at a
jocose angle, scraping the gravel; then she saw that
there was no lock, she would need a padlock, there was
one in the garage somewhere, and in the same instant,
marveling at her stamina, she turned back.

Hurrying up the drive, she thought again of the little
Mexican boy. She saw his luxurious face, that strange
unhealthy grin inside his embracing arms—it sped toward her. Cheeks drawn in as if by age, eyes protruding
with—it must have been hunger, dirty hands like claws
reaching out, grabbing, demanding what? What would
they demand of her? If they were to come and shout for
her out in the road, if she were to offer them—something
—milk, maybe, the chocolate cookies Timmy loved so,
maybe even money? Would they go away then, would
they thank her and run back to their people? Would
they continue their trip north, headed for Oregon and
Washington? What would happen? Violence worried the
look of the house, dizzied Annette! There were the yellow
roses she tended so fondly, rich and sprawling against
the orange brick. In the sunlight their petals, locked
intricately inside one another, were vivid, glaringly detailed, as if their secret life were swelling up in rage
at her for having so endangered their beauty.

There the packages lay against the garage, and seeing
them, Annette forgot about the padlock. She stooped
and picked them up. When she turned again she saw
Timmy standing just inside the screen door. "Timmy,

open the—" she said, vexed, but he had already disappeared. Inside the kitchen she slammed the bags down, fought back the impulse to cry, stamped one heel on the linoleum so hard that her foot buzzed with pain. "Timmy," she said, her eyes shut tight, "come out in this kitchen."

He appeared, carrying a comic book. That was for the look of it, of course; he had not been reading. His face was wary. Fair, like his mother, blond-toned, smart for his age, he had still about his quiet plump face something that belonged to field animals, wood animals, shrewd, secret creatures that had little to say for themselves. He read the newspaper as his father did, cultivated the same thoughtful expression; encouraged, he talked critically about his schoolteacher with a precocity that delighted his father, frightened Annette (to her, even now, teachers were somehow *different* from other people), he had known the days of the week, months of the year, continents of the world, planets of the solar system, major star groupings of the universe, at an astonishing age—as a child he approached professional perfection; but Annette, staring at him, was not sure now that she could trust him. What if, when the shouting began outside, when "Missus! Missus!" demanded her, Timmy ran out to them, joined them, stared back at her in the midst of their white eyes and dirty arms? They stared at each other as if this question had been voiced.

"You almost killed him," Timmy said.

His voice was soft. Its innocence showed that he knew how daring he was; his eyes as well, neatly fringed by pale lashes, trembled slightly in their gaze. "What?" said Annette. "What?"

The electric clock, built into the big white range, whirred in the silence. Timmy swallowed, rustled his comic book, pretended to wipe his nose—a throwback to a habit long outgrown—hoping to mislead her, and looked importantly at the clock. "*He* hit the car. Two times," he said.

This was spoken differently. The ugly spell was over. "Yes, he certainly did," Annette said. She was suddenly busy. "He certainly did." After a moment Timmy put down the comic book to help her. They worked easily, in silence. Eyes avoided each other. But Annette felt feverishly excited; something had been decided, strengthened. Timmy, stooping to put vegetables in the bottom of the refrigerator, felt her staring at him and peered up, his little eyebrows raised in a classic look of wonder. "You going to call Daddy?" he said.

Annette had been thinking of this, but when Timmy suggested it, it was exposed for what it was—a child's idea. "That won't be necessary," she said. She folded bags noisily and righteously.

When they finished, mother and son wandered without enthusiasm into the dining room, into the living room, as if they did not really want to leave the kitchen. Annette's eyes flinched at what she saw: crystal, polished wood, white walls, aqua lampshades, white curtains, sand-toned rug, detailed, newly cleaned, spreading regally across the room—surely no one ever walked on that rug! That was what *they* would say if they saw it. And the glassware off in the corner, spearlike, transparent green, a great window behind it linking it with the green grass outside, denying a barrier, inviting in sunlight, wind, anyone's eyes approachng— Annette went to the window and pulled the draw drapes shut; that was better; she breathed gently, coaxed by the beauty of those drapes into a smile: they were white, perfectly hung, sculpted superbly in generous swirling curves. And fireproof, if it came to that. . . . Annette turned. Timmy stood before the big red swivel chair as if he were going to sit in it—he did not—and looked at her with such a queer, pinched expression, in spite of his round face, that Annette felt a sudden rush of shame. She was too easily satisfied, too easily deluded. In all directions her possessions stretched out about her, defining her, identifying her, and they were vulnerable and waiting, the dirt road led right to them; and she could be lured into smiling! That must be why Timmy looked at her so strangely. "I have something to do," she murmured, and went back to the dining room. The window there was open; she pulled it down and locked it. She went to the wall control and turned on the air conditioning. "Run, honey, and close the windows," she said. "In your room."

She went into the bedroom, closed the windows there and locked them. Outside there was nothing—smooth lawn, lawn furniture (fire-engine red) grouped casually together, as if the chairs made of tubing and spirals were having a conversation. Annette went into the bathroom, locked that window, avoided her gaze in the mirror, went, at last, into the "sewing room" that faced the road, and stood for a while staring out the window. She had never liked the color of that clay, really—it stretched up from Louisiana to Kentucky, sometimes an astonishing blood red, pulsating with heat. Now it ran watery in the sunlight at the bend. Nothing there. Annette waited craftily. But still nothing. She felt that, as soon as she turned away, the first black spots would appear—coarse black hair—and the first splashes of color; but she could not wait. There was too much yet to do.

She found Timmy in the living room again, still not sitting in the chair. "I'll be right back, darling," she said. "Stay here. It's too hot outside for you. Put on the television—Mommy will be right back."

She got the clipping shears out of the closet and went outside, still teetering in her high heels. There was no time to waste, no time. The yellow rosebush was farthest away, but most important. She clipped roses off, a generous amount of stem. Though hurried—every few seconds she had to stare down the road—she took time to clip off some leaves as well. Then she went to the red bushes, which now exclaimed at her ignorance: she could see they were more beautiful, really, than the yellow roses. Red more beautiful than yellow; yellow looked common, not stunning enough against the house. It took her perhaps ten minutes, and even then she had to tear her eyes away from the lesser flowers, over there in the circular bed, she did not have time for them—unaccountably she was angry at them, as if they had betrayed her already, grateful to the migrant workers who were

coming to tear them to pieces! Their small stupid faces
nodded in the hot wind.

Timmy awaited her in the kitchen. He looked surprised
at all the roses. "The big vase," she commanded. In a
flurry of activity, so pleased by what she was doing
that she did not notice the dozens of bleeding scratches
on her hands, she lay the roses on the cupboard, clipped
at leaves, arranged them, took down a slender copper
vase and filled it with water, forced some roses in,
abandoned it when Timmy came in with the milk-glass
vase (wedding present from a remote aunt of hers). The
smell of roses filled the kitchen, sweetly drugged Annette's anxiety. Beauty, beauty—it was necessary to have
beauty, to possess it, to keep it around oneself!—how
well she understood that now.

Finished abruptly, she left the refuse on the cupboard
and brought the vases into the living room. She stood back
from them, peered critically . . . saw a stain on the wood
of the table already, she must have spilled some water.
And the roses were not arranged well, too heavy, too
many flowers, an insane jumble of flowered faces, some
facing one another nose to nose, some staring down
toward the water in the vase in an indecent way, some
at the ceiling, some at Annette herself. But there was
no time to worry over them, already new chores called
to her, demanded her services. What should she do next?
—The answer hit her like a blow; how could she be so
stupid? The doors were not even locked! Staggered by
this, she ran to the front door, with trembling fingers
locked it. How could she have overlooked this? Was
something in her, some secret corner, conspiring with
the Mexicans down the road? She ran stumbling to the
back door—even that had been left open, it could have
been seen from the road! A few flies buzzed idly, she
had no time for them. When she appeared, panting, in
the doorway, she saw Timmy by the big white vase
trying to straighten the flowers. . . . "Timmy," she said
sharply, "you'll cut yourself. Go away, go into the
other room, watch television."

He turned at once but did not look at her. She watched

him and felt, then, that it was a mistake to speak that
way to him—in fact, a deliberate error, like forgetting
about the doors; might not her child be separated from
her if they came, trapped in the other room? "No, no,
Timmy," she said, reaching out for him—he looked
around, frightened—"no, come here. Come here." He
came slowly. His eyes showed trust; his mouth, pursed
and tightened, showed wariness, fear of that trust. Annette saw all this—had she not felt the same way about
him, wishing him dead as soon as he was born?—and
flicked it aside, bent to embrace him. "Darling, I'll take
care of you. Here. Sit here. I'll bring you something to
eat."

He allowed her to help him sit at the dining room
table. He was strangely quiet, his head bowed. There was
a surface mystery about that quietness! Annette thought,
in the kitchen, I'll get through that, I'll prove myself to
him. At first cunningly, then anxiously, she looked
through the refrigerator, touching things, rearranging
things, even upsetting things—a jar of pickles—and
then came back carrying some strawberry tarts, made just
the day before, and the basket of new strawberries, and
some apples. "Here, darling," she said. But Timmy hesitated; while Annette's own mouth watered painfully, he
could only blink in surprise. Impatiently she said, "Here,
eat it, eat them. You love them. *Here.*" "No napkins,"
Timmy said fearfully. "Never mind napkins, or a table-
cloth, or plates," Annette said angrily—how slow her
child seemed to her, like one of those empty-faced children she often saw along the road, country children,
staring at her red car. "Here. Eat it. Eat it." When she
turned to go back to the kitchen, she saw him lifting
one of the tarts slowly to his mouth.

She came back almost immediately—bringing the
package of ice cream, two spoons, a basket of raspberries, a plate of sliced chicken wrapped loosely in wax
paper— She was overcome by hunger. She pulled a
chair beside Timmy, who had not yet eaten—he stared
gravely at her—and began to eat one of the tarts. It
convulsed her mouth, so delicious was it, so sweet yet at

the same time sour, tantalizing; she felt something like love for it, jealousy for it, and was already reaching for another when she caught sight of Timmy's stare. "Won't Daddy be home? Won't we have dinner?" he pleaded.

But he paused. His lips parted moistly and he stared at his mother, who smiled back at him, reassuring him, comforting him, pushing one of the tarts toward him with her polished nails. Then something clicked in his eyes. His lips damp with new saliva, he smiled at her, relieved, pleased. As if a secret ripened to bursting between them, swollen with passion, they smiled at each other. Timmy said, before biting into the tart, *"He* can't hit the car again, it's all locked up." Annette said, gesturing at him with sticky fingers, "Here, darling. Eat this. Eat. *Eat."*

At the Seminary

Mr. Downey left the expressway at the right exit, but ten minutes later he was lost. His wife was sitting in the back seat of the car, her round serious face made unfamiliar by the sunglasses she wore, and when he glanced at her in the rear-view mirror she did not seem to acknowledge him. His daughter, a big girl in a yellow sleeveless dress, was bent over the map and tracing something with her finger. "Just what I thought, that turn back there," she said. "That one to the left, by the hot dog stand. I thought that was the turn."

His somach was too upset; he could not argue. He did not argue with his daughter or his wife or his son Peter, though he could remember a time when he had argued with someone—his father, perhaps. His daughter, Sally, sat confidently beside him with her fingernail still poised against a tiny line on the map, as if she feared moving it would precipitate them into the wilderness. "Turn around, Daddy, for heaven's sake," she said. "You keep on driving way out of the way."

"Well, I didn't notice any sign," his wife said suddenly.

His daughter turned slowly. She too wore sunglasses, white plastic glasses with ornate frames and dark curved lenses. He could see her eyes close. "You weren't watching, then. I'm the one with the map anyway. I was pretty

sure that was the turn, back there, but he went by too
fast. I had to look it up on the map."

"Why didn't you say anything before?"

"I don't know." Sally shrugged her shoulders.

"Well, I didn't see any sign back there."

They had argued for the last hundred miles, off and on.
Mr. Downey tried to shut out their voices, not looking
at them, concentrating now on finding a place to turn
the car around before his daughter complained again.
They were on a narrow black-top road in the country,
with untended fields on either side. Mr. Downey slowed.
"There's a big ditch out there," Sally said. She tapped
at the window with her nails. "Be careful, Daddy."

"How much room does he have?"

"He's got—oh—some room yet— Keep on going,
Daddy. Keep on— Wait. No, Daddy, wait."

He braked the car. He could tell by his daughter's stiff,
alert back that they had nearly gone into the ditch.
"Okay, Daddy, great. Now pull ahead." Sally began waving her hand toward him, her pink fingernails glistening
roguishly. "Pull ahead, Daddy, that's it. That's it."

He had managed to turn around. Now the sun was
slanted before them again; they had been driving into it
all day. "How far back was that road," he said.

"Oh, a few miles, Daddy. No trouble."

They arrived at the crossroads. "See, there's the sign.
There it is," Sally said. She was quite excited. Though
she had been overweight by twenty or twenty-five pounds
for years, she often bounced about to demonstrate her
childish pleasure; she did so now. "See, what did I tell
you? Mom? There it is, there's the sign. U.S. 274, going
east, and there's the hot dog stand."

"It's closed."

"Yes, it's closed, I can see that, it's boarded up but
it's there," Sally said. She had turned slightly to face
her mother, the pink flesh creasing along her neck, her
eyes again shut in patient exasperation.

They drove east on 274. "It's only thirty more miles,"
Sally said. "Can I turn on the radio now?" Immediately
she snapped it on. In a moment they heard a voice ac-

companied by guitars and drums. The music made Mr.
Downey's stomach cringe. He drove on, his eyes searching
the top of the next ridge, as if he expected to see the
handsome buildings of the seminary beckoning to him,
assuring him. His wife threw down a magazine in the
back seat. "Sally, please turn that off. That's too loud.
You know you're only pretending to like it and it's giving
your father a headache."

"Is it?" Sally said in his ear.

"It's too loud. Turn it off," his wife said.

"Daddy, is it?"

He began to shake his head, began to nod it, said he
didn't know. "This business about Pete," he said apologetically.

Sally paused. Then she snapped off the radio briskly.
She seemed to throw herself back against the seat, her
arms folded so tightly that the thick flesh of her upper
arm began to drain white. They drove for a while in
silence. "Well, all right, turn it on," Mr. Downey said.
He glanced at Sally, who refused to move. She was
twenty-three, not what anyone would call fat, yet notice-
ably plump, her cheeks rounded and generous. Behind
the dark glasses her eyes were glittering, threatened by
stubborn tears. She wore a bright yellow cotton dress
that strained about her, the color made fierce by the sun,
as if it would be hot to the touch. "You can turn it on,
Sally," Mr. Downey said. "I don't care."

"It gives you a headache," his wife said. She had
thrown down the magazine again. "Why do you always
give in to her?"

Sally snorted.

"She doesn't care about Peter!" his wife cried. Her
anguish was sudden and unfeigned; both Mr. Downey
and Sally stiffened. They looked ahead at the signs—
advertisements for hotels, motels, service stations, res-
taurants. "Got to find a motel for tonight," Sally muttered.

'She doesn't care, neither of you cares," Mr. Downey's
wife went on. "The burden always falls on me. He wrote
the letter to me, I was the one who had to open it—"

"Daddy got a letter too. He got one right after," Sally said sullenly.

"But Peter wrote to me first. He understood."

"He always was a mommy's boy!"

"I don't want to hear that. I never want to hear that."

"Nevertheless," said Sally.

"I said I don't want to hear that again. Ever."

"Okay, you won't. Don't get excited."

Mr. Downey pulled off the road suddenly. He stopped the car and sat with his head bowed; other automobiles rushed past. "I won't be able to go on," he said. "Not if you keep this up."

Embarrassed, wife and daughter said nothing. They stared at nothing. Sally, after a moment, rubbed her nose with her fist. She felt her jaw clench as it did sometimes at night, while she slept, as if she was biting down hard upon something ugly but could not let go. Outside, in a wild field, was a gigantic billboard advertising a motel. From a great height a woman in a red bathing suit was diving into a bright aqua swimming pool. Mrs. Downey, taking her rosary out of her purse, stared out at this sign also, felt her daughter staring at it, thought what her daughter thought. In the awkward silence they felt closer to each other than either did to Mr. Downey. They said nothing, proudly. After a while, getting no answer, Mr. Downey started the car again and drove on.

The drive up to the seminary was made of black-top, very smart and precise, turning gently about the hill, back and forth amid cascades of evergreens and nameless trees with rich foliage. It was early September, warm and muggy. The seminary buildings looked sleek and cool. Mr. Downey had the feeling that he could not possibly be going to see anyone he knew or had known, that this trip was a mystery, that the young man who awaited him, related obscurely to him by ties of blood and name, was a mystery that exhausted rather than interested him. Mr. Downey had been no more worried by his wife's hopes that Peter would become a priest than he had by her hopes that Sally would enter a convent; he had

supposed both possibilities equally absurd. Yet, now
that Peter had made his decision, now that Mr. Downey
had grown accustomed to thinking of him in the way
one thinks of a child who is somehow maimed and dis-
qualified for life and therefore deserving of love, he felt
as disturbed as his wife by Peter's letters. His son's
"problem" could not be named, evidently; Peter himself
did not understand it, could not explain it: he spoke of
"wearing out," of "losing control," of seeing no one in
the mirror when he went to look at himself. He complained of grit in his room, of hairs in food, of ballpoint
ink he could not wash off his hands. Nothing that made
sense. He spoke of not being able to remember his *name*,
and this had disturbed Mr. Downey most of all; the hairs
reported in his food had disturbed Mrs. Downey most of
all. Nowhere had the boy said anything of quitting,
however, and they thought that puzzling. If he had
spoken in his incoherent letters of wanting to quit, of
going to college, of traveling about the country to observe
"life," of doing nothing at all, Mr. Downey would not
have felt so frightened. He could not parrot, as his wife
did, the words of the novice master who had telephoned
them that week: Peter was suffering a "spiritual crisis."
It was the fact that Peter had suggested no alternatives to
his condition that alarmed his father. It might almost
have been—and Mr. Downey had not mentioned this to
his wife—that the alternative to the religious life had
come to Peter to be no less than death.

God knew, Mr. Downey thought, he had wanted something else for Peter. He had wanted something else for
them all, but he could not recall what it was. He blamed
Peter's condition on his wife; at least Sally had escaped
her mother's influence, there was nothing wrong with her.
She was a healthy girl, loud and sure of herself, always
her father's favorite. But perhaps behind her quick robust
laugh there was the same sniveling sensitivity that had
ruined Peter's young life for him. Sally had played
boisterously with other girls and boys in the neighborhood, a leader in their games, running heavily about the
house and through the bushes, while Peter had withdrawn

to his solitary occupations, arranging and rearranging dead birds and butterflies in the back yard; but in the end, going up to bed, their slippers scuffing on the floor and their shoulders set as if resigned to the familiar terrors of the night, they had always seemed to Mr. Downey to be truly sister and brother, and related in no way to himself and his wife.

The seminary buildings were only three years old. Magnificently modern, aqua and beige, with great flights of glass and beds of complex plants on both the outside and the inside, huddling together against glass partitions so that the eye, dazed, could not tell where the outside stopped and the inside began: Mr. Downey felt uncertain and overwhelmed. He had not thought convincing the rector's speech, given on the day they had brought Peter up here, about the middle-class temperament that would relegate all religious matters to older forms, forms safely out of date. The rector had spoken passionately of the beauty of contemporary art and its stark contrast with the forms of nature, something Mr. Downey had not understood; nor had he understood what religion had to do with beauty or with art; nor had he understood how the buildings could have cost five million dollars. "Boy, is this place something," Sally said resentfully. "He's nuts if he wants to leave it and come back *home*." "He never said anything about leaving it," her mother said sharply.

They were met by Father Greer, with whom they had talked on the telephone earlier that week and who, standing alone on the evergreen-edged flagstone walk, seemed by his excessive calmness to be obscuring from them the fact of Peter's not being there. He was dark and smiling, taller than Mr. Downey and many years younger. "So very glad to see you," he said. "I hope you had an enjoyable ride? Peter is expected down at any moment." Very enjoyable, they assured him. Sally stood behind her father, as if suddenly shy. Mrs. Downey was touching her hair and nodding anxiously at Father Greer's words. In an awkward group they headed toward the entrance. Mr. Downey was smiling but as the young priest spoke, pointing out buildings and interesting sights, his eyes jumped about as if seeking out his son, expecting him to emerge around the corner of a building, out of an evergreen shrub. "The dormitory," Father Greer said, pointing. A building constructed into a hill, its first story disappearing into a riot of shrubs, much gleaming glass and metal. Beside it was the chapel, with a great brilliant cross that caught the sunlight and reflected it viciously. The light from the buildings, reflected and refracted by their thick glass, blinded Mr. Downey to whatever lay behind them—hills and forests and remote horizons. "No, we don't regret for an instant our having built out here," Father Greer was saying. They were in the lobby now. Mr. Downey looked around for Peter but saw no one. "They told us in the city that we'd go mad out here, but that was just jealousy. This is the ideal location for a college like ours. Absolutely ideal." They agreed. Mr. Downey could not recall just when he had noticed that some priests were younger than he, but he remembered a time when all priests were older, were truly "fathers" to him. "Please sit down here," Father Greer said. "This is a very comfortable spot." He too was looking about. Mr. Downey believed he could see, beyond the priest's cautious diplomatic charm, an expression of irritation. They were in an area blocked off from the rest of the lobby by thick plates of aqua-tinted glass. Great potted plants stood about in stone vases, the floor was tiled in a design of deep maroon and gray, the long low sofa on which they sat curved about a round marble coffee table of a most coldly beautiful, veined, fleshly color. Father Greer did not sit, but stood with his hands tightly extended and raised, as if he were blessing them against his will. "Will you all take martinis?" he said. They smiled self-consciously; Mrs. Downey said that Sally did not drink. "I'll take a martini," Sally said without looking up. Father Greer smiled.

Someone approached them, but it was not Peter. A boy Peter's age, dressed in a novice's outfit but wearing a white apron over it, came shyly to take their orders from Father Greer. "Peter will be down in a minute,"

Father Greer said. "Then we can all relax and talk and
see what has developed. And we'll be having dinner
precisely at six-thirty, I hope, in a very pleasant room
at the back of this building—a kind of fireside room we
use for special banquets and meetings. You didn't see it
the last time you were here because it's just been com-
pleted this summer. If anyone would like to wash up—"
He indicated graciously rest rooms at the far end of the
area, GENTLEMEN, LADIES. Mrs. Downey stood, fingering
her purse; Sally said crudely, "I'm all right." She had
not taken off her sunglasses. Mrs. Downey left; they
could smell the faint pleasant odor of her cologne. "He
said he would be down promptly," Father Greer said in
a slightly different voice, a confidential voice directed
toward Mr. Downey, "but he may have forgotten. That's
one of the—you know—one of the problems he has been
having—he tends to forget things unless he writes them
down. We discussed it Tuesday evening." "Yes, yes,"
Mr. Downey said, reddening. "He was never like that—
at home—" "His mind seems somewhere else. He seems
lost in contemplation—in another world," Father Greer
said, not unkindly. "Sometimes this is a magnificent thing,
you know, sometimes it develops into a higher, keener
consciousness of one's vocation. . . . Sometimes it's greatly
to be desired." He made Peter sound mysterious and
talented, in a way, so that Sally found herself looking
forward to meeting him. "If you'll excuse me for just a
minute," Father Greer said, "I think I'll run over to his
room and see how he is. Please excuse me—"

Sally and her father, left alone, had nothing to say to
each other. Sally peered over the rims of her glasses at
the lobby, but did not take the glasses off. She felt hot,
heavy, vaguely sick, a little frightened; but at the thought
of being frightened of something so trivial as seeing Peter
again her mouth twisted into a smirk. She knew him too
well. She knew him better than anyone knew him, and
therefore resented the gravity with which he was always
discussed, while her "problems" (whatever they were;
she knew she was supposed to have some) were discussed
by her mother and aunts as if they were immortal, im-

mutable, impersonal problems like death and poverty, unfortunate conditions no one could change, and not very interesting.

Her mother returned, her shoulders bent forward anxiously as if she were straining ahead. "Where did he go?" she said, gazing from Mr. Downey to Sally. "Nothing happened, did it?" "He'll be right back," Sally said. "Sit down. Stop worrying." Her mother sat slowly; Sally could see the little white knobs of vertebrae at the top of her neck, curiously fragile. When the novice returned he was carrying a tray of cocktails. Another boy in an identical outfit appeared with a tray of shrimp and sauce and tiny golden crackers, which he set down on the marble table. Both young men were modest and sly, like magicians appearing and disappearing. "Suppose we better wait," Mr. Downey said regretfully, looking at the drinks.

But when Peter did arrive, with Father Greer just behind him, they were disappointed. He looked the same: a little pale, perhaps thinner, but his complexion seemed blemished in approximately the same way it had been for years, his shoulders were inclined forward, just like his mother's, so that he looked anxious and hungry, like a chicken searching in the dirt. There were agreeable murmurs of surprise and welcome. Peter shook hands with his father, allowed his mother to hug him, and nodded to Sally with the self-conscious look he always directed toward her. He was a tall, eager boy with a rather narrow, bony face, given to blinking excessively but also to smiling very easily and agreeably, so that most people liked him at once though they did not feel quite at ease with him. In his novice's dress he took the light angularly and harshly, as if he were in strident mourning. And what could be the matter with him, Sally thought enviously, what secrets did he have, what problems that would endear him all the more to their parents? "Here, do have some of this. This looks delicious," Father Greer said, passing the plate of shrimp and crackers around. Sally's mouth watered violently, in spite of herself; she indicated with an abrupt wave of her hand that she did not want any. "Here, Peter, you always loved shrimp, every Friday we had to have shrimp," Mrs. Downey said in a trembling voice. She held the plate out to Peter, who had sat beside her. He hesitated, staring at the shrimp. "The sauce smells so good—" Mrs. Downey said coaxingly. At last Peter's arm moved. He picked up a toothpick and impaled a shrimp upon it; as they all watched, he dipped it into the sauce. Everyone sighed slightly. They settled back and crossed their legs.

They began to talk. Of the weather, first, and of the drive. The good and bad points of the expressway. Of all expressways, of encroaching civilization and the destruction of nature, yet at the same time the brilliant steps forward in the conquering of malignant nature. Peter chewed at the shrimp, Sally saw, but did not seem to have swallowed it. Talk fluttered about his head; now and then he glanced up, smiled, and replied. Sally, finding no one watching her, began to eat shrimp and could not stop. The more she ate, the more angry she felt at the people before her and at the boys who had served the drinks and food and at the seminary itself. She could feel her face freezing into that expression of disdain she hated in her mother but could not help in herself: so she faced everything she disapproved of, flighty vain girls no older than she in fur coats and glittering jewelry, young men in expensive sports cars, gossiping old ladies, old men who drank, young mothers who were obviously so proud and pleased with their lives they would just as soon spit in your eye when you passed them on the sidewalk, pushing baby buggies along as if that were a noble task! Sally did not approve of people talking in church or looking around, craning their bony old necks, nor did she approve of children—any children—who were noisy and restless and were apt to ask you why you were so fat, in front of everyone; she did not approve of people photographed on society pages or on magazine covers, or houses that were not made of brick or stone but were in poor neighborhoods with scrawny front lawns, but also she did not approve of lower-class white people who hated Negroes, as if they were any better themselves.

She did not approve of high school boys and girls who swung along the sidewalks with their arms around each other, laughing vulgarly, and she did not approve of college students who did the same thing. While at college she had been so isolated by the sternness of her disapproval that no roommate had suited her and she had finally moved to a single room, where she had stayed for four years, studying angrily so that she could get good grades (which she did) and eating cookies and cakes and pies her mother sent her every week. She had loved her mother then and knew her mother loved her, since they never saw each other, but now that she was home and waiting for the placement bureau to send her notice of a decent job, something they evidently were not capable of doing, she and her mother hardly spoke and could feel each other's presence in the house as one feels or suspects the presence of an insect nearby. Her mother had wanted her to be pretty, she thought, and deliberately she was not pretty. (And Peter, there, still chewing, was homely too, she had never really noticed that before.) Sometimes she went to bed without washing her face. Certainly she did not wash her hair more than once a week, no matter what was coming up; and she had pretended severely not to care when her mother appropriated for herself the expensive lavender dress she had worn to the important functions at college when she had been twenty or thirty pounds lighter. She wore no make-up except lipstick, a girlish pink, and her shoes were always scuffed and marked by water lines, and she often deliberately bought dresses too large so the shoulders hung down sloppily. Everything angered her: the vanities of the world, the pettiness of most people, the banal luxuries she saw through at once—like this seminary, and the cocktails, when their own priest back home had new missions every week or new approaches to the Bishop's Relief Fund. She picked up the martini and sipped at it; its bitterness angered her. She put it down. She would not drink it and collaborate in this vanity. Even the graceful gleaming glass, finely shaped like a work of art, annoyed her, for beside it her own stumpy fingers and uneven nails looked ugly. What place was there in the real world for such things? She felt the real world to be elsewhere—she did not know where—in the little town they had passed through on the way up to the seminary, perhaps, where the ugly store fronts faced each other across a cobbled main street fifty years old, and where country people dawdled about in new shoes and new clothes, dressed for Saturday, looking on everything with admiration and pleasure. But what were these people talking about? She hunched forward in an exaggerated attitude of listening. Baseball. She was ashamed of her father, who spoke of baseball players familiarly, slowly, choosing his words as if each were important, so making a fool of himself. Father Greer, debonair and charming, was bored of course but would not show it. Mrs. Downey looked puzzled, as if she could not quite keep up with the conversation; the martini had made her dizzy. Peter, beside her, his awkward hands crossed on his knees, stared at something in the air. He was waiting, as they were all waiting, Sally supposed, for this conversation to veer suddenly around to him, confront him in his odd trans- fixed fear and demand from him some explanation of himself. Sally sipped at the cocktail and felt its bitterness expand to take in all of the scene before her. If Peter glanced at her she would look away; she would not help him. She needed no one herself, and wanted no one to need her. Yet she wondered why he did not look at her— why he sat so stiff, as if frozen, while about him chatter shot this way and that to ricochet harmlessly off surfaces.

The subject had been changed. "Peter made some par- ticularly perceptive remarks on the *Antigone* of Sophocles this summer," Father Greer was saying. He had finished his martini and rolled the glass slowly between his palms, the delicate stem turning and glinting against his tanned skin. "We study a number of Greek tragedies in the original Greek. The boys find them strangely intriguing. Puzzles." Mr. and Mrs. Downey were both sitting for- ward a little, listening. "The world view of the Greeks," Father Greer said severely, "is so astonishingly different from our own." Sally drew in her breath suddenly. "I

wouldn't say that, precisely," she remarked. Father Greer
smiled at her. "Of course there are many aspects of our
civilizations that are similar," he said. "What strikes us
as most barbaric, however, is their utter denial of the freedom of man's will." He thought her no antagonist,
obviously; he spoke with a faintly condescending smile
Sally detested because she believed she had been seeing
it all her life. "But that might not be so strange, after
all," she drawled. Her mother was frowning, picking at
something imaginary on the rim of her cocktail glass. Her
father was watching her as if she were performing a
foolish and dangerous trick, like standing on her head.
But Peter, sitting across from her with his long fingers
clasped together on his knees, his back not touching the
sofa, was staring at her and through her with a queer
theatrical look of recognition, as if he had not really
noticed her before. "And their violence," Sally said.
"The violence of their lives—that might not be so strange
to us either." "There is no violence in Greek drama,"
Father Greer said. Sally felt her face close up, suddenly.
Her eyes began to narrow; her lips pursed themselves in
a prim little look of defiance; the very contours of her
generous face began to hunch themselves inward.

An awkward minute passed. "You still on that diet?"
Peter said.

Sally's eyes opened. Peter was looking at her with a
little smile. Her face burned. "What? Me? I—"

"Why, Peter," their mother said. "What do you
mean?"

Peter's gaze plummeted. He examined his fingers.
Sally, more stunned than angry, watched him as if he
had become suddenly an antagonist, an open enemy; she
saw that his hands were streaked with something—it
looked like red ink or blood, something scrubbed into
his skin.

"Sorry," Peter muttered.

In this crisis Father Greer seemed to fall back; his
spine might have failed him unaccountably. The very
light turned harsh and queer; churned about gently in
the air-conditioned lounge, it seemed not to be illumi-

nating them but to be pushing them away from each other, emphasizing certain details that were not to be cherished: Peter's acne, Mrs. Downey's tiny double chin and the network of fine wrinkles that seemed to hold together her expression, Mr. Downey's sluggish mouth, drooping as if under the impact of a sudden invisible blow, even the surface gloss of Father Greer's professional charm dented by a dull embarrassed gleam at the tip of his nose. And Sally was glad of being fat and unattractive, with a greasy nose, coarse skin, a dress stained with perspiration, glad she could delight no one's eyes, fulfill no one's expectations of her—

"I don't believe you've seen our chapel," Father Greer said. He made a tentative movement that was not really tentative but commanding; Sally saw how Peter's shoulders and arms jerked up, mimicking the priest, before he himself had decided to stand. They all stood, smoothing their clothing, smiling down at the martini glasses and what was left of the shrimp and crackers, as if bidding good-by to acquaintances newly made. "It's very beautiful, we commissioned the Polish architect Radomski to design it for us—the same Radomski who did the campus at St. Aquinas University—you might remember the pictures in *Life?*"

They agreed vaguely, moving along. Father Greer seemed to be herding them. Sally, at the rear, caught a glimpse of the young priest's face as he turned, and was startled by the blunt, naked intensity of his concern— an instant's expression of annoyance, alarm, helplessness that immediately faded—and what an attractive man he was, in spite of his deep-set eyes, she thought, what a pity—a pity— But she did not know what the pity was for. Out of spite she kept her martini glass in hand; it was still half full. She wandered at the back of the small group, looking around, squinting through her dark glasses. Several young priests passed them, nodding hello. They walked on. The building smelled like nothing, absolutely nothing. It did not even have the bitter antiseptic smell of soap. Nothing had an odor, nothing was out of place, nothing disturbed the range of the eye: the building and its people might not yet have been born, might be awaiting birth and baptism, immersion in smells and disorder. On the broad flagstone walk to the chapel Sally walked with the martini glass extended as if it were a symbol of some kind, an offering she carried to the chapel under the secret gazes of all those secret boys, cloistered there in that faceless building.

In the chapel they fell silent. Sally frowned. She was going to take off her sunglasses, but stopped. The chapel was gigantic: a ceiling dull and remote as the sky itself, finely lined, veined as if with the chill of distance or time, luring the eye up and forward, relentlessly forward, to the great statue of the crucified Christ behind the altar. There it was. The walls of the building might have fallen away, the veneer of words themselves might have been peeled back, to reveal this agonized body nailed to the cross: the contours of the statue so glib, so perfect, that they seemed to Sally to be but the mocking surfaces of another statue, a fossilized creature caught forever within that crust—the human model for it, suffocated and buried. Father Greer chatted excitedly about something: about that sleek white Christ, a perfect immaculate white, the veins of his feet and throat throbbing a frozen immaculate white. About his head drops of white blood had coagulated over the centuries; a hard white crown of thorns pierced his skin lovingly, rendered by art into something fragile and fine. The chapel was empty. No, not empty; at the very front a figure knelt, praying. The air was cold and stagnant. Nothing swirled here; time itself had run out, run down. Sally felt perspiration on her forehead and under her arms. She had begun to ache strangely, her head and her body; she could not locate the dull throbbing pain. Her head craning stupidly, she stared up at the gigantic statue. Yes, yes, she would agree to Father Greer's questioning glance: was it not magnificent? Yes, but what was it that was magnificent? What did they know? What were they looking at? How did they know—and she thought of this for no reason, absolutely no reason—what their names were, their stupid names? How did they know anything? Her glance fell

in confusion to her parents' nervous smiles and she felt
she did not recognize them. And to Peter's awkward
profile, so self-pitying; was it to tell them he could no
longer believe in Christ that he had brought them to the
seminary? But she understood, staring at her brother's
rigid face, that he could no more not believe in Christ
than she could: that the great milky statue itself could
more easily twitch into life than they could disbelieve
the ghostly contours that lay behind that form, lost in
history—and that they were doomed, brother and sister,
doomed in some obscure inexplicable vexing way neither
could understand, and their parents and this priest, whispering rather loudly about "seating capacity," could never
understand. The three adults walked toward the front
of the chapel, down the side aisle. Peter stumbled as if a
rock had rolled suddenly before his feet; Sally could not
move. She stared up at the statue with the martini glass
in her hand. She and Peter might have been awaiting a
vision, patiently as always. Yet it will only end, she
thought savagely, in steak for dinner—a delicate tossed
salad—wine— And as her body flinched in outrage at this
vision (so powerful as to have evoked in her a rush of
hunger, in spite of herself) she felt a sudden release of
pressure, a gentle aching relaxation she did not at first
recognize. A minute flow of blood. She did not move,
paralyzed, her mouth slowly opening in an expression of
awe that might have been religious, so total and commanding was it. Her entire life, her being, her very soul
might have been conjured up and superimposed upon
that rigid white statue, so intensely did she stare at it, her
horror transformed into a prayer of utter silence, utter
wordlessness, as she felt the unmistakable relentless flow
of blood begin in her loins. Then her face went slack.
She looked at the martini glass, brought it to her mouth,
finished the drink. She smirked. She had known this
would happen, had thought of it the day before, then had
forgotten. She had forgotten. She could not have forgotten but she did, and it was for this reason she grinned
at the smudged glass in her hand. Now Peter turned and
followed the others; she followed him. Bleeding warmly

and secretly. Her gaze was hot upon the backs of her parents, her mother especially, cleanly odored, well-dressed woman: what a surprise! What a surprise she had for her! "I'm afraid this is cloistered," Father Greer whispered. He looked sorry. They headed in another direction, through a broad passageway, then out, out and into a spacious foyer; now they could breathe.

"What beauty! Immeasurable beauty!" Father Greer said aloud. His eyes were brittle with awe, an awe perhaps forced from him; he looked quite moved. Yet what was he moved at, Sally thought angrily, what had they been looking at, what did they *know?* Peter wiped at his nose, surreptitiously, but of course everyone saw him. What did they know? What had they seen? What might they ever trust again in a world of closed surfaces, of panels just sliding shut? She was shaken, and only after a moment did she notice her mother glaring at her, at the cocktail glass and the sunglasses. Her mother's face was white and handsome with the splendor of her hatred. Sally smirked. She felt the faithful blood inside her seeping, easing downward. Father Greer pointed out something further—someone agreed—she felt the hot blood on her legs. She was paralyzed, charmed. The others walked on but she did not move. Her mother glanced around. "Sally?" she said. Sally took a step, precariously. Nothing. Perhaps she would be safe. She caught her mother's gaze and held it, as if seeking help, hoping for her mother to draw her safely to her by the sheer force of her impatience. Then, for no reason, she took a hard, brutal step forward, bringing her flat heel down hard on the floor. Then again. She strode forward, brusquely, as if trying to dent the marble floor. The others were waiting for her, not especially watching her. She slammed down her heel so that it stung, and the blood jerked free. It ran instantly down the inside of her leg to her foot. She was breathing hard, excited and terrified and somehow pleased, waiting for her mother to notice. Why didn't she notice? Sally glanced down, was startled to see how big her stomach was, billowing out in the babyish yellow dress she had worn here out of spite, and saw the delicate trickle of blood there—on her calf, her ankle (which was not too clean), inside her scuffed shoe and so out of sight! At the door the others waited: the slim priest in black, who could see everything and nothing, politely, omnipotently; her father and mother, strangers also, who would see and suffer their vision as it swelled deafeningly upon them, their absolute disbelief at what they saw; her brother Peter, who was staring down at the floor just before her robust feet as if he had seen something that had turned him to stone.

Sally smiled angrily. She faced her mother, her father. Nothing. They looked away, they did not look at each other. Father Greer was holding the door open. No one spoke. Sally wanted to say, "That sure must have cost a lot!" but she could not speak. She saw Father Greer's legs hold themselves in stride, she could nearly see his muscles resist the desperate ache they felt to carry him somewhere—the end of this corridor, through one of the mysterious doors, or back to the cloistered sanctuary behind them. "And these, these," he said, "these are tiny chapels—all along here— Down there the main sacristy—" His words fell upon them from a distance, entirely without emotion. He showed nothing. Sally stomped on the floor as if killing insects, yet he did not look around. She felt blood trickling down her legs, a sensation she thought somehow quite pleasant, and in her shoes her toes wiggled in anticipation of the shame soon to befall them. On they walked. At each of Father Greer's words they leaned forward, anxious not to be denied, anxious to catch his eye, force upon him the knowledge that they saw nothing, knew nothing, heard only what he told them. Sally began to giggle. She wanted to ask Father Greer something, but the rigidity of her hysteria was too inflexible; she found she could not open her mouth. Her jaws seemed locked together. But this isn't my fault, she cried mockingly to their incredulous accusing backs, I never asked for it, I never asked God to make me a woman! She could not stop grinning. What beauty! What immeasurable beauty! It was that she grinned at, nothing else. That immeasurable beauty. Each heavy step, each ponderous straining of her thick thighs, centuries old, each sigh that swelled up into her chest and throat, each shy glance from her brother, all these faded into a sensation of overwhelming light or sound, something dazzling and roaring at once, that seemed to her to make her existence suddenly beautiful: complete: ended.

Then Peter was upon her. He grabbed for her throat. His face was anguished, she was able to see that much, and as she screamed and lunged back against the wall her parents and the priest turned, whirled back, seemed for an instant to be attacking her as well. "Damn you! Damn you!" Peter cried. His voice rose to a scream, a girl's scream. He managed to break away from Father Greer's arms and struck her, his fists pounding, a child's battle Sally seemed to be watching from across the corridor, through a door, across a span of years— "Damn you! Now I can't leave! I can't leave!" he cried. They pulled him back. He had gone limp. He hid his face and sobbed; she remembered him sobbing that way, often. Of course. His habitual sob, sheer helplessness before her strength, her superior age, weight, complacency. She gasped, her body still shuddering in alarm, ready to fight, to kill, her strong competent legs spread apart to give her balance. Her heart pounded like a magnificent angel demanding to be released, to be set upon her enemies. Peter turned away, into the priest's embrace, still sobbing. He showed nothing of his face but a patch by his jaw, a splotched patch of adolescent skin.

Mr. Downey entered the expressway without slackening speed. It was late, nearly midnight. He had far to go. Fortified by alcohol, dizzily confident, he seemed to be driving into a wild darkness made familiar by concrete, signs, maps, and his own skillful driving. Beside him his daughter sat with the map in hand again, but they would not need it. He knew where he was driving them. The expressway was deserted, held no challenge to him, the sheer depthless dark beyond the range of his headlights could not touch him, fortified as he was by the knowledge

of precisely where he was going. Signs, illuminated by
his headlights, flashed up clearly and were gone, they
were unmistakable, they would not betray him, just as
visions of that evening flashed up to him, without terror,
and were gone. They knew what to do. None of this
surprised them. Nothing surprised them. (He thought
of the confessional; that explained it.) A few weeks of
rest, nothing more, the boy would be safe, there was
nothing to worry about. And he felt, numbly, that there
really was nothing to worry about any longer, that everything had been somehow decided, that it had happened
in his presence but he had not quite seen it. The priests
were right: Father Greer and the older priest, a very
kindly Irishman Mr. Downey had trusted at once. Something had been decided, delivered over. It was all right.
In the back seat his wife sat impassive and mindless,
watching the road that led inexorably back home. Beside
him his daughter sat heavily, her arms folded. She
yawned. Then she reached out casually to turn on the
radio. "Please, Sally," her mother said at once, as if
stirred to life. The radio clicked on. Static, a man's voice.
Music. "Sally," her mother said. Sally's plump arm
waited, her fingers still on the knob. "It bothers your
father," Mrs. Downey said, "you know it gives him a
headache." "I'll turn it down real low," Sally said. Out
of the corner of Mr. Downey's eye her face loomed blank
and milky, like a threatening moon he dared not look
upon.

Norman and the Killer

Because he was an ordinary man, whose reflection in mirrors and in incidental windows could have belonged to anyone, Norman had never thought of himself as involved in anything that could attract attention. He had no interest in going to see accidents or fires or other disasters because he would be pushed around by the crowd and would not complain, and because he had no heart to peer in, there, at the very center of the jostling, to see the exposed bleeding flesh suddenly catapulted out of the usual channels of life. Because he was a gentle man, a shy man, no longer exactly young, whose life had attached itself gently to his family, he was surprised at the professional hardness with which he was able to meet customers in the clothing store he managed, and at the violence of the love he was suffering through for a woman his brother-in-law had introduced him to. In his youth he had read much and was able to appreciate the spiritual hardness of the heroes of great fiction, who seemed to him to walk upon ropes stretched over nothing, dazzling and performing endlessly, without fear of death. Their absolution of their humanity made them heroes and for this Norman envied them but could not believe in them; they told him nothing about himself.

The young woman's name was Ellen and she too had read much in her youth, which her dark opaque eyes suggested had been an extension of the life she now led, sternly bleak and self-satisfied, a loneliness that had to be respected because it had been her own choice. She had been married for several years, in her early twenties, but of this Norman did not allow himself to think. He often frightened himself at the anxiety he felt for her: his desperation to protect her from whatever startled her eyes, whatever drew her mind away from him as if he were no more than an accidental accomplice to the caprices of her memory, calculated to remind her always of other evenings, other years. Yet he knew he had no right to that desperation, for she did not belong to him. At times he disliked her for her power over him, but most of the time, during the long identical days at the store, his love for this woman—whom he did not really know—was so absurdly great as to overwhelm him, threaten him with an obscure, inexplicable violence, something that might have been building up in him through the years while he had lived at home, a child grown into a man without anyone really noticing. Waking each morning in his old room, in the old house, he would smell resentfully the odors of breakfast being cooked downstairs and would think that, if he did not marry Ellen, he would wake to this every morning for the rest of his life.

One afternoon they drove out of the city to a summer playhouse. The drive took two hours, and Norman was pleased at Ellen's friendliness. She spoke of the playhouse, some actors she knew, and this made him think idly that she was to him like the women he had been seeing in movies all his life: ethereal and majestic, following a script he did not know, could not anticipate, yet smiling out of the very graciousness of their own near-beauty, welcoming his admiration while not exactly acknowledging it. She wore white; the self-conscious pose of her profile distracted him from the road. She was talking now of her job. Norman thought of marrying her, of living with her, but at this his face flinched, for it seemed impossible that this should ever be; his very reflection, glancing down at him out of the rear-view mirror, the dusty reflection of a rather heavy, polite, stern face, with wisps of damp dark hair curled down on his forehead, caught his eye as if he were sharing a secret with it, a secret of perplexed failure. "I may have to leave this job, after six years," she said. He glanced over at her. "There are complications," she said.

He turned into a filling station to get gas. He did not want to ask her about these complications, but he knew she was anxious to continue. In the bright glare from the sun she looked younger than she was; her youth had always seemed to Norman like a weapon. They waited for the man to put in the gas. "Always complications, involvements," she said. "Personal relationships start off so cleanly but then become too involved. Even business relationships. . . ." She smirked at something, some memory; for a moment her face was unfamiliar, her nose sharp, her eyes darker with the intensity of a bemused unpleasant thought. Norman, unhappy, turned to pay the station attendant. He peered up at a man his own age, of moderate height, dressed in greasy clothes; the man's face was smeared with dirt and perspiration. "Hot day," said the man, with a smirk something like Ellen's. Norman, staring at him, felt his heart begin to pound absurdly. The man's face was familiar, unmistakable. For an instant they stared at each other. The man licked his lips, a stout strong man yet a little startled by Norman's look, and turned away. Norman stared at his back. He wanted to open the door and get out, do something. Beside him Ellen was talking, he could not understand her. Finally she touched his arm. "Is something wrong?" she said. "I think I know that man," he said. As soon as he said this something seemed to assure him: he did not know the man, it was impossible, it did not matter. Nothing mattered. "Know him from where?" Ellen said. "I don't know, nothing. It doesn't matter," he said.

The man returned with Norman's change. Norman tried not to look at him, for the intensity of his feeling had alarmed him: he thought of his uncle, now institutionalized, who had been committed at last by his patient wife, an ordinary man who could not stop talking. In that instant, as he first looked at the attendant's face,

Norman felt a kinship with that other, lost man, whom he had not thought of for ten years. . . . But he did look at the station attendant's face after all. The man was smiling without enthusiasm, a smile that stretched his lips to show discolored teeth, leaving the rest of his face indifferent. He had a rather plump face, he had obviously gained weight, Norman saw, but still, out of that heavy, dirt-streaked face, another face confronted him, unmistakable. It was the face of a boy, maybe seventeen. "Here y'are, thank you," the man said. He had a dirty rag over one shoulder. It was strange, Norman thought, fumbling for the ignition, that the man had not offered to clean his windshield.

He drove away. His heart was pounding furiously. "Why didn't you ask him if he knew you?" Ellen said. "It seems to mean a lot to you." She sounded resentful, but he knew that if he were to continue she would lose interest. "No, nothing. A mistake," Norman said. Yet his mind flashed and dazzled him: he knew the face, of course, he might have been shuffling through a deck of cards to come to it, through a handful of old snapshots, waiting patiently for it to turn up. "You're driving rather fast," Ellen said. He slowed down. He glanced at his watch and was surprised to see that it was so early. A great block of time seemed to have passed, jerked away from him. Back at the garage, was the man staring after this car, his smile abandoned? Norman looked fiercely at the countryside. He shut his mind, pushed everything away. Aside. He would not think, he would not remember.

They had dinner at a country inn near the theater. It was dim and pretentious, but he saw that Ellen enjoyed it. In her white silk dress and dark necklace she looked clean, harshly clean and young, her shoulders poised against an unfamiliar background of rough-hewn wooden walls decorated with old wrought-iron objects Norman could not have identified. Yet Norman heard himself say, "Did you say you had a brother?" Yes, she had said. Why did he ask that? Why at this moment? She had a brother who lived in Europe, what did it matter? She was always antagonistic about families, friends, any re-

lationships that belonged to the past. Norman wanted
to touch her hand, not to comfort her but to ask for
help. The darkness of his mind was released, flowing
steadily, unhurriedly, and out of that flood of old faces
his heartbeat anticipated the anguish of his revelation.
"Excuse me," he said, standing. He caught her glance:
she was thinking that he behaved strangely, he could not
be trusted. He went to the men's room. There, his back
against the tiled wall, he rubbed his eyes and waited until
the turmoil ceased. He remembered the face now. He
knew he had remembered it at once. Now it came clearly,
a boy's face, dirty and hard, and rearing behind it a gray
March morning, an indifferent mottled sky. "My God,"
Norman said aloud. He wanted to rush back to Ellen as
if he had something joyous to tell her. But his legs were
weak; he reached out to get his balance. Or he would
go to a telephone. He would telephone the police. And
his father—but his father was dead, had been dead for
years. He felt strangely peaceful; something might have
been decided. When he returned to their table, where
this attractive young woman awaited him, concerned for
him, he felt his fingers twitch as if he wanted to reach
out to embrace her, to have her draw him to her so that
he would no longer need to think.

One Saturday afternoon when he was fifteen Norman
and his brother Jack were coming home from a movie.
It was about four-thirty: late winter, the day already
ending, a chill bleak wind. The Technicolor of the movie
had dazzled Norman's eyes, so that the warehouses they
passed now seemed to him unsubstantial and deceptive,
not remnants of a world but anticipations of a fuller,
greater world he would grow into. Invisible behind the
vision of that movie had been flights of music, but here
there was no music, only their hurrying footsteps. Jack,
at seventeen, was not much taller than Norman, both
were small for their ages, with meek, dark defensive
faces. There were other boys Norman preferred to be
with—even his younger brother—but Jack never made
friends easily, shrugged away the long days spent at the

high school with a disdainful closed expression, so that only after his death did Norman find out, from other people, that Jack was considered a little strange—not slow, exactly, because he had always been good at mathematics, but not quite quick enough, not right enough, somehow inferior.

They went down by the river, Jack's idea, and here the wind was stronger. An odor of something rotting was in the air. Norman and his brother wore jackets that were alike, the same size, made of material like canvas, a dull faded green. Sitting at the end of one of the old docks was a middle-aged man in the same kind of jacket. He did not look around, he might have been asleep or drunk. "What's he doing out here, he don't have a fish pole," Jack said resentfully. They walked past the dock. Norman shared Jack's resentment, because it seemed to him something was wrong, something adult was out of place, and if this was so, then everything might be out of place. The familiar waterfront had become, in the poor light, parched with heavy clouds that gave to everything a strange lightless glare that hurt Norman's eyes. Jack, as if to comfort him, talked of what they would have for supper that night—he had smelled the spaghetti sauce cooking before they left. But Norman was watching something ahead—movement back by the unloading platform of one of the old warehouses, a giant monstrosity that had been abandoned for years. An immense exhaustion touched him suddenly, for this world was so banal a betrayal of the world of that movie, so unimaginative a failure, that he could not respond to it. A few more years, he thought, and his life would change: he did not yet know just how it would change. He would not be like Jack, begging to quit school, his side of the room cluttered with auto racing magazines. And he thought, glancing at Jack's worried face, that he could not admire him as an older brother, for Jack was not big or strong enough. He did not like Jack because Jack did not bully him; he pitied Jack because Jack at seventeen had to wear the same jacket he wore at fifteen, and the two of them, bored with each other, were doomed to be brothers forever and could do nothing about it.

"There's some guys," Jack said. Norman saw three boys on the dock ahead. Something was tilting, falling over. It was a hollow metal cylinder that was buoyed up for a moment on the water, then sank. "Do you know them?" Norman said. "Are they in your class?" "No, not them bastards," Jack said. As a child, Norman had always taken his responses from other people, and now, at fifteen, he felt Jack's sudden stiffened look pass over him at once. They kept on walking, Jack a little ahead. The three boys were laughing at something, their snatches of words incomprehensible and harsh, as if they spoke a foreign language. One, in a soiled flannel shirt, was lighting a cigarette. They were about Jack's age. As Jack and Norman approached they grew quiet, staring out at the water. Jack was looking straight ahead, but Norman could not help but glance at the boys—absolutely ordinary faces with identical blank, cautious expressions, their hair much too long. They stood with their legs apart, as if posing. The boy in the flannel shirt lit his cigarette and tossed the match out into the water. Jack and Norman passed by, were by them, and Norman felt his legs want to run—he did not know why—but Jack did not hurry. Norman's breathing had quickened. Nothing had happened, no one had said a word, yet just before he was hit something in him shouted at the back of Jack's head: You fool! You goddamn fool for getting us into this!

A board struck Norman on the right shoulder and he spun around, gaping. He saw the three faces lunge at him, serious and quiet. Then the pain exploded again, this time on his chest, and he felt himself falling, falling back into nothing; then he struck the water hard. It swelled upon him and he sank into its frigid softness with his eyes opened in terror at the sky. His arms jerked, his legs threshed, but caught at nothing. It seemed queer to him that the water was cold and hard, yet could not support him. . . . Then he came to the surface, choking. Someone yelled, "Get that one!" and Norman tried

to fling himself backward, anywhere. He did not know
yet that Jack was in the water too. Something struck
the water beside his head, he did not know what, and
disappeared at once. Through the film before his eyes
he saw one of the boys striking at the water by the dock
with a long piece of rusty metal, his face hard and deliberate, as if he were chopping wood and counting the
strokes. Norman pressed backward, out and backward,
his heart pounding so violently that he could not see.
Someone shouted—a word Norman did not recognize—
and it seemed that in the freezing water words were
shattered and had no meaning, did not matter, nothing
mattered.

When he woke, it was with reluctance. Immediately
the air assaulted him: he lay on his back against something hard, faces were peering down at him. Adults. He
had been brought back. In curious alarm they stared at
him and he at them; then he began to vomit. Someone
held him. His body convulsed as if struggling against an
invisible enemy, writhing and fleeing. They spoke to him,
there was a siren somewhere, even a woman's voice, and
though he could now understand their words he felt
himself an intruder, someone returned from the dead
who has no business overhearing anything. It was said
later that he called for Jack at once, but he never remembered this. They had answered by assuring him that
Jack was all right, he was already in the ambulance,
but of course this was a lie.

During the play he could not sit still. He perspired
heavily. Onstage, the actors moved through their lines
without hesitation, pert and skillful, but Norman understood nothing. He might have been drowning again,
drowning in air and words of another language, remote
even from the woman who sat beside him. At intermission
they went outside and he could tell from her silence
that she was not pleased. They stared out together at a
flower garden, some design of grass and flowers murky
in the twilight but heavy with meaning, deliberate and
plotted. "Would you like to go home?" Ellen said softly.

As if guilty, Norman could not meet her eyes. He heard her words but could not make sense of them, for he was staring once again through that cold film at the boys up on the dock—secure and dry—the faces of two of them raw and blurred, but the other face now clear. He recognized it. "Why don't we go home," Ellen said, touching his arm. Norman knew that if he broke down before her he would lose her, of course; her sympathy could not be trusted. "No, I'm all right," he said, almost angrily. "It's nothing."

He stayed at her apartment for only a few minutes. She was tired and distracted and apologetic, and she seemed not to see how he wanted to remain with her, he would have talked of anything, done anything, if only she would protect him against the violence of the past— After he left her he went to a bar for a while and then, dizzy and sickened, he went home. In bed old fragments of prayers taunted his mind, and now and then it seemed to him quite clear that he had made a mistake, that he was perhaps losing his mind. He would do nothing. He would not give in. In the morning he would wake as usual to the pleasant smells from the kitchen below, he would go to the store and call Ellen, he would never drive out to that part of the country again.

But he was unable to call her. He started to dial her number several times, but always something came up and he was relieved to put back the receiver. Once he caught himself walking somewhere very deliberately—to his desk in the back office. He opened one of the drawers and glanced in at the pistol there, half covered with papers. Trembling, he hid it with papers. He stood there, staring down at the drawer for a while. No one came in, nothing happened. The ordinariness of everything, the refusal of life to change at all, baffled and angered him. He felt nauseous but nothing happened. In the rest room, watching himself suspiciously in the mirror, he believed shakily that his reflection was that of a guilty man.

After the store closed he drove out to the country. The drive took less time than it had the other day. While he drove he thought of nothing, not even Ellen, who ought to have been sitting beside him. . . . If he returned to the gas station and saw the man again, and if he could assure himself that it was not the same man he wanted, then perhaps he would call Ellen from the station; he would do that. But as he neared the small junction where the garage was supposed to be, he found himself looking shrewdly around, at houses, down lanes, down side roads. He passed the garage. No one was outside. A shabby garage with dented Coke signs and signs with scrawled numbers on them advertising gas prices, and other signs advertising cigarettes and spark plugs. The drive was just dirt and gravel, not paved. They did little business, he thought, and this was good. Several miles farther he turned down a side road and drove slowly along: country without houses, wild fields unowned by people, woods gone wild. When he saw a shanty by the edge of a woods, half a mile back from the road, he stopped the car and got out.

The shanty was deserted. It was roofed with tar paper and its wood had turned black. Inside there were newspapers on the ground, an old dented pan, some rags, a few tiny ant hills. Weeds blossomed everywhere. Norman tried to imagine what use the shanty had had, who might have built it. It seemed to him a mystery: built, abandoned, now ready for him and his brother's killer.

When he drove back he stopped at the garage for gas. The man who serviced him was not the killer, but Norman saw that there was another man inside, drinking soda pop. "What time do you people close?" Norman said. "Stay open till ten, summer," the man said. Norman hardly glanced at him. His eyes kept moving back to the open door of the garage. "That's all, thanks," he said, smiling. It was the first time he had smiled since having first seen that man.

He called Ellen from his home. At once his voice became anxious and apologetic, and her silence tormented him. "I know, I know what you said that time about not wanting to get involved with people you can't trust," he said hopelessly, "and how you don't want—you don't—" He fell silent. The vision of her that her silence evoked in him was transparent and unfamiliar; was she going to say nothing? How long had they known each other? "I am going to see you again, aren't I?" Norman said. "Yes, of course," she said faintly. "But I think you should get some rest or see a doctor. You don't seem yourself. . . ." "No, there's nothing wrong with me," Norman said sharply. She did not reply, as if startled. "When can I see you? Tomorrow?" Norman said. "No, not tomorrow, I forgot— I have something—" "What are you doing?" she said. "I'm sorry, I just can't make it then. The day after tomorrow?" Norman said. "Can I call you?" "Of course you can call me," she said meekly and coldly. Norman felt in that instant her strange hatred for him, for the force that drew him from her and before which he was so helpless; his eyes smarted with tears. "I'll call you, then," he said. He had the idea as he hung up that perhaps he would never see her again, and yet he could do nothing about it.

The next evening he drove out to the country again. Signs, barns, houses, side roads had become familiar. On the floor of the back seat were a small bag of groceries and two blankets and an old kerosene lamp he had found in the attic. It was nearly ten o'clock when he approached the garage. His heart was thudding dangerously, yet it did not upset him. He knew his body would not fail him, he could drive it as he drove the car. It was when he did not make himself think of the killer, when, out of disgust or fear, he tried to think of other things, that he felt the overwhelming guilt that had become for him the most extraordinary emotion he had ever felt. Now, prepared, everything ready and planned, he felt no guilt at all. With his car headlights off, he parked down the road from the garage, watching. Bushes screened him partly. There was his man—dragging a carton of empty soda pop bottles inside the garage. Norman waited. He had never before felt quite so free: the immensity of freedom to act and to act entirely without consequence. He wondered if that man and the two boys with him had experienced this same sweet suffocating freedom that afternoon sixteen years ago. . . . The garage darkened. Norman had no trouble making out the killer, who was taller than the other man and walked with heavy plodding steps as if he were overcome by the heat or by exhaustion. There was something self-righteous in that walk, Norman saw. The men went to their cars, the car doors slammed shut almost simultaneously, the other man drove off. The killer paused to light a cigarette. He tossed the match onto the gravel and Norman's lips jerked into a grin of recognition.

He stepped on the gas pedal and was able to head off the man's car just as it was about to turn onto the road. Norman leaned across the seat and waved into the glaring headlights. The man yelled, "What do you want? We're closed." But Norman had already gotten out of the car. "Something's wrong with my car, it's an emergency," he said. The man swore. His car engine roared and the car rocked impatiently back on the gravel as the man twisted the steering wheel. "You, wait," Norman said. "Not so fast." He took the gun out of his pocket and approached the man's open window. Behind the headlights he was helpless now, his face sagging at the sight of the gun as if he expected it. Norman's heart thudded viciously and he heard his own words as if from a distance. "I want to talk to you. I don't want to hurt you. You just get in this other car." The man did not move. Norman could hear him swallow. "Did you recognize me the other day?" he said. The man's eyes were fascinated by the gun. "There's no money in there," he said hoarsely. "Just some dollar bills. We made—we made a goddamned four dollars today—" "I don't want money," Norman said. "Get out. Get in my car." The man moved jerkily, then paused. Everything was still except for the noises of the insects. "You don't want any money?" the man said after a moment.

Norman sat beside him and the man drove. They went along slowly, down the dirt road, jerking and bouncing in the ruts. "They're waiting for me at home," the man said cautiously. "My wife and kids." Norman said nothing. When they reached the shanty—he had left a rag near the ditch for a marker—he had the man turn off the road and drive down an old cow lane and into the woods. The car churned and became entangled in underbrush. "Look, I don't know what you want," the man said, bowed over the steering wheel, "but I—I— Why don't you get somebody else for it, not me— My wife is—" "I'm not going to hurt you," Norman said. He was a little embarrassed at the man's fear: he had supposed the man would be the same as he had been sixteen years ago, cold and deliberate, without emotion. "I just want to talk with you," he said. "I want to get the truth from you. Where were you about sixteen years ago?"

He watched the man's damp face. It was an ugly, confused face, and yet its younger image had not been ugly, exactly. "I don't—I don't know," the man muttered. "Please try to remember," Norman said. "What's your name?" "Cameron," he said at once. "Anyone around here would know me— Look, what do you want? I don't know you. With that gun there—" "I'm not going to hurt you," Norman said softly. "Just tell me where you were sixteen years ago." "We come up from Kentucky, first me then my mother and father," he said. Again he swallowed clumsily. "I was maybe twenty then. I don't know. Look, I think you want some other man, I mean, it looks to me you got some other man in mind—" "You never came up from Kentucky," Norman said. "Or if you did you were younger than that." "I don't know how old I was," the man said, "maybe I was younger—" His face rippled nervously. "You remember me, don't you?" Norman said. "You knew me the other day, too, didn't you?" "What other day?" the man said. In his heavy face this new, nervous rigidity contrasted ludicrously with the lazy slabs of flesh close about his jaws. He looked as if he were trying to shake himself free of the weight of his flesh. "I only want to talk to you, then the police will take care of it," Norman said. "Take care of what?" the man said at once. "You know what," Norman said. The man stared across at him. He supposes I am crazy, Norman thought. "So you don't admit it? That you remember me?" he said. He might have been

speaking to a customer in the store, prodding and herding
him on to a purchase, some clothing Norman himself
looked at but did not see, had no interest in seeing
because he had already seen it too many times before.
"I'm not going to force anything out of you," Norman
said. "I give you my word on that. We're going to have
a long talk, nothing hurried. Because I've been waiting
sixteen years—" "What's this sixteen years?" the man
said. His voice was trembling and raw, a voice Norman
had not yet heard from him. There was a certain edginess
there too, a recklessness that made Norman draw back
so he could watch the man more carefully. Nothing was
going to go wrong. He had control. While insects swirled
about the headlights and tapped against the windshield
Norman felt strength course through him as if it were a
sign, a gift, something supernatural. "Sixteen years ago
you killed my brother," he said. "Sixteen years ago last
March." "Killed your brother!" said the man. He made
a whistling noise. "Look, mister, I never killed nobody.
I told you before—it looked like you were after somebody
else, something you said— You got the wrong guy here,
believe me. I never killed nobody. Who was your
brother? Am I supposed to know you? Were you in the
Army with me or something?" Norman let him talk. The
man's words tumbled from him as if stunned with shock;
they meant nothing. Finally he stopped. The insects
flicked themselves lightly against the car windows and
disappeared. "Turn off the lights," Norman said. He
had his flashlight ready. "What do you want?" said the
man. "What are you going to do?" "Turn them off. All
right, now get out. Get out," Norman said. "What are
you going to do?" said the man. "Are you going to—
going to— You said something about the police, why
don't you call them or something? I mean, they got these
things on record, could look it up and see when it was—
they keep a record of all these things, mister, that would
clear it all up— Because I never killed nobody, not even
in the Army when we was overseas, and not even by
accident or anything— Was your brother in the Army?"
"Get out of the car," said Norman. "Then where are we

going?" the man said, gripping the steering wheel. "What are you going to do to me?" "I want to talk to you," Norman said. "You're crazy!" the man whispered.

They went in the shanty, Norman behind the man. Norman put the things down and shone the flashlight around from corner to corner. "What place is this?" the man said. "What are you going to do?" His teeth had begun to chatter; Norman was astonished. "Please sit down," he said. Cobwebs hung dustily from the ceiling. In the glare of the flashlight the weeds were stark and vivid, casting brittle shadows that froze in a complex, teethlike structure against the bottoms of the walls. The man sat, slowly, groping about. He looked gross and foolish sitting in the weeds, his fat stomach straining against his belt. About his forehead dark strands of hair were plastered as if arranged by hand. Norman crouched against the opposite wall. "I want the truth from you," he whispered. "The truth." The man's lips began to move, but he said nothing. "Try to remember," Norman said. "You killed a boy and he's dead, his life was ended in a few minutes, and now you're here with me and alive, you've got to see the difference between the two—He'd be just bones now, everything rotted away if you dug him up, and you're sitting here alive. He was seventeen when you killed him." The man brushed weeds away from him as if they were insects, in terror; then he stopped abruptly. "I think you do remember me," Norman said. "I was with him that day. You and the other two boys—".

"Other two?"

"Other two boys. All three of you. You pushed us in the river and wouldn't let us out. You hit Jack with something—when they found him his face was all slashed. I saw it myself. It was you and two other boys. I know your face."

The man began to shake his head. "My wife is waiting for me," he said faintly, "I can't talk too long. . . ."

"Where are the other two? Did they leave the city?"

"Mister, I got to go home— They're—"

"Shut up about that!" Norman cried. He waited until

his anger died down. "I just want the truth. A boy is dead and you killed him and you're going to tell the truth before you leave here!"

"Mister, I never killed nobody—"

"But I saw you. I saw *you*. I saw your face."

"It wasn't me, it was somebody else."

"It was you."

"I got all kinds of cousins and guys that look like me—"

"Living up here?"

"Sure, around here, in the city too—"

"You said you were from Kentucky."

The man paused. His teeth chattered and he stared at Norman as if a flash of pain had overcome him. Then he said, "I am. They come up too."

"You all came up? When was this?"

"A while ago, I don't know—"

"You're lying," Norman said. "Goddamn filthy liar."

"I'm not lying!"

The man's lips twisted up into a terrified angry grimace. Norman felt his own lips twitch as if in imitation. "I want justice, nothing but justice," Norman whispered. He was shining the flashlight on the man's heaving chest so that the fainter halo of light illuminated the man's face, startling shadows upward from his nose and lips and the deep sockets of his eyes. "I've given up things to get here tonight," Norman said. "I'm going to get an answer from you, going to get justice. We must have justice." He might have marveled at what he said, at his strange talent, for where in the long tedious days at the store and in the evenings at home had he learned such things? Yet he felt the truth of what he was saying. It was true. He had been sent here, he could not turn away from it now if he wanted to. For this man he had given up Ellen, he would never break free and into her world now, he had given her up, killed her in himself. "There are things that have to be finished up, made even," Norman said. "If I turned you over to the police without a confession it wouldn't do any good. Nobody would care. Nobody knows about it any more except

me and my family and you. . . . Are you going to tell
me the truth?"

The man sat staring down at his thick legs, motionless.

"You and two other kids, one Saturday afternoon,"
Norman said softly. "On the docks. You knocked us
both in the water and wouldn't let us out. You hit Jack,
cut up his face. His eye was cut. My brother drowned
but I, I didn't, a man sitting down aways came over and
got me. You read about it in the papers probably. You
and them. You kept on reading it till it was forgotten.
Nobody cared. And even me, I suppose I forgot it too.
. . . Now are you going to tell me the truth?"

After several hours the man was sitting in the same
position. Norman had lit the kerosene lamp and was
sitting with his back against the wall, watching the man
cautiously. When he asked the man about telling the
truth, sometimes he answered and sometimes he did not.
When he said nothing Norman had to fight down an
impulse to strike him. He had to control his anger. "You
son of a bitch," the man whispered. "Going to shoot me
anyway, why not now?"

"I just want the truth," Norman said. "I want it
written down and signed. Your confession."

"My confession . . ."

"On paper. Signed with your name."

"Then what?"

"I told you what."

"Then you're going to shoot me, aren't you?"

"No. I told you."

"Should I write it on paper or what? Do you have
some?"

"Then you did do it?"

The man squinted. "Didn't you say you saw me?"

"Yes, I saw you."

"Then I must of done it."

"Do you admit it?"

The man's face looked paralyzed. "Do you?" Norman
said, leaning forward. The bovine stupidity of that face—
which he felt he had been staring at for years, hating—

was suddenly too much for him. He slashed the back
of the gun against the man's knee, for no reason, without
really knowing what he had done. The blow did not
hurt, the man seemed only baffled by it. Norman's face
burned. "You made me do that," he said accusingly. "I
didn't mean to—I didn't plan— You made me do it."

"Going to shoot me, why not now?" the man said dully.

"Nobody's going to shoot you, for Christ's sake,"
Norman said. "Will you just tell the truth for once?
Will you stop lying?"

"My wife—"

"To hell with that!"

"My wife can tell you. Lots of people could, but you
don't care. You want to kill me."

The man hid his face in his hands. Norman could still
see part of his anguished teeth. "No," Norman said. "I
only want justice." But the word "justice" struck him suddenly as a puzzle: what was he talking about? It evoked
in his mind an uncertain image of a courthouse with a
flag flying over it, not a picture of any court in town but
one out of a movie or a book. The image vanished.
Norman sat up. His head had begun to pound, he had
not eaten that day, he cared about nothing except this
man. "I don't need sleep," he said without pride. "I can
keep going until I get the truth from you. I've waited
sixteen years now."

"Sixteen years," the man whispered. His hands came
away from his face and in that instant Norman saw unmistakably a flash of something like recognition. A drop-
let of perspiration tumbled down the man's face, from
his forehead to his chin and then to his wet shirt front,
as if stunned by this recognition.

"Are you going to admit it?" Norman said.

"I'm not admitting anything!"

Norman's hand, holding the gun, jerked as if it had
come alive. "What the hell do you mean?" he said. "A
minute ago—"

"I'm not admitting anything!"

Norman waited until his heartbeat slowed. He felt on

the precipice of terrible danger. Then he drew his knees up and watched the man silently. The emptiness in his stomach was turning into a kind of strength. While the kerosene lamp flickered indifferently, a cluster of moths and insects reeling about it, Norman and the man faced each other for a period of time. Norman was really not conscious of time passing; he might have been enchanted. "My brother and I were very close," he said softly. "He did things for me, stuck up for me. He looked like me only he was a lot bigger . . . he was going to go to college. Then one day you killed him. Just like that. For no reason." Norman wondered if the man was listening. "Why did you do it? For no reason, nothing, not even for money, just nothing. . . . Something in a murderer's brain must pinch him and make him do it, and everything is ruined. Lives are ruined. Nothing can be right and balanced again until justice is won—the injured party has to have justice. Do you understand that? Nothing can be right, for years, for lifetimes, until that first crime is punished. Or else we'd all be animals. The crime keeps on and on unless it's punished. Somebody like me gets caught in the middle and can't have his own life. Here I have to ruin myself to make it right and never had any choice—" The man's eyes were fascinated by Norman's face; he could not look away. When it began to get light Norman turned off the kerosene lamp. The man, slouched across from him in the weeds, looked rumpled and sick and aged. He really was not Norman's age after all, but quite a bit older. "Here," said Norman. He took an orange out of the grocery bag and tossed it at the man. It struck his knee and fell to the ground. The man seemed not to notice. "Eat that. You need to eat," Norman said. The man pushed the orange away vaguely, yet still without seeming to notice it. Norman wondered if something was wrong. The night had passed quickly for him, yet at the same time something had happened that had cemented him irreparably to this shanty, to this damp ground, to the man's rumpled body; surely it was the same way with the killer. This was something Norman could understand, after all. The woman he had loved—and he could not quite summon up her face—had been in another world where nothing was simple, nothing could be depended upon. Perhaps he had really feared and hated that world. But here, with the man obedient before him, he had only one other thing to keep in mind for both of them: that day in March. Nothing more. He did not need to think of anything further.

The man jerked his head up as if someone had called him. "Eat that orange," Norman said. "That's good for you." The man shook his head slowly. "I said eat it," said Norman. Muscles tensed in his jaw. He waited. The man did not move. "Eat that orange," said Norman, "or I'll kill you." The man's hand dropped and closed over the orange, as if the hand were part of a machine clumsily manipulated. He picked it up and peered at it. "Eat," said Norman. "Eat." The man brought the orange slowly up to his mouth. "Take off the skin first," Norman said. The man hesitated. "I can't eat it," he whispered. Norman saw tears in his eyes. "Take off the skin first," Norman said more gently. He watched the man peel the orange. Juice trickled down his big hands and fell onto his trousers and onto the bent weeds. "Now eat it," said Norman.

When the man finished, Norman said, "Are you ready now to confess?" The man made a sound something like a sob. He wiped his mouth; he stared down at nothing. Norman's heart beat so violently that his arms had begun to tremble. For an instant he felt faint; black spots appeared before his eyes, like insects. But he forced himself to say, evenly, "Are you ready to confess?"

"I never did it," the man whispered.

"But you did. You did something. You killed somebody."

"What?"

"You killed—" Norman paused. "Nothing. That wasn't— Never mind that."

"Look, I never— I never hurt—"

-"Stop lying!" Norman cried. "Do you want to make me hurt you? Is that it? Want to bring me down to your level, a goddamn filthy animal? I waited sixteen years to get the truth from you—"

"What do you want me to do?" the man said. He lifted his sticky palms in a gesture of helplessness. "Where's the paper? What should I write? You said you'd let me go then—"

"I said what?"

"Said the police would have a record of it—"

"I never said that," Norman whispered.

"Yes, you said it, I heard you. We would go from here to the police and they would have some record. Have it written down. In a file. That's how they do it."

"Look, I don't want to do this to you," Norman said. "I don't want to be here. I have my own life, my own life, and here I am, over thirty already, and haven't done anything—haven't started yet—wasting my time with his troubles, and you sit and whine about yourself! You! You gave yourself up to me the day you killed him and there's nothing you can do about it."

"I got proof I wasn't up here—nowhere near here—"

"Like hell."

"We can go out and—"

"Don't you move," Norman said. His eyes throbbed. His vision itself seemed to throb with outrage and dismay. Only now had he begun to realize that this man had tried to kill him too. Had wanted him to drown. At one time that groveling man had stood safe on a dock and wanted him to drown. . . . There was the same face, Norman saw suddenly, as if by magic that young face asserted itself again within the older flabby face.

"If—if you got some paper or something—"

"You'd write it wrong," Norman said.

"No, I'll write it, then you check it, then I'll sign it—"

Norman laughed tonelessly. "You must think I'm crazy," he said.

"What?"

"Who'd believe what you wrote? When you had a gun pointed at you! How can I prove you did it, how can I prove anything? You have me trapped now like you did *then*—I could be drowning out in the water, it's the same thing, I feel like I'm drowning here, there's nothing I can do to get you—to get justice—" Norman's voice had become feverish. His hatred now was impersonal and ubiquitous: he hated without any object, without any catalyst. Even his brother's memory had become an annoyance.

"But what are you going to do?" the man said, licking his lips. "I think they'd believe a note," he said softly.

"They wouldn't. Not a jury."

"If I confessed it out loud to them—"

"No."

"If I said how I remembered it, who was with me, what you two looked like—"

"No, not even then."

"If I—if I got in touch with one of those two guys, and he said—"

"You're lying."

Stunned, baffled, the man stared at him. It seemed to Norman obvious that he was lying now, that he really could not remember anything but was only pretending, as if to make Norman feel better. It was not the lie Norman hated him for but his talent at not remembering: why had Norman not this talent, why had he been cursed with remembering when he had tried so long to forget?

"All right. You can go," Norman said.

The man did not move. "What?"

"You can go. Go."

"You mean leave here?"

His legs moved, experimentally, but he did not get up. He was squinting at Norman. "You want me to go home?"

"Go home to your wife."

"Yes, all right," the man said. He got up slowly. His legs must have ached. Each of his movements was queer and gentle, as if he were still in a dream and feared overturning something fragile. "Yes," he whispered. The man tried not to look at Norman. He moved slowly, even his eyes moved slowly to the door, and it was finally his gesture of absurd fastidiousness—he paused to brush dirt and orange peels off his trousers—that overwhelmed Norman.

"You bastard, you killer!" Norman cried. "Going to walk out like that! It's in the newspapers every day how they kill people and walk out, nothing ever happens, nobody gets punished, nothing gets put right, and people like myself have to live under the shadow of it! Killers! What the hell do I care if you did it or not? If it wasn't you it was somebody else— Or even if nobody did it, if it was an accident or if I never even had a brother named Jack or anything—"

"Named Jack?" said the man.

Norman pulled the trigger. The shot was much louder than he had expected. When he opened his eyes the shanty was empty. He crawled to the doorway and looked out—there the man was, running, through the mist. He aimed the gun again and fired. The man stumbled, fell against a tree with his arms out in an embrace. Still on his knees, Norman fired again. "Everything I did for him," he sobbed, "everything ruined—my life ruined— He wouldn't give a damn anyway, that's how it always is. What do they care? I bring her home money every week, she forgets to say thanks, why should she say thanks? There's always more where that came from. Dirty bastards, killers, a whole world of killers, and that one there sitting all night long telling lies in front of me—as if I didn't know him right away!"

Something in him seemed to collapse. The earth beneath him tilted suddenly, and he felt spiky grass against his face; everything was dizzy, confused. His fingers grasped at the earth as if he believed his weight was not enough to hold him down and keep him from being sucked up into the depths of the morning sky. Minutes passed, Norman waited to regain his strength. "You there," he said bitterly. "Hey, you." The man did not answer. He must have been lying where he fell. Norman made a face, thinking of the day ahead, the airless routine: months, years of ordinary life, so sane and so remote from this field. He closed his eyes and felt his strength course slowly back into his body. Yet still he felt the numbed, beatific emptiness of one who no longer doubts that he possesses the truth, and for whom life will have forever lost its joy.

The Man That Turned into a Statue

They emerged from the bushes at the side of the road. The girl, who was really a child, had a sardonic dazed look that seemed frozen into her face; she wore an orange sweater with an orange cord that tied at her waist and white pedal pushers that were soiled. Each step she took drew wrinkles sharply across these pedal pushers. Her clothes were too tight for her, she had grown out of them in this past year, her body pushing up and out like a vegetable swelling patiently in the earth. Her face was round and hard, with small pursed lips and eyes that seemed to slant in her face like almonds; her brown hair was reckless about her face, snarled from the wind. The man, grunting as he climbed up to the road, was over forty: his dark hair was thin, receding back sharply from his forehead but leaving a patch there right in the center; his face was pale and surprised-looking, this look, too, frozen into him. It was October and chilly; in the bluish light that came at sundown in this part of the country, the narrow road with its cracked pavement and snakelike strips of tar seemed to glow and rise slightly up above the dirt shoulders.

"Now whatcha going to do, you're so smart?" the girl said.

Something had caught across the man's chest, a vine that was entangled in the brush. He paused to tug at it—a slender green vine with tiny ruined flowers—and when

133

he could not get it off at once he tore viciously at it. The girl, watching him with her arms folded and her legs set apart in a pretense of confidence, saw a ripple of fear cross his face. The man muttered something. He had a long nervous nose; his lips were always loose, always about to mutter something, perhaps because his teeth protruded slightly and he could not quite close his mouth.

"Now it's dark so if anybody comes we can see them first. See the headlights," he said.

"Yeah, you're so goddamn smart," the girl said. She wiped her eyes.

"Smart enough to get us out of this, I guarantee that."

But he stood on the road, looking back and forth in both directions and rubbing his hands, and did not seem to know what to do after all. "Spost to be in Canada by now," the girl said. "That map you showed me—"

"Just bad luck," he muttered. The girl watched his hands and felt something prod at her brain: fear, like the touch of a bat's wing. But she hardened her face again and looked down at her shoes, which were new, red-and-white-striped sneakers she had been seeing in the shoe store window for weeks. But this shoe store had been too near home, it was a mistake to think of it. She wiped her eyes again and her mouth turned into a bitter line. "I had bad luck all my life," the man said. She had heard this before. The first time she had seen him, when he was sitting on the steps that led down to his basement apartment, he had started to talk about this out of nowhere, angrily and mournfully, as if his bad luck were something he expected to get hold of with his hands. "Some people get born with it and others don't. Those bastards you see on the expressway, driving out of the city, they don't have it. Got jobs downtown and then drive home out of the city; got born without it. Nobody that gets born without bad luck can understand or give a damn about somebody that has it. . . ." His words ended in a murmur, as if he were no longer paying attention to them. "Okay, come on. This way."

"You're sure, this way?" she said sarcastically.

"Come on."

They walked. It was getting dark and this long day was coming to an end at last, but the end did not mean anything because nothing had been settled. So much had happened, had gone wrong, they were still on foot. . . . The girl remembered suddenly, without wanting to, the door opening and the woman rushing in: the back of the fruit store, smelly and grubby, with empty fruit baskets piled all over, and she standing beside this man as he rifled desperately through a tin box that was supposed to have hundreds of dollars in it but had only a few bills scattered among papers that made no sense. Why had the woman come in just then? She and her old husband had been carrying strips of canvas back along the side of the building, as they did every morning, opening the store up. They lived in two or three rooms on the second floor. But something had gone wrong with the man's plans, though he and the girl had watched the dilapidated back door of the building from the man's basement window across the alley for days. Yet the man had acted like someone in a movie, whirling around and striking the woman without even thinking, he was so fast; the girl's mind was dazzled still at the spectacle of his fist and the woman's surprised face, an image isolated out of the dim jumble of junk behind it; something she would remember all her life. Thinking of it now, she glanced at the man fondly. If only his teeth did not protrude like that and make his jaw slant up to meet them. . . . All his life, he had told her, he had tried to fight his way up and had been pushed back down. His bad luck was like a sickness. The girl, though only thirteen, understood vaguely the difference between her world and the world promised her in movies and in movie magazines, and felt bitterness side by side with her infatuation for this other world. Sitting in the movie house, seeing a movie over for the second or third time, she had often been startled at the way her love for the people on the screen had jerked away, suddenly, to leave her sullen and hateful. When she went home the feeling would get worse, and only in sleep would it vanish; but then she would have to wake up the next morning, another school day, and, lying in bed staring at the gritty windowpane, she could feel the waiting familiar world discharge itself into her mouth and down her throat, into her heart and stomach, turning her heavy and inert with hate as if something had caught there, some seed, and had begun to grow.

"If we try for a ride we'll get picked up," the man said, cracking his knuckles. "That bitch got a good look at me and you both, should of hit her harder. . . . Hell of a chance, hitching for a ride, because some bastard driving by would go and call the cops from a garage or someplace. That's how they are. Nobody asks why you do something or if something made you do it, they don't give a damn. You slip off the road and can't get back on again. They might as well take your name from you and slice off your face, because you can't make it back up again, they don't give a damn, they never think how easy it might be to trade places with you. . . ."

The girl was not listening but dreaming of a field somewhere, of a morning in warm weather, and of herself walking slowly toward this man, who stood leaning against a fence waiting for her. From this distance he looked young and not really familiar. She began to hurry through the grass—which was green and vivid, like grass in a magazine picture—with her arms outstretched to him, her heart racing— "Here comes a car!" the man said. He grabbed at her and they ran clumsily through the bushes and into the ditch. The bottom of the ditch was wet. The girl did not watch the car but stood rubbing her arm. It was not really dark and yet everywhere objects were losing their shapes. The wild field ran back in a tumult to a woods some distance away where trees were dissolved into one another like water in water. The car's headlights seized upon the leaves of the bush and then swept past. "Wonder who's riding in there, lucky bastards," the man muttered.

"I should hitch for a ride myself, I'm tired as hell of walking and hiding," the girl said. "I said, I should get a ride by myself." The man turned to her. She saw in his expression the queer tense bafflement she had seen when the woman had walked into the back room of the store and when the vine had caught across his chest.

"You wouldn't be safe by yourself," he said.

"Yeah?"

"You need somebody to take care of you, a little girl like you—"

"Yeah, sure."

She was ready to step away if he came toward her; he knew this and did not move. The girl followed rules that had come to her out of nowhere—she did not know where—and told her always what to do, when to do it, when it was not right to do anything: in the daylight or when other people were around. She would have been sick to her stomach if he had forced her to break these rules, though she did not know where she had learned them. The man, who had often cringed before her and pressed his wet cheeks against her knees, murmuring things to her she did not hear and after a while did not pay attention to, now stared at her and cracked his knuckles. "I'm going to take good care of you, get some food in you. You're hungry, that's all. You believe all I told you, don't you?"

"Sure I believe you."

"I was married one time and I took care of her too," he said. "Begun all over from a beginning but hit a snag. Three times already I begun over and this is the fourth and last. Going to begin over again up in Canada. Don't you believe me?"

"Sure." The girl ran through the bushes and back up onto the road. A branch had swept across her eye and made it smart, but instead of getting angry she made herself laugh. This was only the second time that she had run away from home. The first time had been a mistake, she had been too young, hadn't any money; she had tried to keep going just on her hatred for her mother and father. But it was different now. She knew what she was doing now. She would keep her hatred for them safe, as if it were a tiny seed she carried greedily inside her, and once away from them and across the shadowy border that separated her from the real world she would let this hatred blossom and so get rid of it. And they would yearn for her across this border, they would keep waiting for her to come home, her mother would be stuffed with baby after baby and yet they would keep waiting for her to come home. . . .

"Something wrong?" the man said.

The girl turned away. She had begun to cry and was ashamed.

"Yeah, it's cold," the man said nervously, "I got to get you someplace warm and safe. Get some food into you. Don't you worry." He slid his arm about her shoulders and they walked along the edge of the road. The girl stared down at the rigid strips of tar in the pavement, one after another across the road like flattened snakes. "I'll change how we are now, don't you worry. Nothing stays the same but has to change. Change is a fact of our life. I read you that part in my book about the laws, didn't I? How they change every place you go and every different person you are?" The girl had forced herself to think of that warm sunlit field again and she resented his question. "Why are you writing that crazy old book anyway," she said. "How the laws change before you even have time to learn them," the man said. He was excited now and could talk to himself as if she were not even there. "Everything changes, won't stay fixed. When my grandmother died I was ten, ten years old, a boy. I was a boy. I went in the bathroom and looked at myself in the mirror for half an hour, maybe. I made faces and looked at my teeth. . . . Do you believe that? I was a boy but I can't remember it, I can remember only a boy in the mirror that I couldn't possibly have been, that was somebody else, a boy who's still a boy . . . not me. . . . And when that boy that was supposed to be me came out of the bathroom he had to think about his grandmother again, because she was dead and the house smelled of it and there was no way to forget. Everybody smelled of it. All this is in my book too. *The Man That Turned into a Statue,* that's what it's called." He touched his coat gently; he must have been carrying the notebook there. "Remember why it's called that?"

" 'Cause that's what you're trying to do," the girl sneered. "Turn into a statue!"

He did not seem to know she was mocking him; immediately she felt sorry. Her face was brittle with resisting something—maybe more tears—and she wondered suddenly if it were not turning to stone.

"Yes, yes," he said slowly.

"It's a real good name—"

"My wife too, she's in there. . . . She was a small woman with hair your color, she had pierced ears. Bluish hands, as if she could never get them warm. She put a crucifix up on the wall that I could feel watching me, tiny little blind eyes in the crucified man, no eyes at all, really, but I could feel them watching me even in the dark. . . . I didn't want to hate her," he said angrily. "I didn't want to hate anyone. Never. Not once. I was always pushed into it, like being pushed into a fire from other people crowding up close. It was like a big whirlpool in the ocean, the deepest part, where everything spins round and round and gets sucked in, and you can't get away from it. If you ran your whole life in the opposite direction you'd get sucked there anyhow, so what the hell? But I never wanted to hate."

He hugged her clumsily and she felt a surge of gratitude. He would take care of her. She did not understand much of what he said, did not even listen to it, but she knew he would take care of her. These shoes she wore, right now, he had paid for; he had not even asked for the change. He had seemed not to know there was any change.

"Another incident in my book," he said in a different voice, a chatty voice, "a man and woman were fighting in a bar. I was there. The man knocked her down right by the juke box, that was all lit up different colors and playing some song. Then he started kicking her and I went over. I said, what the hell are you doing? I told him to stop. But he never paid any attention, and when I pulled his arm he just pushed me away. He never paid any attention. So I went back and sat down. That incident is in there too, with a lot of description. I'm particularly good at description—"

Somewhere close, a dog had begun to bark. The man froze. They could hear the dog running but in the dusk could see only the vague jumbled field beside them. The girl began trembling. "Don't worry," the man muttered. "Bad comes to worst I got this knife."

The dog appeared before them: not a large dog but nervous and wiry, with a dull black coat and dancing paws and ears cringing back alongside its head. "Here, here boy," the man said. "It's okay, boy. We don't want no trouble. It's okay." The dog snarled. It leaped toward them and froze; crouched low, with its mouth twisted up into what looked like a grin. The girl stood behind the man, shivering. She was frightened, not so much by the dog itself as by the way the dog seemed to hate them, as if there were something wrong with them, people the dog had never encountered before. She could feel her own face twisting into a painful mirroring of the dog's look. "Here, boy. Nice boy. Here, here," the man pleaded. He even extended his hand. The dog eyed them suspiciously. For a moment it hesitated, as if thinking; then it leaped at the man's hand. They heard its teeth click. "Bastard," the man said. The dog fell away as if yanked to one side. The man turned to face it, cracking his knuckles. He began again, murmuring to the dog, bending with his hand out, his shoulders hunched and obsequious. The dog crouched snarling against the road. For some seconds it did not move and the man straightened a little. "Maybe if we just keep on walking," he said. "Show him we got somewhere to go. Sometimes they let you go, then."

They walked on. The dog followed them. At first it kept some distance away but then it came nearer; just as the girl glanced around it lunged at the man's leg, its snarls breaking out into harsh barks that sounded like coughs. The man cried out and kicked it away. "The bastard, why don't it let us alone! The bastard!" he said. His voice was profoundly sad. The dog retreated and watched them. After a moment the man put his arm around the girl's shoulders again, to protect her, and they turned to walk on. The girl kept looking back. That dog, she thought, was the kind of dog she had always seen whining at screen doors or looking out car windows, its ears flapping in the wind; it never barked viciously or leaped at anyone. She had been seeing dogs like this all her life but now something was wrong.

Then the dog leaped again. Suddenly it was close behind them and against the man's legs, its muzzle darting from place to place and its teeth flashing. The man kicked it away but it lunged back at once. Something seemed to enliven it, some inexplicable energy that drove it on, snarling maliciously and desperately. The man cried out in pain. He stooped and picked something up— a tree branch—and slashed at the dog. The dog pranced and leaped. "Get back or I'll kill you," the man sobbed. He tried to flick the branch across the dog's face but the dog always ducked away. "I'll kill you, kill you," he said. He threw the branch at the dog and took out of his pocket the knife he used to clean his fingernails and to pick mud off his shoes. The girl could not tell if he threw himself down on the dog or if his knees suddenly collapsed, jerking and terrified.

When the man got to his feet he was panting violently. He stumbled backward. The dog lay writhing; it was bleeding from a wound in its stomach. The man stared as if he could not remember where he was, what had happened. "Well, you got him," the girl said hollowly. She touched the man and he did not seem to notice. "He shouldn't of come after us," she said. She saw that the front of the man's pants was speckled with blood. They would get him, then, she thought, and when they did she would say he had kidnaped her. He had forced her to come with him. And they would believe her, and she would wait for another man to come to her just as she had waited for this one. . . .

"Let's go. Got to keep going," the man said. He began walking fast. The girl hurried to keep up with him. In a while they saw a house ahead, with its porch light on. "That was their dog, I spose," the man said.

"Think they heard him bark?" But no one was out on the porch. The light was an ugly yellow light that fell upon the porch roof and slashed the floor in half, lighting up an old sofa and some junk but leaving the rest in shadow, and lighting up the driveway and a car parked there on a small incline.

The girl felt terror rising stupidly within her at the sight of this house. Each window was lit, even the attic window. Someone lived up there—a child, probably. A little bedroom. She knew they would not go past the house but would go in, and this knowledge pressed down upon her like a giant palm on the top of her head. Her legs were suddenly exhausted under the strain. "We had better hurry on past here," she said.

"But we got to get some food," the man said. He was still trembling and his voice too was trembling. She had known he would say this. "It's not like I don't have the money to pay for it. I do. I'll pay for it. If I just didn't have this bad luck always behind me . . . somebody else would be up in Canada now, all safe, and not make you walk around at night, chased by dogs. . . ."

"I don't want to go in that house," the girl said.

"I never asked for no dog to come, that's for sure," the man said. They were at the end of the driveway now. The girl had stopped shivering. She saw, brushing behind one of the windows, a woman's figure, a flash of color drawing back a curtain and almost immediately releasing it. "You think they might know about us, those people in there?" the man said. "Heard about it on the radio or something?"

"How the hell do I know," said the girl.

"I got to take care of you. I guarantee that. . . ." He took a step forward. She wanted to pull him back but instead stared at the side of his face in fascination. What was there about him that enchanted her, what was it in his humble malicious face that seemed to show how he was enchanted as well? "I bet they're eating in there. Smell it? That's food. Do you smell it?"

"No, nothing."

She smelled something else—an odor of blood and earth and night.

"Sure you smell it. Potatoes or something. Meat. . . ." He put the knife away and went up the driveway. His feet crunched in the gravel. Tediously the girl followed; as he approached the light she saw the bloodstains on his pants, dark wet clots. She was too exhausted to say anything. It did not matter anyway. "We can pay for anything we eat, that's not the trouble. I pay as I go. Always have always will. My word is always been good, you can ask anybody that. . . ."

Before he got to the porch someone was at the door, a fat man in just an undershirt and pants. "Yeah, what do you want?" he said. He loomed up close against the screen door so that his face was dim. "What do you two want?"

"Hello, mister," said the man in a new voice. He waited for the girl to come up beside him; her legs had begun to ache. "We had a accident up the road and had to walk. Had some trouble. Was wondering if we could—"

"Car trouble?"

"Car trouble, yes, and had to walk, and haven't eaten for a long time—"

A child appeared behind the man, a girl with long dark hair. The man turned and said something to her; she went away. The girl's eyes narrowed, seeing her.

"Mister, we had a lot of bad luck and sure would appreciate some help."

The man hesitated. He had a big stomach that strained against his white undershirt and bulged a little over his belt. Then he said, "We got no telephone here."

"If we could have something to eat— I— I'll pay for it—"

"No."

"I got money, look here. Look, that's a fact. I'll pay for it, anything you want. My little girl here—"

"No."

The girl wondered if that fat man had seen the blood. He had begun shaking his head, but the man continued up the driveway and went right up to the porch just the same. He muttered all the way, right through the fat man's angry voice, as if he did not hear it. "I don't run no roadside restaurant here," the fat man said, "I don't have no open house for tramps! What the hell are you doing? What do you think you're—"

Still with his shoulders bent apologetically, the man opened the screen door and plunged the knife into the fat man's chest. The girl's eyes seemed to pinch, jerking her head forward. The fat man had been talking and was now silent. He fell back into the light, his body turning, his arms outstretched, and the girl could see now a brilliant stream of blood emerging out of him as if his words had turned into this. Inside the house, some-one screamed. The man went right in the house, as if he were coming home, and with the knife still in his hand ran through to the next room. He might have known all the rooms in the house, nothing would surprise him. The girl, leaning against the door frame, caught the screen door as it swung idly back to her and stared at the dying man; he stared at her. Coldness enveloped her body like a flame. The dying man gazed at her with a look of angry curiosity over the heaving blossom of blood on his chest. From the other room there were screams; something over-turned. Crashing. Glass, dishes broken. Every sound was another weight added to her body, making her heavy and old, so that she did not think she would ever be able to move again.

After a minute or so the man returned, still hurrying. "Come on," he said. "It's okay. I fixed it." He pulled at the girl's arm and she saw that he was trying to smile. "Okay. Everything okay. I'll take care of you."

She stared at him. She had forgotten how to talk.

"Come on," he said. "In here. I got them dragged out back, it was a woman and a kid, it's okay now. They're out back. They won't bother you now, come on. We better hurry."

She allowed him to lead her into the kitchen. There things were knocked about—chairs, plates, silverware on the floor, a mess of potatoes down by her feet. They had been eating supper, apparently. Most of the dishes were still on the table. "Come on. Sit. Sit down," the man said nervously. Blood had splashed up onto his chest and throat, but he did not notice. There was blood smeared faintly on his forehead. The girl, sitting at the table, looked about and saw blood gleaming on the linoleum, by the sink. A screen door led out back into the darkness; there was blood in great sweep strokes, like angels' wings, to this door and out it, into nothing. The girl sat, slowly. She felt the chair hard beneath her and the table against her cold arms, elbows. "Here, there's this," the man said. He pushed a plate toward her: on it were a piece of meat and some mashed potatoes with gravy on them. The gravy was greasy. She looked up to see the man shaking salt on his food. He tried to smile, nervously, brightly, like a host uncertain of his charm. "Okay, come on. We better hurry. Got us a car now but we better hurry anyway. You know how it is." The girl's gaze fell back down to the plate before her, as if it were suddenly overcome. Her hand groped for something—a fork. She found one and picked it up. Out of the corner of her eye she could see the man eating, his head lowered toward the plate, like a dog, and turned also a little to the side so that he chewed with a look of precise, methodical concentration. The girl tried to remember something but could not. She could not remember what it was that eluded her, just as she could not get hold of the dreams that pleased her so at night when she woke: everything vanished, brushed away. Was something lost or had she simply passed over into the real world, so that now old things were dismissed and new things had names yet to be learned? She could hear the man chewing.

She poked at the mashed potatoes with the fork. The man, raising his head suddenly, said through a mouthful of food, "Here, it needs this," and pushed the salt shaker at her. The salt shaker was in the form of a baby chick, bright lacquered yellow. The girl picked it up and shook salt onto the half-eaten food. She watched the tiny white granules fall; they were not lost but remained there, waiting to be eaten. She set the salt shaker down and her fingers brushed against the man's arm, reaching

out for something else across the table. "Got to be
always in a hurry, sorry for it," he muttered, stuffing
bread into his mouth, "but it ain't always going to be
like this. I guarantee that. Got us a new life coming up."
She could see the faint pale gleam of his skin beneath
his hair, blank and white, something she had never been
able to see before. She felt like a bride awakened to a
body strange and new.

Archways

Klein, a nervous young man whose overcoat in winter hung down far below his knees, felt shame that he was several years older than his fellow students, felt shame that he was seized often by an inexplicable panic, alone or with others, felt shame that he was poor. He was a graduate student in a state university that serviced thirty thousand students, having come to his life's work (he realized with shame) after having been frightened out of other, lesser tasks: clerking, work in the Railway Express, work at his father's filling station. He had slid from one job to another, one segment of his life to another, as if he had been loosed at the top of a great jagged hill and could not control his destiny. Once come to the university, he had known that this was the fate he desired, but he did not feel strong enough to attain it. He imitated others: he bought, he read books (his room was filled with books), he wrote papers for his courses, he studied French and German, he lived alone, lost weight (his mother's mechanical accusation), had few friends, acquaintances rather, he made his own meals up in the room or had them in drugstores, he took notes hour after hour in the library, he appeared, a gentle weary apparition, on the sidewalk before his apartment house with books in his arms. With shame he was familiar: he had grown up with it. Before his father he had had to be ashamed of his mother, who cried endlessly, was

147

endlessly sick, was insulted by his father's mother, a
stout woman with a coat that had a meager fur collar he
had always been fascinated by as a child; before his
mother he had had to be ashamed of his father, who
begged for work around the neighborhood, offering esti-
mates no one wanted, reading up on modern mechanics
so he could compete with other service stations—a desperate attempt that Klein, when no more than a child of
eight, knew to be hopeless. At the garage his father
scurried about in all weather, checking air in tires, checking oil, his face reddened and forlorn. Of his bony wrists
Klein had had to be ashamed, taking the bus downtown
to the library: they had stuck out of his shirt sleeves for
all to see. Of his sister's ruthless blond hair, and of her
language to their mother he had had to be ashamed. Of
their house (they lived over the garage), the stairs on
the outside of the building and enclosed by a feeble tar-
papered canopy: of his thin arms and legs, in gym class
at school: of his shame itself. Now, at twenty-nine, he
took assessment of himself in his room five blocks from
the great university library, sitting on the edge of his bed,
doing nothing, having done nothing all day (it was Sunday), and understood that his shame for his life had
grown so great that he must die: but he had ten weeks
to go before the semester was over, and he did not like
to betray the people who had hired him, trusted him,
given him fifteen hundred dollars for the year and the
title "emergency help."

He attended classes during the day and taught two
classes of his own, remedial composition, in the late
afternoon and evening, three days a week. Before each
class he was visited with panic, terror that he would
break down before the hour ended. This never happened, but his panic did not end. He was perhaps
ashamed of the old building to which his classes had
been assigned, and he understood that the dank, dusty
air of the basement room had come to suffuse him, had
been breathed into him, had come to define him. His
students were desperate, doomed young people, many
of them from the country, remote incidental rural sections

of the state, bewildered at their failure (they were assigned to this course because they were far below average in English), unable to comprehend his teaching, his encouragement, his love. Their failure had widened their eyes, giving them the alert, electric look of animals to whom all movements signal danger. Like animals, they appeared mild and obedient until, knowing themselves trapped, they slashed out at him as if he were the crystallization of the forces that had maimed them— the obscure, mysterious spirit of the famous university itself, so available to them (they, with their high-school diplomas) and yet, as it turned out, so forbidden to them, its great machinery even now working, perhaps, to process cards, grades, symbols that would send them back to their families and the lives they supposed they had escaped.

Standing before his classes, eraser and chalk in hand, Klein sometimes deluded himself into thinking that his students' grave, attentive expressions were related to his presence; that they were actually learning, changing before his eyes. He wrote sentences on the board in his nervous handwriting: they watched. There in the first row, in the four-thirty class, the usual girls, crowded in close, staring and sightless—the lank handsome girl with the blond braids coiled ascetically about her head, chill and feigning attention, absolutely illiterate; the plump, smiling, perpetually astonished little girl in the pink sweater, also illiterate, with a baby's tiny handwriting and circled dots over her i's; the thin bespeckled girl who mentioned often in her compositions that she had been a JV cheerleader back in high school, back in Oriole, whether he, Klein, would believe it or not—he could not take that away from her. Behind them, the three other girls in the class, pens poised, and when he asked who could improve this sentence, at once the older girl with the dark, dissatisfied face would shoot her hand up. He thought her part Negro; she was almost pretty, attractive in a hard, frowning way. Beside her one of his troublemakers, a wise guy not from the country but from the city, illiterate despite his handsome sweaters

and bored, bland expression; and behind him adolescents
with blemished faces, huge hands and feet, educated
now into knowing their unworth, torn between despising
him (their "Mr. Klein") or falling before him to embrace his knees, begging aid, magic. The pipes in this
basement room groaned with effort; it was too hot; yet
the students went on, drugged and brave, improving sentences by hit or miss, staring at compositions shot into
vicious clarity by the opaque projector for their criticism
(all were interested in this: charmed and hypnotized by
the procedure's resemblance to the form of a movie, which
they knew they liked), accepting red-inked papers back,
ceremoniously, at the end of each Monday's class, walking out alone, quickly, or dawdling behind to speak with
him, sad-eyed or coquettish or swollen with gratitude
depending on their grades. When Klein thought of his
life, his essential life, nothing came to him except an
image of his class. The classes he himself took, sat in
wearily and hopefully, faded away as if they were no
more than dreams. He pitied his students and feared
them. Of course they hated him, they had no one else,
and yet he would have expressed his sorrow for them
had he not known they would have rejected it angrily—
for he was to them a transparent obstacle, a blemish,
something between them and their "careers" (in confer-
ences they talked familiarly of their "future careers" as
if these ghosts were real, actually existed somewhere and
had only to be located), and he did not possess any
meaning in himself. He yawned at the thought of his
students, they at the thought of him. If he died they
would not mourn him, would not miss him, in a month
would be unable to recall his name. And he accepted
their justified indifference, and the probable indifference
of his professors, as two more reasons why he should
die—if no one cared, why keep on?

His room was dirty. He cleaned it but it was dirty just
the same. It looked as if no one lived in it, as if the
clutter had accumulated noiselessly over the years,
knocked about by anonymous intruders. His books, which
he loved, the seven-dollar Van Gogh print above the

desk, the little braided rug he had bought at a sale, these things should have made his room his own, but they did not. The worn, shredding paperback books were not related to the print; the arty print not related to the modest rug; the rug not related to the paint-splashed floor; none of them related to him. The curtains at the window, feebly imprinted with green geometrical designs, could not have been purchased by Klein, who had better taste. A mistake. The wastebasket beside the desk was a glaring blue metal, stamped with the university's official animal (a kind of rodent he did not recognize): another mistake. His bedspread, costing eleven dollars, had been put away in the closet because it was too much trouble to make the bed. The thought of his room exhausted him, as did the thought of his classes (he met them again tomorrow, the weekends flew by); in fact, the only thought that nourished him was the thought of his death. This he felt to be truly his, as nothing else was. This alone was personal, private. It would perhaps not be magnificent, but no one would laugh. He need not be ashamed of it at least. To insure this he must choose a proper means of suicide: nothing violent, nothing theatrical. He had narrowed his choices down to two, either sleeping pills or hanging. For a while he had considered slashing his wrists (he lingered over the word "slashing"), but it would have to be done in the bathroom and there was no dignity there. Or if he did it in bed, in the landlord's bed, the blood might seep through the floor and drip from the ceiling below, an ambulance would arrive, and he would wake in a hospital thwarted and under arrest. . . . He got up and put on his overcoat and went out for a walk.

The sidewalks were deserted. Sundays were tedious, deadly, one had too much time to think on Sundays. He would do it on a Sunday, then, after his final examinations were graded and the grades turned in. Years ago he had supposed Sundays sacred, his family had gone to church, but what happened there seemed to him never related to anything else: a game, a bore. Then his family had stopped going and he had stopped. He had not been

told why. Perhaps there had been no reason. . . . Yet
that was what terrified him, he thought angrily, stopping
on the sidewalk with his hands clenched into fists: no
reason, nothing explained. His childhood was without
explanation. Why this particular failure (his father's poverty), why his mother crying at the kitchen table, why
that particular argument, why footsteps up and down
the stairs that night? What were these mysteries? Why
could he understand nothing? Why was he always the
victim, always the silent one, absorbing all blows, all
pain, all indifference? Why could he control nothing? And
why, now, was he here—standing before a slummy shoe
repair shop—what had brought him here? Had he willed
it, had he anything to do with it? He was furious at himself. Only his death would be meaningful, yet was he not
fearful of this? His most shameful knowledge was that,
ugly as his life was, part of him did not want to leave it.

He went back to his apartment house at that moment
and his life was changed.

On the stairs going up he met the dark girl from his
afternoon class. She was alone; she wore a red coat that
looked new. Seeing him, she stiffened and her hand rose
from the railing, hesitantly, as if the gesture were rehearsed. "Hello, Mr. Klein," she said in her student's
voice. He greeted her irritably. He had tried to look
past her, around her, but had not been able to avoid her
gaze. She stepped aside to let him pass and he went by.
But, inside his room, he felt oddly agitated and did not
want to take off his coat. Something was wrong, something would happen. He went to the window and looked
out: below, on the walk, strangers passed by in their
gloomy winter coats. In a minute someone knocked at
his door.

Klein, turned, arguing with himself. His lips framed
words but he went to the door and opened it: the girl.
"Yes?" he said coldly. He had been too kind to them in
class. He had failed to suggest the distance between
them. The girl touched her nose with a tissue, a nervous
gesture she might have been hiding behind. "It's a coinci-

dence meeting you like this," she said, "but a friend of mine lives upstairs." She waited; Klein looked behind her, did not help her. "I wanted to see you anyway to explain something."

He sighed. He surrendered, stepping back. "Come in."

She looked everywhere and nowhere, the tissue prominent in her hand. "Do you have a roommate?"

"No, none."

"That's nice—there," she said, pointing at the print. She stared at it. Then she turned. "No, my coat's all right, I'm only going to stay a minute. I'm sorry to barge in like this, I didn't mean to—" She ran out of breath suddenly.

"Sit over there, the desk chair," Klein said.

She pulled the chair out and sat as if participating in a ritual. "It's about the theme I handed in on Friday, Mr. Klein. I thought I better explain it a little, so you don't get the wrong idea."

"I haven't read them yet," Klein said.

"Haven't?"

She watched him awkwardly. A peculiar girl, he thought, older than the other students, carrying about with her like a disfigurement the weight of obscure, remote disappointments: she could have been one of the girls he often saw waiting at bus stops, working girls, cheaply glamorous and forlorn. She had a full face, eyebrows too thick, eyes worked over with black pencil, not exactly beautiful but stern and bright enough to attract the approval of random city boys—not college boys. Despite her open, generous face she had a habit of squinting (he recalled from class) that emphasized her deep-socketed eyes and gave her a look of doubt, disbelief. Her hair was black and thick and heavy, not lustrous. From under the cheap red coat her legs emerged muscular and stubborn, crossed primly at the ankles. She came to him in fragments: nervous as he was, and hungry (he had forgotten to eat), Klein fumbled with the buttons of his coat as if she had asked him to stay.

"May I ask if you're Jewish?" she said.

"I am not."

Was she disappointed? Her face shifted to show emotion, but Klein wondered if it was not planned. Then she went on, as he had somehow expected, "Some of the kids wondered." Vaguely she called up the magical, censorious presence of the classroom; Klein was disarmed. He remained where he was, standing, with his coat in his arms.

"Are you from around here?" the girl went on.

"What?"

"Are you from around here? The city?"

"No," he said. His words were straining up to the surface, pulling themselves up from a great obstinate distance. "Are you?"

She smiled slightly at his question. She had relaxed a little; her legs were now crossed at the knee. "I have a sister that lives here but I don't see her much. My folks are moved away—I don't see them much either. I get kind of lonely sometimes."

"Yes, well." Klein's face had grown warm. Despite his irritation, he felt a tenderness for the girl: for this clumsy loneliness, for the clenched tissue that was probably to her a vague, desperate attempt at feminine ornament. On campus, on the sidewalks between buildings, she would walk solidly on her heels, unaccustomed to the aloof competitive grace of the college girls; she would walk with her strong shoulders thrust slightly forward, as if to show her courage. Klein's voice was abrupt when he spoke. "Did you want to see me about something?"

"Look, I'm sorry to take up your time, I know you're busy. I just wanted to explain something about the paper, so you won't think it's—"

"Yes, what?" He glanced over at the untidy pile of themes on the floor beside his bed. Saddened by the stupidity of the first theme he had looked at, Klein had let them all fall to the floor. "What about it?"

"I guess I'm taking up your time. I'd better leave."

"No, it's all right. As long as you're here—"

"I wouldn't want to take up any of your valuable time."

Klein's heart had begun to pound at the change in the girl's tone.

"I mean, you're a teacher and all, you're pretty important. I wouldn't want to take up any of your precious time that you don't get paid for by the school."

"Look—"

"Look, I'm tired of being treated like dirt by everybody around here," she said quietly. "Nobody here is better than me. I know that. I've been told that enough times. Is it true or not?"

Klein sighed. "True."

"Yes, like hell it's true."

He lay his overcoat on the bed and sat beside it. "Do you want a cigarette?" he said.

"Sure, thanks."

They lit cigarettes. "What's your problem?" said Klein.

She was staring at the floor and he feared she would begin to cry. "Well, it's hard to begin, I—I don't know. Or which one is the worst one, but anyway that's not why I'm here—like I said, I happened to be visiting this friend of mine—"

"Should I read your theme now?"

"No, please, that's all right," she said shakily. She looked away. "Maybe I better leave. I made a mess of this."

"A mess of what?" Klein laughed. "What's wrong? I've got time."

"And I'm grateful for it, I mean I really know you are busy, I didn't mean what I said before— I'm sort of confused. I never was at college until now." She looked at him, squinting against the smoke from her cigarette. "This is all pretty new to me. I didn't finish school when I was supposed to, but had to quit for a reason, and I just got my diploma last year. Went at night."

"Your writing isn't bad," Klein offered.

"Yeah, that's a surprise. I'm doing better than I hoped," she said, and Klein felt another absurd rush of tenderness. "I work forty hours, you know, at a store, and I don't get enough time. You know, it's pretty hard to come back like this—nobody here cares if you make it or not. Nobody cares."

"Yes, that's life." But the banality of his remark startled

Klein, for he had meant to be sincere. "That's the way life is," he said, clearing his throat.

"I'm going into psychology."

"That's nice—"

"You're thinking how stupid that is, how I'll never make it," she said. "Okay. Maybe I know it myself. But I'm going to try just the same."

"I don't think—"

"It's all right, it doesn't matter. Maybe I should act like I'm in class and pretend something, I don't know. I'm too dumb to know what to do. And I guess I better go now, to hell with the theme." She was dabbing at her eyes with the delicate shredded tissue. "If you think it's worth talking about later, okay, but otherwise I'm just wasting your time, right?"

He was helpless before her heavy, obstinate passivity. She seemed older than he, and stronger; he could not compete with her. All he could do was wave her remarks aside weakly. "Of course not. It's what I'm here for."

"Here? Up here in your room?" She stood. The tissue had disappeared; her coat protected her. "I guess I'll see you tomorrow."

"Yes, tomorrow," he said. He went to open the door for her. Her slowness, which was not graceful, and her calculating averted gaze made him awkward; he was relieved when she left. Yet he stood, his hand on the doorknob, as if listening for her footsteps to return. Perhaps he should open the door, call her back? But he had nothing to say to her. He stood, he listened. She had left.

He read her theme at once. It was a description, in small slanted proper handwriting, of childbirth. Klein became weakened at her words, his stomach cringed at her dramatic underlined conclusion: "That was how I knew that I was really alone."

Monday he returned the papers. She was there, waiting, and he tried not to watch her. Like the others, she opened the paper to the back, read the grade, and without expression folded it again and left. He was disappointed, though he had not really wanted her to talk to him again; talking with students exhausted him, made him nervous. The prospect of teaching that day for some reason had been terrifying—more than ever his panic had come upon him, for had he not perhaps given away some of himself to that girl, however unwillingly? He had been unable to eat, and now the girl's behavior disappointed him (he could not deny this), he would take refuge in thoughts of his death: he had decided upon sleeping pills the night before. He would go to a doctor and complain of sleeplessness. . . .

Someone awaited him in the hall. Late afternoon, and stuffy and dark in the basement, the corridor with its cracked plaster and dirty floor—he looked around to see the girl approaching, shy and pleased. His heartbeat startled him. "Well, I guess you didn't think too bad of it," the girl said.

She and Klein both looked at the paper she held. "Your writing isn't bad," Klein said after a moment.

"Well," said the girl. Her coquetry was clumsy yet touching: she seemed to release herself to a gesture, a rehearsed mannerism, yet draw back at the last moment as if frightened at her daring. Now she had been about to raise her eyes from the paper to Klein's face, but she froze with her gaze in mid-air, fixed and surprised. She said, "Are you going out that way?"

"Out that door? Yes," Klein said abruptly, as if surrendering himself to something grim. They walked down the corridor together, acutely conscious of each other. "I'm going over to the clinic," Klein heard himself say.

He had not been prepared for this remark, nor had the girl. She frowned as he opened the door for her, leaning against the tarnished brass bar so that the door swung open with a mechanical violence. They ascended the stone steps into a gray afternoon. Limply the girl caught up his words, as if they had been precious: "Going over to the clinic? Is there something wrong?"

"Nothing much," Klein said.

They walked slowly. Klein did not know where he was going. The girl walked with her gaze downcast, watching her feet perhaps, as if she did not know either and were waiting to be told. "Look," Klein said, his eyes half shut, "if you want to explain this paper to me, all right. I would like to hear about it."

She looked up. "What about the clinic?"

"It can wait," said Klein.

They had coffee together and were still in the restaurant, a dingy campus place, at six. Klein offered, as if spontaneously, to buy her dinner. The sudden intimacy of their sitting together, coats off, books aside, had made him a little giddy. While they talked, the girl's abrasive coarseness ebbed; he felt in her hesitant speech and her occasional abrupt vulgarity something that seemed familiar. Did she remind him perhaps of his sister? But his sister's grittiness had no humor, no fragility, no hint of being vulnerable. In the presence of his occasional smile, her flirtation lapsed and she looked at him frankly. "Sure, I was married when the baby was born and that made a big difference to my mother," she told him, a dreary predictable story that seemed to him also familiar, as if it were a memory of his as well as of hers. "I didn't have any illusions about it and I turned out to be right. I thought maybe it would be a change—not so lonely as before. But it wasn't, but I wasn't surprised. I had the baby put out for adoption and we got divorced; he used to bother me for a while, then he quit—went out of town or something. If anything like that happens to me again. . . ." He was sympathetic but not surprised. Nothing about her could surprise him. Her failure made him angry, not at her but at the closed, paneled world that excluded her as it excluded him.

They returned to the same restaurant the next evening, some change in their relations having occurred (she smoking airily; he patient with the clumsy waitress), and he understood that the other people in the restaurant and those who had passed them languidly out on the street constituted for her, as they did for him, one aspect of the enemy, that great impersonal block of humanity whose surfaces were slick and impenetrable. The multiplicity of planes these surfaces suggested did not fool him: he longed to rescue her. "We all feel that way," he said quietly. Their glances, their kindnesses, their words were unmistakable; Klein felt himself drifting. "We all feel lonely. There are some people . . ." But he did not want to talk about other people. He veered back to the girl at once, who sat across the table from him listening with her deep-set eyes, the flesh slightly shadowed beneath them, perhaps pleased with her hair, which had been recently washed. "You must understand that it's nothing to be ashamed of," he said. "I've got to understand it myself. Some people get loneliness as if it were a disease. It makes them sick. I suppose I'm one of them." She nodded. They looked not at each other but toward each other, their gazes offset, sightless, pretending distraction: someone was arguing at the counter. Suddenly Klein thought of the sleeping pills he had yet to acquire and his heart pounded. He could not eat. "This place is a dump, isn't it?" he said.

They went to his apartment. He had to teach the next day, he had reading to do, but he did not care. Opening the door, he became dizzy. He had not wanted any of this to happen, yet it had happened; they were mute and warmed before it. The girl was a little nervous and sat at his desk, smoking, with the ash tray on her lap. They talked for hours: Klein could see his raw young voice prod at her eyes, her mouth. "I try not to show it in class," he said. She was deeply moved, he could see. He sensed in her silence and in the affected mannerisms of her smoking a generosity he was not accustomed to, which alarmed him because he was not certain he could meet it. "No, you don't show it, it's a surprise to me," she said slowly. He had been telling her of his nausea before classes. "Nobody thinks of teachers like that. Though I had a teacher in high school once, a woman . . . Most of the teachers here, you know, they separate themselves from you, they take care of your work for the course but outside of that they don't give a damn. You could be lying on the sidewalk and they'd go around you. They don't want to waste their time. What they're afraid of is getting mixed up with you. I suppose I don't blame

them, because somebody like me, somebody that's out
of place here . . . " "Why do you feel out of place?"
Klein said. "I don't know, I was born that way," she said.
"I was born out of place." He did not know whether
the mirroring of his plight in her evoked in him contempt
or love.

They awoke at three-thirty. Klein had left the meek
desk lamp on, channeling its light into a halo on the wall.
His room looked different, ghostly and rich: why not? The
girl was shy, softened, younger; he believed he loved her.
Words suggested themselves to him, but he rejected them,
they were not adequate, they would be embarrassing.
He wanted to feel that she shared this magical intimacy—
that was why she said little, hushed as if at church—yet,
walking her to her apartment (in a darkened building
on a side street), he was jealous of her distraction when
she glanced up at an automobile passing, jealous of her
failure to hint to him, however insincerely, that she was
at all surprised at what they had done: that they had
even done anything extraordinary. Klein felt like a person
in a dream. "Good night," he said, not going up the
stairs with her, and was overcome by an impulse to laugh.
The girl herself smiled suddenly. Yet he became immediately dissatisfied, for he thought ahead to the next day,
the next morning, the girl alone in her room (he imagined
it a room exactly like his own, just as anonymous), having
forgotten him.

Back home he had time now to feel shame for the
soiled sheets he had had for her. Dreamily, his hands
trembling as he remade the bed, he recalled that he had
planned that morning to do something profound; but
he could not remember what it was.

In class she was no different, though quieter. He could
not always count on her to answer the questions he sent
out to the class, hopeful and indefatigible. She did not
wait for him afterward, but they had dinner together,
at his place or at hers: a room smaller than he had
imagined, decorated with travel posters. "They're just
junk," she said of the posters, "but they look like windows

or something. It isn't just the wall there but openings
looking out—that's how I think of pictures." They were
able to work together, as if relieved of the necessity of
thinking about each other; Klein did not have to imagine
her, and so he was freed. She did not let him read her
work for his class until she handed it in, and he read her
compositions eagerly, before leaving the classroom,
his eyes racing along the neat handwritten lines as if
looking for something he could not identify. She wrote
of her family, their poverty, and he muttered, "Yes, yes,"
to each cliché, each undignified detail of the uninteresting
truths by which both their lives had been shaped.

This was November: the last week of the month, one
weekday morning, he saw her in a drugstore buying
something. She wore the red coat, though it did not look
so new any more, was wrinkled slightly behind, and she
stood fingering her hair nervously while the clerk reached
down to get something beneath the counter. Klein was
about to go to her when he stopped. He waited for her to
turn around and see him, but she did not; then he stepped
aside, out of the way, until she turned to leave. What
had she been buying? She had been at the cosmetics
counter. Klein strolled by, his eyes dazzled by the gold
and silver displays: the tubes of lipstick, studded with
rhinestones, the little dressing table mirrors, the pencils,
brushes, mysterious tubes. These things were fictions,
he thought, they were not real. They were fictions, but
his own world—he thought of his room, of the girl and
her bowed, attentive head—was real and would not
betray him.

That night they admitted to loving each other. Klein
had been drinking wine, was extremely agitated, not
quite himself. The girl looked different: different lipstick? They ate spaghetti she had made. "I was never
taught anything, how to cook," she said. "I learned it
all by myself. So don't be surprised what it tastes like."
Yes, she did love him: he knew now that she had loved
him for some time. Why else those frightened glances,
that uncomfortably comfortable domesticity here in this
room? Her staying with him that first night, far from

being casual, had been to her a tremendous event; he saw that now and the knowledge urged him to tell her again that he loved her. He loved her. Suffused with her love for him, he towered above her, protective and kind, his gaze distracted toward the shaded window as if lured to contemplate the future: no sleeping pills, no death after all, only a new life.

The first week of December, bitter cold. Klein returned from the library with an armload of books. Excited, he ran up the stairs as if he believed something awaited him in his room, some adventure. He let the books fall on his bed. Lately he had been reading a great deal, sometimes at the girl's room, sometimes here. His hair had been cut the day before, he had bought new shoes. He and the girl saw each other every evening; but already his interest in her had begun to wane, he wanted to read while she talked, telling him in detail of her life (her trouble with neighbors in the apartment house, with teachers). He was patient with her. That afternoon, after his composition class, he had known that he did not love her and that he had never loved her; that he did not especially want to see her again; that perhaps she had freed him, giving herself and thereby freeing him to himself— he did not quite understand. He was in a hurry. She was to come that evening for dinner, and he sat down to write out the note she would find taped on the door: the problem was how to be kind, considerate, to take it seriously (for already his thoughts were running wild, seizing upon the scattered lines of the medieval poetry he was to write an essay on, upon the respectful answer of one of his professors when he had asked a question in class that day). There was too much to think of. He could not concentrate.

She did not come to the next class meeting. Klein, nervously anticipating her gaze, was relieved; his gratitude made him eloquent and he believed he could see some of the students reappraising him. He understood that matters like that between the girl and himself happened often, perhaps daily, at this great university. Pity he felt for her, but not love, not even interest any more (she with her dreary half-smiling recollections of past insults, past pain, which impressed upon him too persistently the shabby detours and stumblings of his own life). If their relationship had begun in a dream, its termination woke Klein into something further: complexity, excitement, a new anxiety about his life, his future, even his personal appearance. He had bought the shoes with money saved week by week; he looked forward to buying something else—a suit, an overcoat. He spoke to his colleagues and appreciated their response to his humor, forced though it sometimes was. The secretaries in the English department knew him; he was able to be heard joking with them carelessly, like anyone else. The girl did not come to class. He did not see her. He contemplated writing another note, a letter this time, but he did not get around to doing it. Too much had happened between them, or perhaps too little had happened. He did not know. Between his classes he joked with the secretaries or dawdled with his colleagues or talked with his professors about things he had just discovered in his reading: ideas he hoped were his own, original ideas that excited him immensely. In his composition class he thought himself eloquent, and the desk at which the girl had once sat became for him not a depressing sight but (though he disliked himself for this) a symbol of something he possessed—perhaps power, the power of his new freedom. He had been loved. He had been worthy of love. The semester ended, the girl did not appear, he was forced to fail her in the course, though he talked the problem over seriously with another teaching assistant, a young married man given to a rather pleasing, keen, intellectual recklessness, popular in the department, talked it over discreetly and without embarrassment or humor, simply as a problem. The young man saw no choice, she would have to be failed, and he reminded Klein that maneuvering for grades was common at the university and that he himself suspected the girl's motives, really, though perhaps she liked Klein well enough. He said he would have supposed Klein wiser than to have been involved in such a dangerous situation; Klein, chagrined, in a way disappointed to know it was probably true she had only wanted a good grade from him, had to agree. The semester ended and she did not appear, he put an F beside her name (which did not look familiar), and supposed he would forget her, which he did.

That spring two students committed suicide; one, a girl but not the girl he had known, someone else, the other an Indian student, and Klein was reminded of the peculiar state of his own feelings months before: he recalled them in alarm, as if they had been the insane impulses of a stranger, someone in a novel. The girl had not appeared, he had not met her on the street or anywhere, and he never met her again. Perhaps she left school. In any case he never met her again and went on with his work, doing well, as well as any of the second-best students (for he recognized his limitations honestly), committing much to memory, grateful for and humble to the great academic tradition in which he would live out his life. With his degree he left for a comfortable though not well-known little college, married, had children, achieved happiness, did not seriously join in with his colleagues' criticisms of their lives, did not call attention to himself, bought a brick home, was proud of his wife for her chic competent womanly look, was proud of his children (two boys), took up sailing as a hobby since there was a fair-sized lake near the college. What possibility of happiness without some random, incidental death?

Dying

"Come closer, sit here on the edge of the bed. Or are you afraid of me?"

"Why should I be afraid of you?"

"You might catch my disease."

"You don't have any disease."

She saw that he was irritated, in spite of his smile. It was too warm in this room again, everything crowded and musty; as usual he had not opened the window. Each time she came to visit him she felt herself more tediously familiar with the furniture of his life, now narrowed strangely to this room in a half-empty old apartment building with a TV-Radio repair shop on the first floor. Things lay where she had seen them last: a pile of old newspapers, books from the city library, dirty trousers collapsed on the floor. The man himself, sitting propped up in bed, watched her distaste with a kind of malicious triumph, as if he were proud of residing over this particular kingdom.

"Well," she said, setting down the bag she carried, "how much do you weigh today?"

"I didn't bother weighing myself."

She sat at the little kitchen table, only a few yards from his bed. As she crossed her legs she could not help but glance down at them, and this annoyed her; she said coldly, "What's wrong with you now? As soon as I came in you were irritated."

"That isn't true—"

"It's true."

He scratched at his bare chest. She could hear his fingernails against his skin and smiled at the familiarity of the sound. "So I suppose you won't be coming any more," he said.

"Please, not that again."

They were silent. She could hear the sound of machines from somewhere, not far away. These sounds and even the sight of his room pleased her, as if she were coming home to something, and now their routine disagreement seemed to fit in precisely with what she had expected. He made a sound of impatience. His hair was tousled, yet she could see clearly that he would be bald soon; that sandy boyish hair was a disguise that had never fooled her. They had met years ago at college, both of them dissociated from the larger social world of the university by their having the wrong clothes, the wrong mannerisms, the wrong nervous intensity. To her he seemed to have changed little. To him, she guessed, she was more attractive than she had been; surely her blond hair wound in thick braids about her head and her expensive clothes must draw all the light of this shabby room to her. "Here, look what I brought you today," she said suddenly. "Why should we always fight?"

"Is that all for me?"

"Of course, everything." She sat with her back arched as if she were a princess, elegantly conscious of sitting this way as he watched her, and began to take things out of the bag. "Some wonderful fresh fruit; look at these colors. Look at this apple, isn't it beautiful? No, seriously. Do you want an apple now?"

"I don't like the skins on apples. The noise they make—"

"How preposterous," she said, laughing.

"I can't help it."

"But how can you be so weak?"

"Are you going to start that again?"

"No, no, look at these bananas—but they're not ripe.

I bought you some eggs, here. And some oranges, do you want an orange?"

"I don't care."

"Well, do you want it or not?"

"Oranges make a mess."

"Do you want me to peel it for you?"

He shrugged his shoulders. She watched him through her lowered lashes, as if trying to reconcile this man with the man she had once known, whose shoulders and arms had been broad—not muscular, exactly, but solid—while in this man hints of bone had begun to assert themselves fragilely beneath his flesh. "I'll put these things away and peel one for you," she said. She looked around; he said, "You can use that newspaper there." She nodded and put the paper on the table. Peeling the orange with her short chipped nails, she smiled at him as if she were performing an intimate gesture, parodying some intimate gesture. "Of course I'm coming to see you again," she said. "Why do you always ask that? Of course I'm coming. I like to take that bus, I even like to walk past that damn construction area. Those men in the white helmets—"

"What are they doing for so long?"

"I told you, widening the street. Putting an overpass in too."

"What about the men in the helmets?"

"The sun glares off the helmets, the men work with their shirts off, they're very tanned—"

"Not like me."

"When it's sunny, like today, everything is hot and gleaming. On overcast days it's something else again, another scene. All the light drains out and everything is sluggish, even the machines seem slower."

"How have you been this week?"

"Oh, fine. Wonderful. And you?"

"The same."

"You didn't get out, I suppose."

"No."

"I'm glad you're so pleased with yourself."

"What do you mean by that?"

"You promised you'd get out somewhere, go down-town or to the park, any goddamn thing. Now you tell me you stayed here."

"I wasn't up to it."

"You'll never be up to it, then."

"Look, for a bag of fruit I don't have to put up with this. I'm not your husband."

She frowned; then she laughed. Her laughter surprised her, for she knew it was not the right response to his eager, sullen tone. "No," she said. If she were to look at him, she knew, he would be staring at her with his big angry eyes, grown larger now that his face was thin, trying to involve her in some mysterious hurt. But this was familiar. Always he led her to talk about her husband, angrily and wistfully, as if trying to trap her in a lie.

"What do you mean by that 'no'? Is the idea so absurd?"

"Certainly not."

"You do mean it."

"Here's the orange, it smells wonderful. Do you want a plate or something? I'd better get you one." Dishes were piled in the sink, some still dabbed with food. She took a saucer and rinsed it and brought it to him. "I suppose I could wash those dishes for you, but I don't want to. I can't stand to do dishes."

"Okay, thanks," he said. He put the saucer on his thigh and picked up the orange carefully. "Why don't you sit here? On the edge, there's room."

She sat on the edge of the bed. "My feet ache, I wore these shoes without stockings. It's so hot, even for July. Can I ask you why this window is never open?"

"Noise from outside."

"But you open it at night?"

"Yeah." He was eating a section of the orange, self-consciously. She saw him glance at her crossed legs. "Your shoes got dirty."

"All that dust out there, yes."

"Do you wear high heels like that to attract attention?"

"Whose attention?"

"I don't know, anyone's. Is that why women wear them?"

"I don't know."

"How stupid!"

"Yes, stupid. Why don't you get out of bed?"

He ate the orange angrily. Now a spurt of juice appeared on his chin. "Why don't you come in here with me?" he said.

She smiled and looked vaguely away—at a calendar on the wall with half its numbers X'd out. "You don't really want that," she said.

"Look, I'm sick as hell of your telling me you know what I want. You know me better than I know myself, crap like that. Maybe you talk to your husband like that, but—"

"I never talk to him like that."

"Then to your friends."

"No, only to you." She paused. "You're my only friend."

He laughed. Then an unpleasant mottled flush appeared on his face. She was fascinated at his embarrassment, which came and went for reasons she could never understand. It was true, she thought, watching him eat, that he was her only friend; only to him could she talk, he existed for her as a face and a voice, a presence, a spirit, as no one else existed. Yet it was her husband she loved. Her love for her husband was so secure that it could be neglected and returned to, forgotten, and nothing would ever happen to it. Now this strange man, lying in his rumpled bed and supposing himself sick, was so moved by her having said that he was her friend that he could not for a moment even look at her. He ate the orange, slowly and deliberately, sullenly, as if it were a duty he did to please her. "Yes, my only friend," she said, touching his shoulder. At his look of irritation she withdrew her hand. "You were my only friend at college, too. Later on, when I didn't see you much any more, I still thought about you. That was what upset me—I always thought about you, you were always there. I didn't always want you so close to me, do you understand? You created something in me that stayed alive. . . . And just last year I thought that you couldn't be dead, nothing could have happened to you or I would have known it. And then our meeting like that, by magic. . . ."

"Magic, hell. Accident."

"By accident . . ."

"Did you ever tell your husband about me?"

"I told him about every man I had been involved with."

"What do you mean, involved with?"

"Made love with."

He stared down at the saucer. She felt his muscles tense as if he were stiffening himself against a blow. "We didn't make love," he said.

"Yes."

"We didn't, no, for Christ's sake. You say that now—you've imagined that now—to keep us apart. We never did."

"We did, yes. I remember."

"Look, this is ridiculous, every time we argue about it! We never made love, you never let me touch you, you were never any closer than this and you know it. What the hell are you trying to pull?"

"You've forgotten it, that's all."

"I've forgotten nothing!"

"Why are you so angry?"

"Because you're lying—it's a trick to keep us apart now, when you know how I feel about you—"

She lowered her gaze. When he talked like this she felt a peculiar comfortable lassitude overtake her, as if he were safely set upon a speech already written and memorized, something she might have helped write herself. "No, honey," she said, taking the saucer from him, "that's not true. I don't involve myself with other men now. I'm not interested. You don't seem to understand about my marriage; you have the idea that marriage is—"

"You've never admitted the truth about your marriage."

She set the saucer on the bureau. There were a number of bottles there, a stained spoon, an ash tray. "What's this?" she said. She picked up a small blue bottle filled with capsules. "Is this new?"

"No. Herzog's tranquilizers. He said nothing was wrong with me, just to keep calm. No anxiety."

"Well?"

"The fat old bastard! Seven dollars for those things."

She set the bottle down and forgot about it. "Well, let's not argue; I don't want to waste time that way. Why do you always want to talk about my marriage when it only upsets you? It has nothing to do with you, nothing at all. I shouldn't have told you about him that time, but I thought you'd be pleased to know what my life is like now. After all, when we knew each other I wasn't very happy. Would you like me to be that way now?"

"Yes."

"But that's a—" She stared. Before her gaze little bluish lines seemed to appear beneath his eyes and at the sides of his nose, near his nostrils. "That's selfish," she said.

"So what? Who isn't selfish?"

"How am I selfish?"

"You talk to me about him, to make me miserable. You lie. You lie to me and you won't—you won't—"

"But I said it wasn't going to be that way, the first time I came. I love you as a friend. Don't you know how important that is, what it means to me? What does a lover mean beside a friend? Doesn't that mean anything to you?"

"Christ, you really believe that." He drew his hand across his eyes; she could hear the slight elastic sound of his eyeballs being rubbed. "I hate that, stop it," she said, pulling at his wrist. "That noise—"

"Huh?"

"Oh, nothing."

"What noise?"

"Oh, nothing, it's silly. Nothing."

He stared at her, saw she was embarrassed about something. After a moment he said, "Doing any painting?"

"No."

"Anything wrong?"

"Of course not."

"Well, I just asked."

"I'm not angry, I'm sorry. I haven't been working but I think I have an idea. For two weeks or so . . ."

"You never did a portrait of your husband, did you?"

"No, I'm past that stage. Anyway, I wouldn't call it that, I never did portraits. That thing of you wasn't a portrait."

"Did you really see me that way?"

"Oh, I don't know."

"You never talk about your painting, why is that?"

"I don't know anything about it, I suppose."

"How old are you now?"

She laughed. "Why do you ask? You know I'm thirty-four."

"You're still young, then."

"Why do you say that, that way? You're the same age."

"Well, the success you've had with it, without trying, and you're so healthy—" Nervously she caressed his wrist, avoiding his sticky fingers. She could feel waves of hatred in the stuffy air between them. "If that magazine had carried that story of you last year, how do you know what might have happened?"

"I never expected them to run the story."

"So you were crowded out, but look how close it was, that stupid news magazine with the artsy-craftsy color section! Just like that. Some half-wit takes a liking to a painting and there you go, easy as that."

"It hasn't been easy, I wouldn't say that."

"For Christ's sake don't tell me that. You've never worried about it, not once. You don't give a damn about it."

"But it isn't my life, I'm not like you—"

"Not your life!" He drew away from her. Now he did look ill: perhaps he was not imagining everything after all. His lips were dry and loose and contemptuous. "Of course it isn't your life. You're married. You're in love. You've got money. You've even got a friend you can show off to, that you visit surreptitiously."

"What a foolish word—"

"Surreptitiously? What else should I say?"

"Nothing."

"You've got everything, why should you worry about your work? Your career? You worry about nothing. You sleep at night. You have no headaches, no fears, no moments of darkness when you know absolutely that everyone is going to die and that you—you can't escape it."

"But you're not going to die. Don't torture yourself with it."

"I wasn't talking about myself, what makes you think that!"

"You never talk about anything but yourself."

"And look at my work, all scattered around here, those goddamn papers on the floor there . . ."

"Oh, have you been working?"

He grinned contemptuously. "What do you think?"

"But you said last week you had an idea."

"No good."

"But if you started to write, something might happen. It used to be that way, didn't it? I still remember one of your stories, the one that was dedicated to me— About that German woman who worked for the family—"

"Forget it."

"But I liked that story."

"I didn't. So forget it."

"What was wrong with it?"

He had begun to breathe heavily. His eyes narrowed as if resisting pain. "I should think you'd play some music, at least," she said softly. "Should I put something on?" He seemed not to hear her at first; was he truly in pain, did he imagine it or did he pretend? "No, thanks, no," he said rigidly. "Don't you like the records I bought? Is something wrong with them? That fifth symphony is supposed to be a perfect cutting—" "No, forget it," he said. "Are you all right?" she said. He nodded impatiently. "But you don't want any music on?" she said. "Not while you're here." "But in the background—to blot out that noise—" "I don't put music on to blot out noise!" he said shrilly. He closed his eyes. She touched his chest and was surprised at how cool and damp his skin was. "That goddamn orange," he muttered.

"Do you want a pill? Anything?"

"No."

She bowed her head and caressed his chest vaguely. While she waited for his pain to pass she looked down at the floor—unfinished boards painted an ugly brown. Something had been spilled near the bed. "I'm going to exhibit some things in Chicago, by the way," she said. "In September. *He's* going to go down with me and help."

He pushed her hand away. "I'm all right."

"Are you going to see the doctor this week, then?"

"I suppose so."

"But how have you been, worse?"

"I weigh a hundred fifty-six."

"Oh."

"So that crap you made me eat, that goddamn nutritious cereal, didn't work. Matter of fact it made me throw up."

"Maybe if you went out sometime—went for a walk—"

"Out here?"

"You could move closer to the city. Near a park, why not? How did you ever find this apartment; it isn't in the city or in the country, there isn't anything here but vacant lots and buildings half torn down and that factory, or whatever it is, down that way— What a stupid place! It's inconvenient for me, too, since I don't drive—"

"Inconvenient for you!"

"Well, I mean—"

"I thought you liked to take that bus. Liked to walk by the men working out there so they can watch you. In your high heels."

"What's wrong with you?"

"Nothing."

"If I took a taxi out here next time, would you come back with me? We could go to that doctor near my house; I told you about him. I think your doctor at the clinic is too busy."

"Near your house? I couldn't afford it."

"Don't be silly."

"What? On that check they send me? How could I afford it?"

"I mean, don't be silly, I'd pay for it myself. Of course I'd pay for it. I always said that examination they gave you wasn't complete—"

"Your husband would pay for it."

"I have my own money."

"And his money too, you have his money! I saw his ads in the paper, real estate in a commercial area, will build to suit tenant— I was proud to see it."

"Don't talk about him, please. Be sensible, be nice. We've got to do something about your health. You keep losing weight, we've got to do something about it. Why don't you look around at me?"

"What do you want from me anyway? Why do you keep coming here?"

His face was brittle with anguish. She knew in that instant that she had never been apart from him during all those years, but that they had been regarding each other with this same inexplicable anguish, always, confusing other faces with the one face they desired, confusing other voices with that single unique voice neither of them could quite reject. She was humiliated by her bondage to this whining, helpless man.

"Why do you keep coming here?" he said.

She stood. She turned away. "I don't know."

"You never know anything!"

"Leave me alone. I'm going now."

"What time is it?"

"I'm going."

"Is it time for the bus?"

"You exhaust me, for God's sake—"

"But don't go yet, I mean it isn't time for the bus, is it? What time is it?"

His desperation shamed her. She stared over at the sink. "I know, I'll do your dishes for you," she said.

"No, the hell with them—"

"It's dirty this way, you'll make yourself sick," she said. "Don't you ever want to get well?" She inhaled slowly, feeling tears about to come into her eyes. She waited. Nothing happened, no tears. "Don't you ever want to get well?" she repeated, as if this remark were a cue that would inspire her to sorrow.

He had heard her coming on the stairs and opened the door for her. "Well, hello," she said. "How good you look! What's happened?"

"Oh, the weather change after the heat wave, I guess," he said. He was leaning back against the sink, smiling. Behind him the grimy window faced nothing—she could not tell if it looked out upon another anonymous building or upon the gray sky. "Come on in, sit down. Sorry about last time."

"Last time?"

He glanced at her. She was still smiling, pleased at his being out of bed and dressed, but now she saw that she had said something wrong. "Oh, yes, last time," she said. She recalled their argument vaguely—he had refused to come with her to a doctor. "Then I know what," she said, not sitting in the chair he had offered her, "let's go out for a walk. Not that way, where they're working, but up this other way. . . ."

He hesitated. She saw that his hair had been dampened and combed recently, that it looked thin. For a moment he was about to agree; then, as if terrified by something, he turned away slightly. "Maybe later on."

"Please, a nice walk. You said yourself the weather is nice. Come on."

"No." He went past her and sat on the edge of the bed. His movements were cautious, even rigid, as if he were in some kind of danger. She sat in the chair and felt the atmosphere of the room go heavy with failure. "So," he said, "how's your work been going?"

"I've started a painting." She saw that he was barefoot. His long, bony white toes cringed as she spoke. "I've been working on it for three days."

"Yeah, how is it? Anything like the last one?"

"I guess not." Watching his toes, she heard her voice go thick with embarrassment. "Men working on a road, a lot of white, in fact everything's white or black or gr..y.

No colors. The weeds alongside the road have been whitened by dust . . . they look like bones of something, skeletons. . . ."

He smiled sourly. "Not putting this place in, are you?"

"Well, no. I don't want any buildings."

"Why not? This is a picturesque dump and you like picturesque things. Television antennae on the roof. Quaint things."

"What do you mean, quaint?"

"You like quaint things, don't you? Men working, with white helmets. What happened to their suntans? Transfixed weeds, transfigured weeds—"

"Just what do you mean, quaint? What do you mean?"

He was still smiling but she knew he was nervous, ready to back down. "Forget it," he said. "I'm doing some work too."

Her heart was beating rapidly. For a moment she did not hear what he had said. Then she said, "Oh, that's nice. Really. Are you going to let me read it?"

"Maybe, when it's done."

"What is it?"

"A story."

"Oh, a story," she said. The flatness of her voice startled her. "But how are you? How do you feel?"

"The same."

"I'm so glad to hear you're working. . . ." She glanced over at the kitchen table, which was cluttered with dishes and newspapers, as if seeking out evidence of his work. "A story, did you say? About what?"

"A man and a woman."

"A love story?"

"Yes."

"You'll let me read it when it's finished?"

"Sure."

"I always liked what you wrote. In college . . . I thought you were the most intelligent man I ever met."

"Now you know better, huh?"

"I didn't mean that."

"You think I've changed some?"

"No. But we've all changed. . . ."

"Some of us for the better."

"We've grown older. Grown into adults. Surely there's nothing wrong with that."

"What are you suggesting?"

"I don't understand you."

"Are you suggesting I haven't grown up?"

"I didn't say that, my God. How touchy you are! As far as I'm concerned you were always grown up. You had no childhood." And now she could see that he was not well, really, that she had imagined when she first came in that his being up, his smiling so confidently, had meant much more than it did. "How much did you say you weigh?"

"A little less."

"But how much?"

"A hundred forty something. I don't know."

She winced. Her hand came up before her in a gesture of pity, or defense, as if she supposed he expected some movement from her. "Please tell me what you're doing for yourself."

"I'm resting. Thinking."

"Be serious, will you? This is important."

"How can anything about me be important?"

"It's important to me!"

"But why to you? Who are you?" He stood up, excited. Then he sat down and lay back on the bed, laughing. "My God, if you could explain that to me. Why you bother with me."

"Because you're my friend," she said contemptuously.

"I'm your friend," he said. "But why? Why? If this is the last time you come, everything should be settled between us. Right now you're thinking—"

"You don't know what I'm thinking."

"You're wishing you hadn't come. A sick man isn't a man at all."

"But what has that got to do with it?"

He swung his legs around off the bed. "What has what got to do with it?"

"What you said—"

"What? What?"

"Oh, I don't know. You're giving me a headache. And I wish you'd open that window, noise or no noise, it smells in here—"

"A sick man isn't a man, huh? That's what you think?"

"I never said that!"

"You don't let me be a man!"

"Look, please, if you're—" She made a gesture of rising that was insincere; he did not respond. They were silent for a while. "So you lost more weight," she said. She looked over at his little calendar, something from a service station, on which the new month was being X'd out. For some reason this pleased her, as if it were a landmark.

"Yes. And you, you're looking very good."

"With these lines under my eyes?"

"What? Let's see. I don't see anything."

"You never notice anything. I was up until four last night, drawing weeds. Don't laugh. Then I couldn't sleep when I did go to bed." As she spoke, a wave of excitement rose in her that she had to hide from him. His narrow glittering eyes were hostile.

"You're looking very good just the same. Very healthy."

Her excitement was transformed suddenly into a sensation of dismay. She put her hands to her eyes in a melodramatic gesture. "Why do you hate me so," she said.

"What?"

"You hate me, I can feel it. You hate me. There's something inside me that was born when I met you— when a woman meets any man, it happens—and this thing, this creature that becomes me when I'm with you, you're killing it, you hate it and want to destroy it—"

"That's not true," he said quietly.

"You want me to come to bed with you so you can kill it. We're fighting each other, I bring you love and we're antagonists; what's wrong with us? The other time it wasn't like that. We were close to each other and it was beautiful—" He said nothing. She went on, in spite,

"But of course you don't believe that ever happened. You've forgotten it, like all men."

He made a gesture that indicated nothing. He looked confused and ill. A hand might have been pressing against his chest, pushing him back down on the soiled pillow that was propped up against the headboard. He took a package of cigarettes out of his pocket, as if for something to do.

"Anyway," she said, "you should open that window."

"I open it at night."

"You're so remote here; my God, this is the end of the world. That window is all you have, and you keep it closed. How can you live like this?"

He lit a cigarette. "You're very generous, then, to come here in spite of everything. To come here and let me admire you. See what I can't have."

"Do you think that's why I come here?" she said sharply.

"How do I know? Why you began, or why you're stopping—"

"Why I began? When I saw you downtown that day I couldn't have walked away. Are you serious? Don't you know what you mean to me? You looked so sick— I guess I thought you were drunk— There was never any question about my coming to see you."

"Is that true?"

"Yes."

"And about stopping?"

"Why do you always bring that up?"

"Because I'm afraid."

She got up slowly. In spite of his watching her, she stretched her arms and stifled a yawn. "I'm still sleepy. I got up at seven this morning. . . . Now you, you say you're afraid, afraid of what? How strange you are—" She came to sit by him on the edge of the bed. He was pleased at this; she saw the cunning rigidity of his face relax. "Afraid of what?"

"The usual."

"But what nonsense—something you can't even explain—" She watched him closely, as if jealous of something. He took hold of her arm and caressed it without affection. She smiled sharply. "Tell me what you're afraid of."

"I'm not sure."

"Not that thing that bothered you once before, I hope. That awful accident—"

"Oh, that. The woman by the bus? No, not that, but I still dream about it sometimes. No. Something else. Earlier than that, years ago. . . . But hell, I don't want to talk about it."

"I want to talk about it. I want to know."

"Do you? I was working at the hospital then, I told you about that. I was twenty-seven— Where were you at twenty-seven?"

"Married."

"To him?"

"I've only been married once."

"At the hospital, then. . . ." But he said, with a harsh burst of laughter, "Hell, I'm crazy, what's the difference? Do you think I don't know absolutely every truth about myself, even how I look to you?"

"That's not possible."

"Do you suppose your mind is so impregnable? I can see everything—everything. And if I say I'm crazy, do you think I don't prefer this to something else? Huh?"

His fingers had become hard against her arm. She seized his hand and brought it to her lips. "Don't hurt me," she said.

"Don't hurt you! You come to watch me suffer and you're afraid of getting hurt yourself!"

"Do you think I come to watch you suffer?"

"Why else? Why? You could let me lie in bed and rot, what the hell does it matter? It occurs to me now that you won't let me alone until I'm dead, dead and stinking. Then you'll go back home and wash your hands."

"Please don't talk like that—"

He jerked his hand away. "And I didn't do any writing either. A lot of crap; I was lying. I did nothing."

"I know."

"I wish I could tell you what I thought when I heard you coming up the stairs. I feel I'm learning a new language, that this is a prison and I have to talk in code. You have a key that lets you in and out and you're a spy they've sent in here, and I have to talk to you, I can't help it, I lie here and wait for you and think, What if she doesn't come! What if she's left me! And then when you leave I feel worse, I wish you had never come. And you're a spy, you want to get that secret from me and show it to them, paint it up, transfigure it so that it becomes symmetrical and quaint—ending up in five colors, reproduced in that news magazine! Do you think I don't know you? Everything about you? You might be a character in something I've written, that's how well I know you! A woman, a devouring woman—"

"If that's so, then you wanted me that way. If you created me, you created me that way."

He smiled bitterly at this. "To hell with that psychological crap! And you want me to go for a walk—as if I can go for a walk! As if I can walk down those stairs! And so sympathetic with suffering—other people's. So appreciative of suffering. So sweet, solicitous. And all you ask in return is that I love you. And if I did tell you what I dreamt about, could you understand it? No. Could you feel it? Only as a picture. You'd get a vision, a sight, the picture of what happened, but you wouldn't know what I know. You weren't there. People like you never happen to be there."

"Tell me about it."

"And then what?"

"What do you mean?"

"What will you do for me?"

She half-closed her eyes as if seriously thinking. Then she said, "What I've always done for you."

He turned away with a grunt. His hatred for her made him shudder; she watched with fascination the convulsive jerking of his hand. "So I'm your jailer now," she whispered.

"I didn't say that."

"I'm a spy, then. That your jailers have sent."

"Hell, I know I'm crazy, that was just talk. No one cares about me except you. Forget it." He shivered. She was frightened, physically frightened, by the shift in his expression: His anger had been overwhelmed by a look of passive terror. "But what's wrong with you?" she wanted to cry. "What is it? What do you know that I don't know? Why are you dying?" But she said nothing. She held his hand and pressed it against her throat and would not let him pull it away.

She believed she heard something, it must have been him telling her to come in. So she opened the door. He lay in bed, evidently just waking, his eyes narrowed and vague as if out of focus. A stale, sharp odor was in the room. Immediately she began to breathe shallowly, as if in the presence of danger. "Did I wake you?" she said. She had brought him a bag of groceries and some magazines; she put the things down slowly on the cluttered table. A coffee cup was nearly overturned—still half filled with coffee, with a cigarette butt floating in it. "Are you all right?" He raised himself on his elbow. The sheet fell away to show his pale, bluish chest. He stared at her and began to smile. She faced his smile with fear, for it seemed to her ghastly, its very eagerness terrifying. "You didn't forget I was coming, did you?" she said coquettishly. But the lilt of the remark was ludicrous in this musty room and she felt her cheeks burn with shame. He did not notice. "Come in, sit down," he said. "I guess I was asleep." She came to him and stood nervously by the bed as he sat up and tried to smooth his hair down. She wanted to pull the sheet up about him, to protect him. "God, what a taste in my mouth," he said, making a face. "Could you get me some water or something?"

She brought him a glass of water. He drank it eagerly. The side of his face was crisscrossed with reddened wrinkles from the pillow. She took the glass from him when he finished. "I was lying here thinking about you, I

wasn't asleep," he said, touching her arm. "I was thinking how I loved you. And if you didn't come this time
. . . If I thought it was the wrong day or something. . . ."
Then in mid-sentence his tone changed; she could see
him swallow and then struggle not to show something—
anxiety, malice. He tugged at her wrist. "Come down
here with me. Just this one time, will you? It isn't too hot
in here. I can brush this off the bed—crumbs or something, what is it?" He began brushing something off
angrily. "I've been thinking about you ever since you
left last time. And a whole week in between—that goddamn exhibit you had to go to— Of course you had to
go to it. Come on here."

She laughed nervously and tried to pull away. "I
brought you some magazines—"

"Look, goddamn you, you—" But he stopped. He
grated his teeth. "You don't know how I've been waiting
for you," he said softly.

"Please, let go. What's wrong with you?"

"With me?"

"I come in here and see how you've let yourself go—
see what you've done to yourself— There's nothing wrong
with you, don't you know that? Nothing! You're weak,
whining, and now you want—"

"What?"

She turned away from him. She was overcome with
disgust and shame and could not look at him. "How can
you think I'm like that, that I would want to make love
with a dying man!" she said.

And, as soon as this was said, the tension between
them dissolved; even the foul air of the room seemed to
weaken. She looked over her shoulder at him. He was
sitting up, the wrinkled sheet fallen down to his stomach,
his body hunched and skeletal and contemplative. So
that is what he looks like, she thought sharply, and could
not remember if he had really changed or if she had
never seen him before. After a moment he glanced up
and smiled shakily. "Magazines, huh?" he said. "What
kind?"

She brought them to him. She sat on the edge of the bed. He looked at the glossy covers, smiling, and leafed through the pages perfunctorily. "And how have you been this week?" she said. She saw that his vague familiar smile did not change, that he had not heard, and she had to repeat her question.

What Death With Love Should Have to Do

At last she said, "I'm bleeding," and in fear tightened her hold around him, her arms high against his ribs and her legs locked around his body as if she believed he would try to escape her. The motorcycle crashed through a thicket; stiff branches snapped back at them, across the dark green plastic of their goggles, stinging their cheeks. He would hear nothing.

They were in the open again. The motorcycle leveled suddenly, the sun slashed at them as if lurching precariously in the sky. Mae clung to Vale, her face against his wet back. They were in a lane, a cow path. Dust billowed up behind them, and flecks of straw, and churnings of grass. The sun tilted again and remained level. They were alone. The other cyclists were nowhere in sight; Vale had left them behind. The air smelled of empty heat, of hot, dry grass. There was a fine golden glow to the air that reminded Mae dreamily of love, and the roar of the motorcycle swelled out to obliterate all other sound: the usual country noises, birds and insects and dogs barking forlornly in the distance. Again the motorcycle dipped and recoiled up out of a rut. Mae cried out with pain. Vale absently caressed her hand and released it, as if he had just recalled her.

A fine day: they had noted it earlier, avoiding each

other's eyes. Clumsy acting, in the diner (an old trolley up on blocks) down the street from the big dirty house in which they now lived: it made Mae suddenly conscious that she was young, after all, after so many years. Vale had said, frowning at his cigarette, "Are you sure you want to do it?" And Mae, thin and exhausted from the hot sleepless nights, had said, "For Christ's sake, *yes.*" Why did he have to be prodded always to do what he wanted to do? Staring at him, she imagined she could see the little flecks of his failings, his weaknesses, appear like pimples on his tanned face. "It wouldn't be your fault if anything went wrong," she said bitterly. "Went wrong?" said Vale. "You know things like that happen all the time." Later, out in the country, he had made her drink beer with him and the others. They joked; they danced around in their excitement. Mae drank the beer with her eyes closed, as if it were medicine. Now she could feel it in a tight hot circle in her stomach, waiting to force its way up.

She looked around, awakened by pain. Behind them the countryside jiggled crazily. They had cut down through someone's wheat field, down a hill, and their path was idly vicious—she stared back at it, as if she expected it to reveal some truth about herself and Vale. No one else was in sight; Vale would be proud. He was in the lead and straining to go faster. In moments of loneliness or terror (she did not know which this was) Mae murmured to herself *love, love,* that magic incantation, and there would come to her mind not just Vale's face (Vale sleeping: his boy's face, innocent and brutal, lips open slightly, a thread of saliva on his chin) but the faces of the other men, sometimes hopelessly mixed together, the eyes of one and the mouth of another, and even the faces of her brothers and sisters and the reserved, shadowed, secret face of her mother: an audience that stared in silence. As if resisting them, Mae pressed her mouth against Vale's back. Her lips were parched with dust, and yet she saw a faint spider-web pattern of blood on his shirt: she must have been cut somehow, by those branches probably. Vale strained forward, up-

ward, the muscles in his shoulders and back asserted
themselves, he shouted something back at her—she embraced him desperately, just in time, for there was another
crash, a jolt that hit her in the stomach. They had
abandoned the lane and were crossing a field, bumping
from rut to rut. She could feel Vale's chest expand with
joy.

As always, the confusion of the race obscured all
memories leading up to it. Once begun, all races were
alike: they were perhaps the same race: their noises
dispelled all mornings, all previous nights, fused them
into a sameness that seemed a broad, thick, muddy
stream to which everyone had to return. Vale had
taught her to love these races, but he had also taught
her to hate the return to rigid ground. Though she had
been in love with Vale for only a few months, it seemed
to her that her life had been a practice for such times: this
dissatisfaction with the calm earth, this hatred of familiar
things, of her own face in mirrors or reflected back to
her from store windows, or (and this baffled her) even
the delirious struggles of their love. At this thought her
insides churned; she could feel the warm blood again,
as if awakened. She closed her eyes and pressed the
goggles against Vale's back, though she knew this irritated him, and for some reason thought immediately of
her mother, who might be standing with the screen door
pushed open as she often did, frowning out into the
sunlight, waiting for Mae, able to hear—fifty miles
away?—the insane roaring of Vale's motorcycle.

Another hill. They reared up out of the earth to land
with great agility on a hillside well worn, pasture land
with stumps of old trees here and there, not enough to be
dangerous. No cows in sight; the farmers might have
known about the race. Mae expected vaguely to see one
appear out from behind a tree with a shotgun. Vale had
been shot at more than once, so she had been proudly
told; he had made his escapes down anonymous roads
on this same motorcycle, not stopping, as he put it, to
pass the time of day. Now the sun swerved again. Were
they falling? No, for Vale was in control, they had

turned and were plunging downhill. Mae saw a creek
ahead. Her eyes refused this; she turned aside. She would
tell him, would shout it at him. She would tell him she
was bleeding. He had not heard. . . . And yet she said
nothing, dreamily she closed her eyes and thought, for
some reason, of an accident she had witnessed once:
blood on the blue motorcycle, on the grass around it,
flicked up onto the dusty indifferent weeds and even
onto insects on these weeds, so that their hard black
little shells were flecked with blood as they crawled
lazily about.

Her muscles jumped by themselves. She gripped him
in terror so that he grunted and slashed at her arm,
without thinking. Her body had learned to resist, to draw
itself back as if refusing to see what awaited; that was
wrong. That was stupid. Vale's body, by contrast, urged
itself forward, lunged forward into everything. He was
not jolted because he became the jolting itself, became
the careening, the speed. On the open road his body
joined itself to the motorcycle as in love it joined itself
to hers; he could not be hurt. She knew, jealously, that
his mind dissolved out into the windy sunshine, into the
roar of the motorcycle. There was no alien, unknown
space to threaten him. He resisted nothing. She pretended to give herself, yet always resisted, and now as
they rushed to the creek bank she held herself rigid as if
hurtling through a dream that had betrayed her. The
wheels churned viciously, striking bottom. Water surged
against them, warm startled waves against their legs.
Early September: the creek was shallow, and parched
white rocks, flat rocks with moss baked onto them,
dipped on either side and seemed to stare up, flat faces,
in white, frenzied terror at what Vale was doing. Vale
shouted something—she could not hear. Then something
happened and she clawed at him and was knocked off
the seat.

She did not know what had happened. She was sitting
in the creek, leaning over clumsily to vomit in the dirty
water. Vale splashed over to her. He shouted something
but his words seemed to come to her through water,

dazed and blurred. He loomed over her, began pulling
her up. "Goddamn it, Mae, we got no time for it! No
time!" he said. She could not get her breath. He yanked
her to her feet and over to the motorcycle, not looking
back at her. Please help me, aren't you going to help
me? she thought, staring at his back, his strong shoulders.
He had forgotten. He did not know her.

They went on. Heading for a road now, up a long
incline choked with weeds. The air was not so warm as
it should have been. The motorcycle strained coyly, this
was dangerous, they might tip back except that Vale knew
what to do, knew how to snake about, to dance with it,
tease it, to balance and unbalance it. Tall grass crackled
about their feet as if it were on fire, torn by the wheels
and sucked into the spokes. They ascended slowly to
the road. At the top they barely moved. Mae groaned
and urged them forward. "Come on!" she cried angrily.
Then she felt Vale's sigh of relief: they had made it.
They turned and moved on. How level this was! Mae
had forgotten what roads were like. Now Vale fled as if
death itself were pursuing him, or perhaps some cheap
embarrassment (being beaten by one of his friends),
leaning forward into the wind as if he were urging himself
out of his body, weary of it, and away from Mae too, at
last weary of her and her fragility. Behind them ex-
plosions of dust, great clouds of dust. The other cyclists
could see the dust now from across the creek; they
would know where Vale was. At the thought of them
Mae's mind snapped back to the memory of that accident,
last week, and to the knowledge of herself now, bleeding
so secretly. She closed her eyes. She could not curse it
because it was what they had wanted. Two months
along, and to get rid of it so easily! Vale already had a
child, a son, fifty miles away. That was why, perhaps,
he had forgotten about her, could not guess her pain,
would not cut the engine and drift along quietly and
curve off the road so he might turn to her. She would
tell him nothing.

Their speed was intoxicating; she would think of this.
The wind and the sunlight were transformed into a golden

buzzing, like liquid. Mae let her head fall back gently and opened her mouth to it. But it was just air, nothing more. She groped for something to hang onto: a memory, something. What came to her was the morning last April when she had gone over to the garage where Vale worked to get a Coke. He had been inside, squatting by his motorcycle, his eyes blinking at her through beads of sweat. She had wanted him and had gone to get him. She had been watching him for years, a boy much older than she; and, back from the city where she had been living for a while, rested and home, sworn at and slapped and forgiven by her mother, allowed back in her old room, she had decided that Vale would be next. She had always liked his lean hard face, his muscular arms and shoulders, his nervous long legs and big feet. She remembered him from school, years ago. He had scowled then, imitating someone, and he scowled often now, even in his sleep, because of his work at the garage and his hatred for the people he had to give gas to, put air in tires for, check oil for. He hated them and so he had two vertical lines on his forehead. He spoke in bursts of words, often shouted, was vain and unsure of himself, was infatuated with Mae as (so he was told) he had once been infatuated with his wife, before she became his wife.

The countryside was blurred with their speed. Mae watched it through her lashes, distrusting it. Speed taught her that no sight was real: no appearance demanded faith in itself, since it changed so easily, flowed in and out of itself. Nothing stayed. Noise shattered Mae's thoughts, rattled and vibrated in her throat. She glanced down at her legs and was surprised to see no blood there. Her slacks were wet. She could not see her feet. The dirt road, clotted with pebbles, sped along. The air was suddenly thick with dust: someone was ahead of them. They rounded a turn too fast. Vale pulled out of the skid and they saw a pickup truck ahead of them, with children in the back. A boy scrambled to his feet as Vale overtook them. In envy he stared; the seriousness of his look reminded Mae of one of her brothers, her favorite brother, now fourteen, a boy who hated her, she supposed, as they all did, who could not understand—as she herself could not understand—what she was doing. The boy on the truck platform hardly glanced at her. He was interested only in Vale.

Vale roared past. Mae slyly and contemptuously peered over at the driver of the truck, who stared at her (a middle-aged farmer with a large, brutal bald head) with hatred. She met his gaze solidly as they passed. Those looks were familiar: everyone looked at her that way. She was reminded of her father, that remote, dying old man, dead for years now, coughing into his handkerchief, and of her mother, still waiting at that screen door, waiting and listening and smelling the air. Mae had been gone for five months now, but her mother awaited her. Every morning, every night. At the dinner table no one would speak of her but, shivering with dread, everyone would think of her; she knew this; she did not have to be told. "Will you forgive me this time?" Mae thought. She would ask her mother this. "Will you let me in again?" The last time she had come home one of her younger brothers had been using her room, that closet behind the stairs she had once been so proud of, and the bed had been soiled from his dirty feet. The magazine pictures she had taped up on the wall were gone. "If you don't want me here I'll go back," Mae had said. "I'll catch the bus at the corner and go back!" Her mother would not speak to her for days: cold and pale, silent and suffering, a rosary entwined in her fingers. The other children hated her. They were afraid of her. But on the third day, so early in the morning it had not yet become light, her mother had come to her as always. Her eyes rimmed with shadow, her skin aging, coarse: never had she been so pretty as Mae! She had knelt at the bed and buried her face in the blanket. Mae, terrified, wanted to push her away, wanted to cry out that she hated her mother, hated her! That she did not know why she had come home! At the memory she dug her nails into Vale's chest. She had always hated her mother, and once Vale had said that he was sick to hell of her muling and puking, that she thought of her mother more than she did of him, did not hate her mother but loved her, more than she did him, and that he would not stand for it. She had slapped his mocking face. What did he mean, what did he know? He was brutal and ignorant, at the end of these races he would stagger about, drinking beer, laughing, showing everyone the nicks and scratches on his face and hands, as if there were something about blood that was funny. . . . But what has this to do with love, Mae thought dizzily, what has blood to do with love and why did they go together? Why were they related? She opened her eyes and saw trees with hazy leafed branches floating overhead, so blasted with Vale's deafening roar that they reared up as if in terror, straining to get away.

She embraced Vale but he did not notice. Her muscles, small and hard, would always relax, release, after a moment. She could not sustain an embrace. She was capable of strength, but only for seconds: passion reared her body, animated it as dying animates creatures wounded, blasted by shot, but left her then exhausted, panting, minutes closer to death. Mae rubbed her sunburned face against Vale's back and felt her strength flow into him, surging up into his arms, down into his thighs. They worked together. She leaned against him, her body groaning with the strain of the race; she sighed and let her head fall back again so that the sharp air slashed across her nose and parched lips. Vale swerved; pebbles were thrown up against the spokes; Mae leaned with him, felt the motorcycle respond gratefully to their skill. Ahead, the road dipped out of sight, bushes and nameless trees leaned to them, in patches the sky appeared, and, mottled and indistinct, the gray-green mountains wavered behind miles of sunny mist. They slammed into a shallow, were stunned by something there—a rock, probably—careened up, swerved, skidded. But Vale had control. Mae gripped him, indifferent as always when there was real danger, staring sightlessly at nothing. At such times she understood she was alone. Everything drifted from her, memories of her past and of herself (for she saw herself, without regret, as the anonymous

hard-faced girl surrounded by men, on tavern porches at
night, at filling stations, in disreputable automobiles going
past, jostling about street corners, taut and coquettish and
frightened, stared at by safe, secure women with destina-
tions who could feel only pity and hatred for her), memories even of Vale's body, his muscles, leaning away,
away. She remembered the blood and her mind leapt at
it. That was real. She knew what it meant. No baby this
time, they had been too clever, no one had fooled them:
Vale would want to celebrate. The first time they had been
worried, he had taken her to a doctor in town and she
had lain on the kitchen table, awake all the time, ten
minutes (so Vale had told her later, proud of her), chewing on her agony, keeping it in. The doctor had been pale,
shaken, not so much at Vale's threats as at Mae's stern
sullen rigidity, her refusal to admit pain. Then the last
time, which evidently had not been serious, on a turkey
run like this, it had happened and without much pain:
she had time then to be ashamed. The old shame of her
young girlhood overtook her and she had thought, in the
midst of Vale's delight, that this could not really be
happening to her: she could not really have become this
person. But this time it was different, somehow. Her body
was exhausted. She knew that it had surrendered and
that only the momentum of the race kept her going. She
would say nothing to Vale, she would never tell him.
As if in mockery of her pride, her teeth rattled suddenly.
She clamped her jaws together. Her mouth was dry and
filled with dust. She had seen Vale rinse his mouth out
after a race, spitting out the mud with breathless boyish
laughs. . . .

Suddenly she could not remember where they were.
She did not know how far they had to go or how long
they had been driving. Had they been this way before?
Nothing was familiar. Why had she seen so little with
Vale after all, when it was Vale she loved, or almost
loved? She felt her eyes burn suddenly behind the goggles.
A bitter lament began itself, like a song (she was always
haunted by songs, snatches of melodies heard on juke
boxes and radios), a formless wail she wanted to deny,

in panic and shame. This was not like her: this was someone else. Mae was not like this. She regretted nothing. She was afraid of nothing, nothing, not the operation that time, not that man, years ago, with the black hair frizzed and queer on his body, not her mother who waited for her so patiently. None of these frightened her, for she had chosen them. She had wanted them just as she wanted now this race and this stubborn pain. But everything was confused. She could not recall which race this was. . . . Did they really wait for her, sisters and brothers, the lost, dead father, the mother weeping in that helpless perpetual grief?

She fell. Her arms betrayed her, she was not strong enough to keep hold of Vale. She fell back slowly as the motorcycle sped on, and before she hit the ground she had time to wonder if he would notice, if he would glance around. Then she struck, hard on her side, and something snapped in her shoulder, some tiny brittle bone teased beyond patience. She did not lose consciousness but lay quietly and stared up at Vale's young panicked face. He leaned over her. His eyes were pale inside the goggles, white hollows against his dirty skin. Something in his face, some twitching muscle, could not acknowledge the end of the race. "Hey, honey, are you for Christ's sake okay?" he said. He took off his goggles. "Why'd you let go? Look, are you bleeding or something? Did it happen?" He pulled her up, propped and prodded her into sitting, as if that would make her all right. He squatted on the road and stared into her face as if staring into an abyss. "Honey," he said, shaking his head sadly, "I forgot about it, you ought to of told me. . . . Honey, look, don't die, I mean you're not going to die, are you? You're not hurt that bad, are you?"

Vale was a young man of twenty-six, newly married when he met Mae. He and his wife lived with their month-old son in a trailer not far from the girl's father's garage, an Esso service station on the outside of a village named Frothing. A small river bounded the village on one side; there was a sawmill, an old cider mill shut

down, and a tavern with a water wheel lit up at night
to attract tourists. Because a new highway had been
opened north of the village, not so many tourists on
their way to the mountains drove slowly through town
as they once did. The Esso station had never done well
anyway with tourists—they would brake and coast curiously by, staring at the dirt drive and the greasy, leaning
garage with its array of tin signs advertising soft drinks
and cigarettes and gasoline. Vale, who worked for his
father-in-law, would sit smoking on a stump in front of
the garage and stare coldly at the tourists—often middle-
aged men and women—who showed such caution. He
could see at the back of their minds a clumsy inert fear
and would have liked to seize this fear and drag it out
into the daylight.

Frothing was about half a mile long. There were a few
stores and some boarded-up buildings and several frame
houses that faced the old state highway; then the Esso
station; then the bridge over the river, which was lively
in the spring, showing flashes of white as the water
streamed over the flat black rocks, but shallow the rest
of the year. Vale had always hated Frothing.

He worked on his motorcycle when there was nothing
else to do, though his father-in-law grunted in disapproval
at this. He loosened parts and tightened parts, back and
forth. Sometimes his wife ambled over with the baby. His
wife was a tall girl with long brown hair. She wore
colorful jeans or slacks, blouses without sleeves that
showed her long, muscular, hair-flecked arms. She was
eighteen but looked older; Vale thought of her as older
than he was. Now that she was a mother she did not
seem any different to Vale, who realized that she had
always been one really, had always been so competent
and controlled, so that the baby's crying did not weary
her as it did Vale and did not even provoke her into
answering Vale's aimless insults. Like her mother, she
was robust and healthy, partial to bracelets and wide
belts, imitation leather belts with rhinestones on them,
that gave her a brusque cowboyish look. She had always
been ready to laugh at remarks people, especially men,

would make: that was what Vale had liked about her at first, the way she grinned and laughed, sometimes giggled helplessly, at his jokes. Now she often said, "Yeah, that's very funny, ha ha," and smirked at him, keeping her boyish laughter for Vale's friends. She did not laugh much around the garage, not down with Vale as he worked endlessly at his motorcycle without taking much notice of her (there was nothing to say any more, and she stood around shifting her weight from foot to foot, cracking gum, sighing) or upstairs with her mother, who always had the radio on. Vale could hear his wife's heavy tread upstairs, and often the baby's crying, but he never could make out what his wife and her mother said, nor did he hear them laugh.

One morning Mae walked into the garage. The front door was always kept open and Vale glanced up to see her there with the dazzling glare from the dirt drive behind her. "You still got Cokes for sale here?" she said. Though her face was shadowed by the glare behind her, Vale recognized the taut suspicious expression she had always, even as a child, displayed. Vale, wiping the sweat out of his eyes, waved her over to the machine in the corner. "Yeah, well I need change," the girl said, holding out her hand, palm up. Vale felt his face go hot as he stood. He took the quarter from her and went over to the cigar box his father-in-law kept money in (the cheap old run-down bastard, Vale thought) to get change. The girl waited with one foot out slightly in front of the other, her ankles crossed. Vale gave her the change without smiling.

She drank the Coke in front of him. She had pale brown hair that had been cut jaggedly and was combed by her to stick out around her face stiffly, like doll's hair. She was small, thin, nervously agile; Vale sensed a peculiar tension in her movements as she lifted the bottle to her lips and brought it down again, watching him, a tension he understood. Even her features were stiff and arch, as if held rigid purposely. She had fine, intricate eyes, thickly lashed and outlined skillfully with black pencil; her eyelids had crescents of silvery blue. Her lips, deeply pink, sucked at the soft drink and pursed themselves with modesty and cunning. "Come home, huh?" Vale said finally. He did not know how to talk to her because he had always thought of her as a child. "Had enough of the city, huh?" he said, grinning without humor. She shrugged her small shoulders. "Here, you want some?" she said. She thrust the bottle out at Vale, who accepted it before he had time to think. He gulped it down; while drinking, some germ of childish revenge suggested itself to him and he finished the Coke, so that he handed the bottle back to her empty. "Yeah, thanks," he said, wiping his mouth. Their eyes met and they smiled. Then they looked away, laughing in embarrassment. "You're some sort of a pig, I guess," Mae had said, staring past him at the motorcycle. Vale looked down at her bare legs. "Are you glad you came home?" Vale said. She laughed again and turned away. Vale followed her out into the sunshine, still holding the empty bottle. "Hey, you," Vale said, swallowing, "you, Mae," as if he were reciting an incantation or something, not listening to what he was saying. Mae glanced back at him over her shoulder, showing her little white teeth in a smile, but did not stop; she was going home. Vale was seized by a sensation of alarm and despair—he could not understand. "You pig, little pig," he muttered, watching her.

Mae had run away from home four or five times, always with men, various men who worked in Frothing or were just on their way through. She ran off on Greyhound buses, in trucks, in automobiles. She came home the same way after a few months, and would appear with her family in church for Sunday Mass, sitting alone in new clothes and a new hat and lipsticked meditation while the rest of the family filed docilely out into the aisle and up for communion. When the girl had come home this time, jumping out of a car right in the middle of the street on Saturday afternoon, everyone had noticed but had not had much to say—there was nothing to say about her, and even those who hated her, like Vale's wife, shrugged their shoulders and said they "felt sorry" for her. There was something wrong with her. Vale always agreed, but now he knew it must be true: there was something wrong with her, her very stiffness, her self-conscious, deliberate cheapness, even the poised sweetness of that stupid, stupid innocence. His face stiffened at the thought of her into an expression of distaste. He wanted nothing to do with her.

That night he went out for a walk, something he never did, and walked the two miles down to Mae's mother's house. It was a warm spring night. Sounds of crickets, night birds, owls, dogs barking forlornly. Vale knew little about Mae's mother, who was a small, tidy woman of about fifty. She had married an old man with children half grown and her first child had been Mae; after her had come a succession of boys and girls, poking relentlessly out, sticking up their heads to be counted. The stepchildren were gone away, married. The old man had died when Vale was still in school. Vale had never paid any attention to them, having been busy with his own life. He remembered his own mother talking about Mae, telling of how her mother and the old man had beaten her, trying to make her behave, and, later, after the old man's death, how her mother had beaten her alone, furiously and hysterically, so that people on either side of them could hear. Apparently none of it worked. Mae was expelled from school when she was thirteen. She hung around the sawmill and around the bar. She took no notice of other children but had been interested only in men, at first men much older than she; but then as she grew older she would accept younger men, until Vale was the youngest of all: Mae then was sixteen. There were other bad girls, but Mae was somehow different. The others were stupid, some of them mentally retarded, or spiteful, or malicious, or desperate to leave home. Mae was happy with her home, showed no spite or malice, took care of her younger sister lovingly, went to church every week with her family, and to the world that was not made up of the certain men she wanted showed a hazy, smiling expression, more absent-minded than innocent.

The next night Vale returned. He had left his wife crying in the trailer, the baby in the plywood box crying harmoniously with her; but as soon as he had run out to the road he had forgotten about them. He could think only of Mae. He waited around on the road, went down to the tavern where he drank beer with some farmers, came back and prowled around in the field behind the house. Nothing. This went on for several nights. She did not peek out the window or come to the door. Though he waited patiently, she did not come to the garage. He waited. Her childish smile had magnified itself in his brain so that he could click it on at once and become intoxicated by it, blotting out the tedium of the garage and his father-in-law and his wife's doomed, bright chatter, her gestures of passion as he made love to her, pretending she was Mae.

Yet when she did come again he was not surprised. He had the motorcycle ready: it might have been for this that he had been preparing it. *"He's* been after me to sell it, the old bastard," Vale had whispered to Mae, nodding upstairs to indicate his father-in-law. "Wants me staying around. Don't want me driving off somewhere!" Mae carried a straw purse with a felt kitten on it, in white. Vale was so excited beneath her smiling, still gaze that he could not keep his hands still. "You ever take anybody for a ride on that?" Mae said. Vale sighed and was afraid to touch her; his blood pounded. They looked at each other. Mae giggled at his discomfort. They kissed and Vale had to step back, putting his hand down flat on the white fur seat of the cycle. "Christ, I don't know if I can drive," he said. "I'm not kidding." He was able to think clearly, though, as if he had planned this in advance: he took his transistor radio off the shelf and put it in the saddlebag, and went over to the cigar box and took the money inside (twelve dollars and some change). Because he felt it would be more of an insult, hours later when his father-in-law came in for the afternoon, he left the cigar box in its place on the shelf with the smudged cover closed.

That evening they were in the city (a town of about

fifteen thousand people), where Vale felt they disappeared, sucked into it and each other. Vale had some friends there; Mae might have had, but said nothing. She was a secretive, quiet girl, embarrassed sometimes by Vale's passion for her but sometimes gloating over it, asking him about his wife and what she had been like. She would not say the word *love;* she taught Vale to be ashamed of it too. After they had been there a month he and another man drove her to a doctor they had heard of, in the same city. The doctor was sardonic, sallow, had a drooping, indifferent face. Confronted with Vale and the other man, he had sat at the old-fashioned table in his kitchen, rested his elbows on the oil cloth cover, and had covered his sunken eyes with his hands. "I don't do it for nothing. I don't do it any more," he said. "Who sent you here?" Mae had stood behind them, shivering. Vale was forced to take hold of the man by what remained of his hair, at the very crown of his head, before he agreed. "She better not get hurt," Vale said. "You know what risk there is," the doctor whined, staring sideways at Mae. "You do a nice clean job and we won't bother you no more. See you get left alone," Vale said. "She may die," the doctor said. "No she don't," Vale said, as if he had been waiting for this. "No she don't, doctor. You'll see to that."

The next time she had not really believed she was pregnant, but Vale was nervous about it; he did not like the thought of her having a baby, of her body being changed. He was not sure he would be attracted to her so strongly afterward and something close to bitter tears threatened him at the thought of this loss, as if it were a part of himself, of his youth. They had practiced a turkey run until Mae, ashamed, had said, "It's enough. It's enough," and baby or no, pregnant or not, they had got by safely. It was Vale's theory that she had been pregnant just a little and that their acting so quick had brought it off; Mae herself said nothing. She would lie sleepy and sleepless for hours, her eyelids heavy, her lips slightly parted, oblivious to him. At these times she looked patient: as if she had been waiting for centuries.

When they ran out of money she did not seem to care. Vale's wife had always fought with him about money, but Mae hardly noticed. He always got money when he needed it, working part time at garages or driving trucks, and a few times he and another young man had helped themselves to money lying unattended here and there, though they drew the line (he swore to Mae, who probably did not care) at real robbery; they did not like the risk of meeting people face to face, of having the temptation to hurt these people, maybe even kill them. "I wouldn't trust myself," Vale said honestly. "I got a bad temper and I just wouldn't trust myself. I draw the line at that."

He never thought of his old life. He felt cleansed and young again. After a few weeks he could not always remember his wife's face. He thought of the baby as a younger brother, perhaps. Mae stunned him into remembering himself only once in a while, asking as she did (as if it were not a joke), "What year is it? Sometimes I can't remember what year it is." She spent time looking at the calendar, which had a picture of Niagara Falls on top. What she found there puzzled him; she lingered on dates, ran her fingers along the numbers, not really counting but caressing. Sometimes Vale thought of her while driving alone and it was odd that his mind skipped past her as she was now (as if there were nothing there, really, but someone he had imagined) and settled upon her as a child, though at that time he had never noticed her in particular. He kept rummaging through these memories, sifting the garbage of his own late childhood, but could discover nothing more than a thin child with hair long and snarled underneath, as if someone in authority— her mother, no doubt—had insisted upon such long hair for the child's beauty, at the expense of her suffering. But he could not remember her before she had become "bad"; it seemed to him that even then, as a child of four or five, she had been as she was now, collaborating some- how in being "bad." This thought discomforted him, for he felt he could not understand her. But most of the time he thought of her with warmth. This had been her last flight from home, he thought, this flight would be permanent. He supposed that after a while his wife would get a divorce and he and Mae would get married. He never thought much about it. When an image of their future life suggested itself to him it was just another picture of their present, that furnished room with the open stairway outside and this particular stretch of road, reaching out dazedly into the future, obscured by dust.

While Mae was dying inside her mother's old farmhouse, Vale waited patiently down the road, smoking and drinking beer. The feed mill was closed down for the day. In front of it a rusted truck was parked, had been parked for years, surrounded by weeds and small prickly bushes. Out of a mound of clay atop its streaked hood small fine weeds grew, delicate as lace. Vale sat on the running board of the truck and waited. He was heavy with beer. Friends of his, one of them a cousin of his wife's, hung out down the road at the tavern (the Mill-Side Inn) and came out from time to time to look down at him. Now it was dark: they jostled each other in the gravel parking lot of the tavern, inside the halo of insect-dotted pink light. "Hey, you, Vale," one of them called. "Hey, you still there? Going to get yourself kilt?"

Vale had thrown up right on the road, but he could not stop drinking. He had bought six cans of beer and still had more to drink. He thought bitterly that inside the house the family was eating; he thought he could smell food, meat and potatoes. But he was not sure. The idea of food made him vomit again. When his vision cleared he saw the windows of the old house wink at him. The curtains inside hung filmy and rigid. The old house was lit by a sweet, stale, damp light, as it had always been lit, even before they had had electricity. All farmhouses looked alike. The doctor's car was in the driveway, parked near the front, and whenever Vale's eye happened upon it his brain flinched. There was a pickup truck there too, belonging to some relative, one of the stepbrothers probably; he knew he had serviced it but

could not remember. It was not from nearby. Vale sat on
the running board again, lighting a cigarette with his
trembling fingers. He knew nothing. No one came to the
door, no one looked out the window. He could see
nothing through the curtains. Someone had warned him
of trouble (Mae's stepbrother was furious) but nothing
would come of that: they had forgotten him. He leaned
over to spit. His mouth was sour. A quarter of a mile
away, out by the sparkling water wheel, two men stood
and waved their arms and yelled drunkenly at him. Their
harsh young voices came to Vale through a mist.

When someone opened the door of the house at last,
Vale got to his feet. It was late now and the countryside
was quiet. His head pounded. "Hey, hey you there," he
called, stumbling onto the road. A boy ran out to the
driveway. Vale crossed to him. "Hey, you. Is that you,
Eddie?" The boy stared. He wore jeans and a shrunken
undershirt; Vale could see his chest bones shadowed in
the moonlight. "You tell me what's going on," he said.
His voice was loud and frightened.

The boy considered running past Vale; Vale put out
his arms in a vague, threatening embrace. "You got no
right here," he whispered. "Ma said—"

"What happened to her?" said Vale.

The boy started to run by and Vale grabbed his arm.
Vale could feel him shivering. "She's dead," he whispered. "I got to go down there to call the sheriff."

"What?" said Vale.

"I got to go use their phone," the boy said, and his
voice broke into a whine. "She told me to go call! We
got to report it right! The doctor said—"

"You little bastard!" Vale said. He began shaking the
boy. "What are you lying for—you and that old bitch
of a mother in there— Trying to tell me—" The boy
jerked away in terror; Vale saw that he looked guilty.
"Yes, you! You and them other ones and that bitch of a
mother of yours! I never saw it till now, that *you* did it
to her and not me—she didn't remember me, did she?
Forgot me! She never paid any attention to me, she was
always thinking of someone else that she loved better—

all of you in there, bastards, son-of-a-bitches— Who
sucked the blood out, got in there and sucked it out—"
He threw something against the house: the can of beer.
It rolled up onto the shadowed roof, approached the
peak, paused, and turned to roll silently back down; it
fell into the grass. Vale and the boy watched it. "You
know but you won't let on," Vale said bitterly to the boy.
He was exhausted; his mind buzzed; he could not get
things straight. Already the little lights inside the trailer,
peeking out from behind safety-pinned curtains, beck-
oned to him—he must rest so that he could understand
what happened, so that he would know who had killed
Mae. He must sleep. "There's so much of it I don't
know," he said. "But those bastards. Those killers," he
said, swaying, waving his empty hand vaguely as if he
were conjuring shadows out of the unfamiliar night.

Upon the Sweeping Flood

One day in Eden County, in the remote marsh and swamplands to the south, a man named Walter Stuart was stopped in the rain by a sheriff's deputy along a country road. Stuart was in a hurry to get home to his family—his wife and two daughters—after having endured a week at his father's old farm, arranging for his father's funeral, surrounded by aging relatives who had sucked at him for the strength of his youth. He was a stern, quiet man of thirty-nine, beginning now to lose some of the muscular hardness that had always baffled others, masking as it did Stuart's remoteness, his refinement, his faith in discipline and order that seem to have belonged, even in his youth, to a person already grown safely old. He was a district vice-president for one of the gypsum mining plants, a man to whom financial success and success in love had come naturally, without fuss. When only a child he had shifted his faith with little difficulty from the unreliable God of his family's tradition to the things and emotions of this world, which he admired in his thoughtful, rather conservative way, and this faith had given him access, as if by magic, to a communion with persons vastly different from himself—with someone like the sheriff's deputy, for example, who approached him that day in the hard, cold rain. "Is something wrong?" Stuart said. He rolled down the window and had nearly opened the door when the deputy, an old man with gray eyebrows and a slack, sunburned face, began shouting against the wind. "Just the weather, mister. You plan on going far? How far are you going?"

"Two hundred miles," Stuart said. "What about the weather? Is it a hurricane?"

"A hurricane—yes a hurricane," the man said, bending to shout at Stuart's face. "You better go back to town and stay put. They're evacuating up there. We're not letting anyone through."

A long line of cars and pickup trucks, tarnished and gloomy in the rain, passed them on the other side of the road. "How bad is it?" said Stuart. "Do you need help?"

"Back at town, maybe, they need help," the man said. "They're putting up folks at the schoolhouse and the churches, and different families— The eye was spost to come by here, but last word we got it's veered further south. Just the same, though—"

"Yes, it's good to evacuate them," Stuart said. At the back window of an automobile passing them two children's faces peered out at the rain, white and blurred. "The last hurricane here—"

"Ah, God, leave off of that!" the old man said, so harshly that Stuart felt, inexplicably, hurt. "You better turn around now and get on back to town. You got money they can put you up somewheres good—not with these folks coming along here."

This was said without contempt, but Stuart flinched at its assumptions and, years afterward, he was to remember the old man's remark as the beginning of his adventure. The man's twisted face and unsteady, jumping eyes, his wind-snatched voice, would reappear to Stuart when he puzzled for reasons—but along with the deputy's face there would be the sad line of cars, the children's faces turned toward him, and, beyond them in his memory, the face of his dead father with skin wrinkled and precise as a withered apple.

"I'm going in to see if anybody needs help," Stuart said. He had the car going again before the deputy could protest. "I know what I'm doing! I know what I'm doing!" Stuart said.

The car lunged forward into the rain, drowning out the deputy's outraged shouts. The slashing of rain against Stuart's face excited him. Faces staring out of oncoming cars were pale and startled, and Stuart felt rising in him a strange compulsion to grin, to laugh madly at their alarm. . . . He passed cars for some time. Houses looked deserted, yards bare. Things had the look of haste about them, even trees—in haste to rid themselves of their leaves, to be stripped bare. Grass was twisted and wild. A ditch by the road was overflowing and at spots the churning, muddy water stretched across the red clay road. Stuart drove, splashing, through it. After a while his enthusiasm slowed, his foot eased up on the gas pedal. He had not passed any cars or trucks for some time.

The sky had darkened and the storm had increased. Stuart thought of turning back when he saw, a short distance ahead, someone standing in the road. A car approached from the opposite direction. Stuart slowed, bearing to the right. He came upon a farm—a small, run-down one with just a few barns and a small pasture in which a horse stood drooping in the rain. Behind the roofs of the buildings a shifting edge of foliage from the trees beyond curled in the wind, now dark, now silver. In a neat harsh line against the bottom of the buildings the wind had driven up dust and red clay. Rain streamed off roofs, plunged into fat, tilted rain barrels, and exploded back out of them. As Stuart watched, another figure appeared, running out of the house. Both persons— they looked like children—jumped about in the road, waving their arms. A spray of leaves was driven against them and against the muddy windshield of the car that approached and passed them. They turned: a girl and a boy, waving their fists in rage, their faces white and distorted. As the car sped past Stuart, water and mud splashed up in a vicious wave.

When Stuart stopped and opened the door the girl was already there, shouting, "Going the wrong way! Wrong way!" Her face was coarse, pimply about her forehead and chin. The boy pounded up behind her, straining

for air. "Where the hell are you going, mister?" the girl
cried. "The storm's coming from this way. Did you see
that bastard, going right by us? Did you see him? If I see
him when I get to town—" A wall of rain struck. The
girl lunged forward and tried to push her way into the
car; Stuart had to hold her back. "Where are your folks?"
he shouted. "Let me in," cried the girl savagely. "We're
getting out of here!" "Your folks," said Stuart. He had
to cup his mouth to make her hear. "Your folks in
there!" "There ain't anybody there— *Goddamn* you,"
she said, twisting about to slap her brother, who had
been pushing at her from behind. She whirled upon
Stuart again. "You letting us in, mister? You letting us
in?" she screamed, raising her hands as if to claw him.
But Stuart's size must have calmed her, for she shouted
hoarsely and mechanically: "There ain't nobody in there.
Our pa's been gone the last two days. *Last two days*.
Gone into town *by himself*. Gone drunk somewhere. He
ain't here. He left us here. LEFT US HERE!" Again she
rushed at Stuart, and he leaned forward against the
steering wheel to let her get in back. The boy was about
to follow when something caught his eye back at the
farm. "Get in," said Stuart. "Get in. Please. Get in."
"My horse there," the boy muttered. "You little bastard!
You get in here!" his sister screamed.

But once the boy got in, once the door was closed,
Stuart knew that it was too late. Rain struck the car in
solid walls and the road, when he could see it, had
turned to mud. "Let's go! Let's go!" cried the girl, pounding on the back of the seat. "Turn it around! Go up on
our drive and turn it around!" The engine and the wind
roared together. "Turn it! Get it going!" cried the girl.
There was a scuffle and someone fell against Stuart. "It
ain't no good," the boy said. "Let me out." He lunged
for the door and Stuart grabbed him. "I'm going back
to the house," the boy cried, appealing to Stuart with
his frightened eyes, and his sister, giving up suddenly,
pushed him violently forward. "It's no use," Stuart said.
"Goddamn fool," the girl screamed, "goddamn fool!"

The water was ankle deep as they ran to the house.

The girl splashed ahead of Stuart, running with her head up and her eyes wide open in spite of the flying scud. When Stuart shouted to the boy, his voice was slammed back to him as if he were being mocked. "Where are you going? Go to the house! Go to the house!" The boy had turned and was running toward the pasture. His sister took no notice but ran to the house. "Come back, kid!" Stuart cried. Wind tore at him, pushing him back. "What are you—"

The horse was undersized, skinny and brown. It ran to the boy as if it wanted to run him down but the boy, stooping through the fence, avoided the frightened hoofs and grabbed the rope that dangled from the horse's halter. "That's it! That's it!" Stuart shouted as if the boy could hear. At the gate the boy stopped and looked around wildly, up to the sky—he might have been looking for someone who had just called him; then he shook the gate madly. Stuart reached the gate and opened it, pushing it back against the boy, who now turned to gape at him. "What? What are you doing here?" he said.

The thought crossed Stuart's mind that the child was insane. "Bring the horse through!" he said. "We don't have much time."

"What are you doing here?" the boy shouted. The horse's eyes rolled, its mane lifted and haloed about its head. Suddenly it lunged through the gate and jerked the boy off the ground. The boy ran in the air, his legs kicking. "Hang on and bring him around!" Stuart shouted. "Let me take hold!" He grabbed the boy instead of the rope. They stumbled together against the horse. It had stopped now and was looking intently at something just to the right of Stuart's head. The boy pulled himself along the rope, hand over hand, and Stuart held onto him by the strap of his overalls. "He's scairt of you!" the boy said. "He's scairt of you!" Stuart reached over and took hold of the rope above the boy's fingers and tugged gently at it. His face was about a foot away from the horse's. "Watch out for him," said the boy. The horse reared and broke free, throwing Stuart back against the boy. "Hey, hey," screamed the boy, as if mad. The horse turned in mid-air as if whirled about by the wind, and Stuart looked up through his fingers to see its hoofs and a vicious flicking of its tail, and the face of the boy being yanked past him and away with incredible speed. The boy fell heavily on his side in the mud, arms outstretched above him, hands still gripping the rope with wooden fists. But he scrambled to his feet at once and ran alongside the horse. He flung one arm up around its neck as Stuart shouted, "Let him go! Forget about him!" Horse and boy pivoted together back toward the fence, slashing wildly at the earth, feet and hoofs together. The ground erupted beneath them. But the boy landed upright, still holding the rope, still with his arm about the horse's neck. "Let me help," Stuart said. "No," said the boy, "he's my horse, he knows me—" "Have you got him good?" Stuart shouted. "We got—we got each other here," the boy cried, his eyes shut tight.

Stuart went to the barn to open the door. While he struggled with it, the boy led the horse forward. When the door was open far enough, Stuart threw himself against it and slammed it around to the side of the barn. A cloud of hay and scud filled the air. Stuart stretched out his arms, as if pleading with the boy to hurry, and he murmured, "Come on. Please. Come on." The boy did not hear him or even glance at him: his own lips were moving as he caressed the horse's neck and head. The horse's muddy hoof had just begun to grope about the step before the door when something like an explosion came against the back of Stuart's head, slammed his back, and sent him sprawling out at the horse.

"Damn you! Damn you!" the boy screamed. Stuart saw nothing except rain. Then something struck him, his shoulder and hand, and his fingers were driven down into the mud. Something slammed beside him in the mud and he seized it—the horse's foreleg—and tried to pull himself up, insanely, lurching to his knees. The horse threw him backwards. It seemed to emerge out of the air before and above him, coming into sight as though out of a cloud. The boy he did not see at all—only the hoofs—and then the boy appeared, inexplicably, under the horse, peering intently at Stuart, his face struck completely blank. "Damn you!" Stuart heard, "he's my horse! My horse! I hope he kills you!" Stuart crawled back in the water, crab fashion, watching the horse form and dissolve, hearing its vicious tattoo against the barn. The door, swinging madly back and forth, parodied the horse's rage, seemed to challenge its frenzy; then the door was all Stuart heard, and he got to his feet, gasping, to see that the horse was out of sight.

The boy ran bent against the wind, out toward no-where, and Stuart ran after him. "Come in the house, kid! Come on! Forget about it, kid!" He grabbed the boy's arm. The boy struck at him with his elbow. "He was my horse!" he cried.

In the kitchen of the house they pushed furniture against the door. Stuart had to stand between the boy and the girl to keep them from fighting. "Goddamn sniffling fool," said the girl. "So your goddamn horse run off for the night!" The boy crouched down on the floor, crying steadily. He was about thirteen: small for his age, with bony wrists and face. "We're all going to be blownt to hell, let alone your horse," the girl said. She sat with one big thigh and leg outstretched on the table, watching Stuart. He thought her perhaps eighteen. "Glad you come down to get us?" she said. "Where are you from, mister?" Stuart's revulsion surprised him; he had not supposed there was room in his stunned mind for emotion of this sort. If the girl noticed it she gave no sign, but only grinned at him. "I was—I was on my way home," he said. "My wife and daughters—" It occurred to him that he had forgotten about them entirely. He had not thought of them until now and, even now, no image came to his mind: no woman's face, no little girls' faces. Could he have imagined their lives, their love for him? For an instant he doubted everything. "Wife and daughters," said the girl, as if wondering whether to believe him. "Are they in this storm too?" "No—no," Stuart said. To get away from her he went to the window. He could no longer see the road. Something struck the house and he flinched away. "Them trees!" chortled the girl. "I knew it! Pa always said how he ought to cut them down, so close to the house like they are! I knew it! I knew it! And the old bastard off safe now where they can't get him!"

"Trees?" said Stuart slowly.

"Them trees! Old oak trees!" said the girl.

The boy, struck with fear, stopped crying suddenly. He crawled on the floor to a woodbox beside the big old iron stove and got in, patting the disorderly pile of wood as if he were blind. The girl ran to him and pushed him. "What are you doing?" Stuart cried in anguish. The girl took no notice of him. "What am I doing?" he said aloud. "What the hell am I doing here?" It seemed to him that the end would come in a minute or two, that the howling outside could get no louder, that the howling inside his mind could get no more intense, no more accusing. A goddamn fool! A goddamn fool! he thought. The deputy's face came to mind, and Stuart pictured himself groveling before the man, clutching at his knees, asking forgiveness and for time to be turned back. . . . Then he saw himself back at the old farm, the farm of his childhood, listening to tales of his father's agonizing sickness, the old peoples' heads craning around, seeing how he took it, their eyes charged with horror and delight. . . . "My wife and daughters," Stuart muttered.

The wind made a hollow, drumlike sound. It seemed to be tolling. The boy, crouching back in the woodbox, shouted: "I ain't scairt! I ain't scairt!" The girl gave a shriek. "Our chicken coop, I'll be gahdammed!" she cried. Try as he could, Stuart could see nothing out the window. "Come away from the window," Stuart said, pulling the girl's arm. She whirled upon him. "Watch yourself, mister," she said, "you want to go out to your gahdamn bastardly worthless car?" Her body was strong and big in her men's clothing; her shoulders looked muscular beneath the filthy shirt. Cords in her young neck stood out. Her hair had been cut short and was now wet, plastered about her blemished face. She grinned at Stuart as if she were about to poke him in the stomach, for fun. "I ain't scairt of what God can do!" the boy cried behind them.

When the water began to bubble up through the floor boards they decided to climb to the attic. "There's an ax!" Stuart exclaimed, but the boy got on his hands and knees and crawled to the corner where the ax was propped before Stuart could reach it. The boy cradled it in his arms. "What do you want with that?" Stuart said, and for an instant his heart was pierced with fear. "Let me take it. I'll take it." He grabbed it out of the boy's dazed fingers.

The attic was about half as large as the kitchen and the roof jutted down sharply on either side. Tree limbs rubbed and slammed against the roof on all sides. The three of them crouched on the middle beam, Stuart with the ax tight in his embrace, the boy pushing against him as if for warmth, and the girl kneeling, with her thighs straining her overalls. She watched the little paneless window at one end of the attic without much emotion or interest, like a large, wet turkey. The house trembled beneath them. "I'm going to the window," Stuart said, and was oddly relieved when the girl did not sneer at him. He crawled forward along the dirty beam, dragging the ax with him, and lay full length on the floor about a yard from the window. There was not much to see. At times the rain relaxed, and objects beneath in the water took shape: tree stumps, parts of buildings, junk whirling about in the water. The thumping on the roof was so loud at that end that he had to crawl backwards to the middle again. "I ain't scairt, nothing God can do!" the boy cried. "Listen to the sniveling baby," said the girl. "He thinks God pays him any mind! Hah!" Stuart crouched beside them, waiting for the boy to press against him again. "As if God gives a good damn about him," the girl said. Stuart looked at her. In the near dark her face did not seem so coarse; the set of her eyes was almost attractive. "You don't think God cares about you?" Stuart said slowly. "No, not specially," the girl said, shrugging her shoulders. "The hell with it. You seen the last one of these?" She tugged at Stuart's arm. "Mister? It was something to see. Me an' Jackie was little then—

him just a baby. We drove a far ways north to get out of it. When we come back the roads was so thick with sightseers from the cities! They took all the dead ones floating in the water and put them in one place, part of a swamp they cleared out. The families and things—they were mostly fruit pickers—had to come by on rafts and rowboats to look and see could they find the ones they knew. That was there for a day. The bodies would turn round and round in the wash from the boats. Then the faces all got alike and they wouldn't let anyone come any more and put oil on them and set them afire. We stood on top of the car and watched all that day. I wasn't but nine then."

When the house began to shake, some time later, Stuart cried aloud: "This is it!" He stumbled to his feet, waving the ax. He turned around and around as if he were in a daze. "You goin' to chop somethin' with that?" the boy said, pulling at him. "Hey, no, that ain't yours to —it ain't yours to chop—" They struggled for the ax. The boy sobbed, "It ain't yours! It ain't yours!" and Stuart's rage at his own helplessness, at the folly of his being here, for an instant almost made him strike the boy with the ax. But the girl slapped him furiously. "Get away from him! I swear I'll kill you!" she screamed.

Something exploded beneath them. "That's the windows," the girl muttered, clinging to Stuart, "and how am I to clean it again! The old bastard will want it clean, and mud over everything!" Stuart pushed her away so that he could swing the ax. Pieces of soft, rotted wood exploded into his face. The boy screamed insanely as the boards gave way to a deluge of wind and water, and even Stuart wondered if he had made a mistake. The three of them fell beneath the onslaught and Stuart lost the ax, felt the handle slam against his leg. "You! You!" Stuart cried, pulling at the girl—for an instant, blinded by pain, he could not think who he was, what he was doing, whether he had any life beyond this moment. The big-faced, husky girl made no effort to hide her fear and cried, "Wait, wait!" But he dragged her to the hole and tried to force her out. "My brother—" she gasped. She seized his wrists and tried to get away. "Get out there! There isn't any time!" Stuart muttered. The house seemed about to collapse at any moment. He was pushing her through the hole, against the shattered wood, when she suddenly flinched back against him and he saw that her cheek was cut and she was choking. He snatched her hands away from her mouth as if he wanted to see something secret: blood welled out between her lips. She coughed and spat blood onto him. "You're all right," he said, oddly pleased. "Now get out there and I'll get the kid. I'll take care of him." This time she managed to crawl through the hole, with Stuart pushing her from behind; when he turned to seize the boy, the boy clung to his neck, sobbing something about God. "God loves you!" Stuart yelled. "Loves the least of you! The least of you!" The girl pulled her brother up in her great arms and Stuart was free to climb through himself.

It was actually quite a while—perhaps an hour— before the battering of the trees and the wind pushed the house in. The roof fell slowly, and the section to which they clung was washed free. "We're going somewheres!" shouted the girl. "Look at the house! That gahdamn old shanty seen the last storm!"

The boy lay with his legs pushed in under Stuart's and had not spoken for some time. When the girl cried, "Look at that!" he tried to burrow in farther. Stuart wiped his eyes to see the wall of darkness dissolve. The rain took on another look—a smooth, piercing, metallic glint, like nails driving against their faces and bodies. There was no horizon. They could see nothing except the rushing water and a thickening mist that must have been rain, miles and miles of rain, slammed by the wind into one great wall that moved remorselessly upon them. "Hang on," Stuart said, gripping the girl. "Hang on to me."

Waves washed over the roof, pushing objects at them with soft, muted thuds—pieces of fence, boards, branches heavy with foliage. Stuart tried to ward them off with his feet. Water swirled around them, sucking at them, sucking the roof, until they were pushed against

one of the farm buildings. Something crashed against
the roof—another section of the house—and splintered,
flying up against the girl. She was thrown backwards,
away from Stuart, who lunged after her. They fell into
the water while the boy screamed. The girl's arms
threshed wildly against Stuart. The water was cold, and
its aliveness, its sinister energy, surprised him more than
the thought that he would drown—that he would never
endure the night. Struggling with the girl, he forced her
back to the roof, pushed her up. Bare, twisted nails raked
his hands. "Gahdamn you, Jackie, you give a hand!" the
girl said as Stuart crawled back up. He lay, exhausted,
flat on his stomach and let the water and debris slosh
over him.

His mind was calm beneath the surface buzzing. He
liked to think that his mind was a clear, sane circle of
quiet carefully preserved inside the chaos of the storm—
that the three of them were safe within the sanctity of
this circle; this was how man always conquered nature,
how he subdued things greater than himself. But whenever he did speak to her it was in short grunts, in her
own idiom: "This ain't so bad!" or "It'll let up pretty
soon!" Now the girl held him in her arms as if he were a
child, and he did not have the strength to pull away. Of
his own free will he had given himself to this storm, or
to the strange desire to save someone in it—but now he
felt grateful for the girl, even for her brother, for they
had saved him as much as he had saved them. Stuart
thought of his wife at home, walking through the rooms,
waiting for him; he thought of his daughters in their twin
beds, two glasses of water on their bureau. . . . But these
people knew nothing of him: in his experience now he
did not belong to them. Perhaps he had misunderstood
his role, his life? Perhaps he had blundered out of his way,
drawn into the wrong life, surrendered to the wrong role.
What had blinded him to the possibility of many lives,
many masks, many arms that might so embrace him? A
word not heard one day, a gesture misinterpreted, a level-
ing of someone's eyes in a certain unmistakable manner,
which he had mistaken just the same! The consequences

of such errors might trail insanely into the future, across miles of land, across worlds. He only now sensed the incompleteness of his former life. . . . "Look! Look!" the girl cried, jostling him out of his stupor. "Take a look at that, mister!"

He raised himself on one elbow. A streak of light broke out of the dark. Lanterns, he thought, a rescue party already. . . . But the rain dissolved the light; then it reappeared with a beauty that startled him. "What is it?" the boy screamed. "How come it's here?" They watched it filter through the rain, rays knifing through and showing, now, how buildings and trees crouched close about them. "It's the sun, the sun going down," the girl said. "The sun!" said Stuart, who had thought it was night. "The sun!" They stared at it until it disappeared.

The waves calmed sometime before dawn. By then the roof had lost its peak and water ran unchecked over it, in generous waves and then in thin waves, alternately, as the roof bobbed up and down. The three huddled together with their backs to the wind. Water came now in slow drifts. "It's just got to spread itself out far enough so's it will be even," said the girl, "then it'll go down." She spoke without sounding tired, only a little disgusted—as if things weren't working fast enough to suit her. "Soon as it goes down we'll start toward town and see if there ain't somebody coming out to get us in a boat," she said, chattily and comfortably, into Stuart's ear. Her manner astonished Stuart, who had been thinking all night of the humiliation and pain he suffered. "Bet the old bastard will be glad to see us," she said, "even if he did go off like that. Well, he never knew a storm was coming. Me and him get along pretty well—he ain't so bad." She wiped her face; it was filthy with dirt and blood. "He'll buy you a drink, mister, for saving us how you did. That was something to have happen—a man just driving up to get us!" And she poked Stuart in the ribs.

The wind warmed as the sun rose. Rain turned to mist and back to rain again, still falling heavily, and now objects were clear about them. The roof had been shoved against the corner of the barn and a mound of dirt, and eddied there without much trouble. Right about them, in a kind of halo, a thick blanket of vegetation and filth bobbed. The fence had disappeared and the house had collapsed and been driven against a ridge of land. The barn itself had fallen in, but the stone support looked untouched, and it was against this they had been shoved. Stuart thought he could see his car—or something over there where the road used to be.

"I bet it ain't deep. Hell," said the girl, sticking her foot into the water. The boy leaned over the edge and scooped up some of the filth in his hands. "Lookit all the spiders," he said. He wiped his face slowly. "Leave them gahdamn spiders alone," said the girl. "You want me to shove them down your throat?" She slid to the edge and lowered her legs. "Yah, I touched bottom. It ain't bad." But then she began coughing and drew herself back. Her coughing made Stuart cough: his chest and throat were ravaged, shaken. He lay exhausted when the fit left him and realized, suddenly, that they were all sick—that something had happened to them. They had to get off the roof. Now, with the sun up, things did not look so bad: there was a ridge of trees a short distance away on a long, red clay hill. "We'll go over there," Stuart said. "Do you think you can make it?"

The boy played in the filth, without looking up, but the girl gnawed at her lip to show she was thinking. "I spose so," she said. "But him—I don't know about him."

"Your brother? What's wrong?"

"Turn around. Hey, stupid. Turn around." She prodded the boy, who jerked around, terrified, to stare at Stuart. His thin bony face gave way to a drooping mouth. "Gone loony, it looks like," the girl said with a touch of regret. "Oh, he had times like this before. It might go away."

Stuart was transfixed by the boy's stare. The realization of what had happened struck him like a blow, sickening his stomach. "We'll get him over there," he said, making his words sound good. "We can wait there for someone to come. Someone in a boat. He'll be better there."

"I spose so," said the girl vaguely.

Stuart carried the boy while the girl splashed eagerly ahead. The water was sometimes up to his thighs. "Hold on another minute," he pleaded. The boy stared out at the water as if he thought he were taken somewhere to be drowned. "Put your arms around my neck. Hold on," Stuart said. He shut his eyes and every time he looked up the girl was still a few yards ahead and the hill looked no closer. The boy breathed hollowly, coughing into Stuart's face. His own face and neck were covered with small red bites. Ahead, the girl walked with her shoulders lunged forward as if to hurry her there, her great thighs straining against the water, more than a match for it. As Stuart watched her, something was on the side of his face—in his ear—and with a scream he slapped at it, nearly dropping the boy. The girl whirled around. Stuart slapped at his face and must have knocked it off—probably a spider. The boy, upset by Stuart's outcry, began sucking in air faster and faster as if he were dying. "I'm all right, I'm all right," Stuart whispered, "just hold on another minute. . . ."

When he finally got to the hill the girl helped pull him up. He set the boy down with a grunt, trying to put the boy's legs under him so he could stand. But the boy sank to the ground and turned over and vomited into the water; his body shook as if he were having convulsions. Again the thought that the night had poisoned them, their own breaths had sucked germs into their bodies, struck Stuart with an irresistible force. "Let him lay down and rest," the girl said, pulling tentatively at the back of her brother's belt, as if she was thinking of dragging him farther up the slope. "We sure do thank you, mister," she said.

Stuart climbed to the crest of the hill. His heart pounded madly, blood pounded in his ears. What was going to happen? Was anything going to happen? How disappointing it looked—ridges of land showing through the water and the healthy sunlight pushing back the mist.

Who would believe him when he told of the night, of the times when death seemed certain . . . ? Anger welled up in him already as he imagined the tolerant faces of his friends, his children's faces ready to turn to other amusements, other oddities. His wife would believe him; she would shudder, holding him, burying her small face in his neck. But what could she understand of his experience, having had no part in it? . . . Stuart cried out; he had nearly stepped on a tangle of snakes. Were they alive? He backed away in terror. The snakes gleamed wetly in the morning light, heads together as if conspiring. Four . . . five of them—they too had swum for this land, they too had survived the night, they had as much reason to be proud of themselves as Stuart.

He gagged and turned away. Down by the water line the boy lay flat on his stomach and the girl squatted nearby, wringing out her denim jacket. The water behind them caught the sunlight and gleamed mightily, putting them into silhouette. The girl's arms moved slowly, hard with muscle. The boy lay coughing gently. Watching them, Stuart was beset by a strange desire: he wanted to run at them, demand their gratitude, their love. Why should they not love him, when he had saved their lives? When he had lost what he was just the day before, turned now into a different person, a stranger even to himself? Stuart stooped and picked up a rock. A broad hot hand seemed to press against his chest. He threw the rock out into the water and said, "Hey!"

The girl glanced around but the boy did not move. Stuart sat down on the soggy ground and waited. After a while the girl looked away; she spread the jacket out to dry. Great banked clouds rose into the sky, reflected in the water—jagged and bent in the waves. Stuart waited as the sun took over the sky. Mist at the horizon glowed, thinned, gave way to solid shapes. Light did not strike cleanly across the land, but was marred by ridges of trees and parts of buildings, and around a corner at any time Stuart expected to see a rescuing party—in a rowboat or something.

"Hey, mister." He woke; he must have been dozing.

The girl had called him. "Hey. Whyn't you come down here? There's all them snakes up there."

Stuart scrambled to his feet. When he stumbled down-hill, embarrassed and frightened, the girl said chattily, "The sons of bitches are crawling all over here. He chast some away." The boy was on his feet and looking around with an important air. His coming alive startled Stuart—indeed, the coming alive of the day, of the world, evoked alarm in him. All things came back to what they were. The girl's alert eyes, the firm set of her mouth, had not changed—the sunlight had not changed, or the land, really; only Stuart had been changed. He wondered at it . . . and the girl must have seen something in his face that he himself did not yet know about, for her eyes narrowed, her throat gulped a big swallow, her arms moved slowly up to show her raw elbows. "We'll get rid of them," Stuart said, breaking the silence. "Him and me. We'll do it."

The boy was delighted. "I got a stick," he said, waving a thin whiplike branch. "There's some over here."

"We'll get them," Stuart said. But when he started to walk, a rock slipped loose and he fell back into the mud. He laughed aloud. The girl, squatting a few feet away, watched him silently. Stuart got to his feet, still laughing. "You know much about it, kid?" he said, cupping his hand on the boy's head.

"About what?" said the boy.

"Killing snakes," said Stuart.

"I spose—I spose you just kill them."

The boy hurried alongside Stuart. "I need a stick," Stuart said; they got him one from the water, about the size of an ax. "Go by that bush," Stuart said, "there might be some there."

The boy attacked the bush in a frenzy. He nearly fell into it. His enthusiasm somehow pleased Stuart, but there were no snakes in the bush. "Go down that way," Stuart ordered. He glanced back at the girl: she watched them. Stuart and the boy went on with their sticks held in mid-air. "God put them here to keep us awake," the boy said brightly. "See we don't forget about Him."

Mud sucked at their feet. "Last year we couldn't fire
the woods on account of it so dry. This year can't either
on account of the water. We got to get the snakes like
this."

Stuart hurried as if he had somewhere to go. The boy,
matching his steps, went faster and faster, panting, waving
his stick angrily in the air. The boy complained about
snakes and, listening to him, fascinated by him, in that
instant Stuart saw everything. He saw the conventional
dawn that had mocked the night, had mocked his desire
to help people in trouble; he saw, beyond that, his
father's home emptied now even of ghosts. He realized
that the God of these people had indeed arranged things,
had breathed the order of chaos into forms, had animated even Stuart himself forty years ago. The knowledge
of this fact struck him about the same way as the nest of
snakes had struck him—an image leaping right to the
eye, pouncing upon the mind, joining itself with the per-
ceiver. "Hey, hey!" cried the boy, who had found a
snake: the snake crawled noisily and not very quickly up
the slope, a brown-speckled snake. The boy ran clumsily after it. Stuart was astonished at the boy's stupidity,
at his inability to see, now, that the snake had vanished.
Still he ran along the slope, waving his stick, shouting,
"I'll get you! I'll get you!" This must have been the sign
Stuart was waiting for. When the boy turned, Stuart was
right behind him. "It got away up there," the boy said.
"We got to get it." When Stuart lifted his stick the boy
fell back a step but went on in mechanical excitement,
"It's up there, gotten hid in the weeds. It ain't me," he
said, "it ain't me that—" Stuart's blow struck the boy
on the side of the head, and the rotted limb shattered
into soft wet pieces. The boy stumbled down toward the
water. He was coughing when Stuart took hold of him
and began shaking him madly, and he did nothing but
cough, violently and with all his concentration, even
when Stuart bent to grab a rock and brought it down
on his head. Stuart let him fall into the water. He could
hear him breathing and he could see, about the boy's lips,

tiny flecks or bubbles of blood appearing and disappearing with his breath.

When the boy's eyes opened, Stuart fell upon him. They struggled savagely in the water. Again the boy went limp; Stuart stood, panting, and waited. Nothing happened for a minute or so. But then he saw something —the boy's fingers moving up through the water, soaring to the surface! "Will you quit it!" Stuart screamed. He was about to throw himself upon the boy again when the thought of the boy's life, bubbling out between his lips, moving his fingers, filled him with such outraged disgust that he backed away. He threw the rock out into the water and ran back, stumbling, to where the girl stood.

She had nothing to say: her jaw was hard, her mouth a narrow line, her thick nose oddly white against her dirty face. Only her eyes moved, and these were black, lustrous, at once demanding and terrified. She held a board in one hand. Stuart did not have time to think, but, as he lunged toward her, he could already see himself grappling with her in the mud, forcing her down, tearing her ugly clothing from her body— "Lookit!" she cried, the way a person might speak to a horse, cautious and coaxing, and pointed behind him. Stuart turned to see a white boat moving toward them, a half mile or so away. Immediately his hands dropped, his mouth opened in awe. The girl still pointed, breathing carefully, and Stuart, his mind shattered by the broken sunshine upon the water, turned to the boat, raised his hands, cried out, "Save me! Save me!" He had waded out a short distance by the time the men arrived.